Seaside Secrets

A Pastor Clarissa Abbot Mystery

by

Glen Ebisch

For information, email **Cozy Cat Press**, cozycatpress@aol.com or visit our website at: www.cozycatpress.com

COZY CAT
P R E S S

Editor: Jaimie Patterson
ISBN: 978-1-946063-69-4
Printed in the United States of America

10 9 8 7 6 5 4 3 2 1

For Marie and Joe Flahive: good friends.

Chapter One

Clarissa Abbot stood in the hospital hallway, sweat beading on her forehead. Granted, it was a surprisingly warm day for the middle of May, but the building was well air-conditioned, and Clarissa knew that she was perspiring from nervousness, not heat. She was just finishing up her first week as pastor at Shore Side Community Church in Shore Side, New Jersey. It had been a week of firsts for her, especially since the previous pastor, Reverend Warren Hollingsworth, had spent only a short afternoon with her going over how the church was run before leaving with his son for a new life of retirement in western Pennsylvania. His last words as he went out the door were to blithely say that the church secretary, Mrs. Dalrymple, would fill her in on anything he'd overlooked, which were, in Clarissa's opinion, most of the essential details.

Unfortunately, Mrs. Dalrymple's daughter had phoned the next day to say that her mother had to quit her position out of ill health, and she was immediately moving to be with family in northern New Jersey. The gossip around the church, which Clarissa tried— unsuccessfully—to ignore, said that Mrs. Dalrymple had carried a decade-long torch for the old Reverend, a distinguished-looking widower, and was crushed when he suddenly picked up sticks and decided to leave the area without giving her more than a day of warning. There were even some who thought that the Reverend's sudden decision to move came about as a result of the widow Dalrymple's increasingly aggressive attentions.

Whatever the cause, all of these desertions, as Clarissa found herself morosely thinking of them, had left her without any help at getting up to speed in her new position. Oh, she had preached a good enough sermon on her first Sunday, and struggled after church to learn the many names of those who came to her welcoming luncheon, but the business side of running the church was locked inside the office computer, which she had so far been unable to access. She had called Reverend Hollingsworth several times during the last week to ask for the computer password, but he had yet to be available—due to spending most of his time out on the links with his son.

But the computer was a problem for another day. Today, Clarissa was doing hospital rounds for the first time since her assignment as a trainee assistant pastor. Fortunately, there was only one member of her congregation in the hospital, a man named David Ames. As she walked into his room, she hoped that he would be as hale and hearty as one could be in the hospital. It was always hard to offer comfort to someone who was both suffering and a complete stranger.

The blinds were pulled back halfway from the windows at the end of the room, offering a glimpse of the Atlantic Ocean a few blocks away. The first bed she came to was occupied by a man who was either asleep or unconscious, and the other had a curtain pulled around it.

Clarissa waited discreetly for a couple of minutes for the curtain to be removed, but eventually decided that she could be waiting there all day. "Hello?" she called out softly.

A middle-aged woman in a nurse's uniform popped out from around the curtain. She was almost as tall as Clarissa and more heavily built. "I'm just finishing up

Mr. Ames' sponge bath," she said, giving Clarissa a suspicious look. "Are you a member of his family?"

Clarissa, like a lot of women in the ministry, had mixed feelings about wearing a clerical collar. On the one hand, it defined who you were—which was often helpful if you were, like herself, a young woman and didn't look particularly ministerial—but it also established a distance between yourself and the people you were trying to serve. Since seminary, she had settled for wearing a dark blouse and black slacks along with a short-length jacket. Her light brown hair, which tended to bleach out to blond in the summer, was cut in a short bob. She was twenty-seven, but knew she looked younger, so she was accustomed to being challenged while doing her job.

"I'm the minister from the Shore Side Community Church," she replied.

The nurse still looked skeptical. "I thought the minister from that church was an older, respectable-looking man."

Clarissa wondered if she fell short as a woman or because she was somehow less than respectable.

"He retired," she said. "I'm his replacement." She stuck out her hand. "Pastor Clarissa Abbot."

"Nice to meet you," the nurse said, taking her hand. "I'm Wanda Bascomb. No offense intended, we just have to be careful about security nowadays."

"I understand."

"Let me just get Dave straightened up, and you can talk to him. But he gets tired very quickly, just so you know." She gave Clarissa a meaningful glance as if to suggest that Dave was in dire straits.

A few moments later, the curtain slid back with dramatic speed, and David Ames was revealed, propped up in bed. It was hard to tell his size under the bedclothes, but Clarissa's guess was that he was tall and thin. He had a fringe of white hair that was clearly losing the fight against baldness, and an equally white mustache which was flourishing, as if to offset the hair loss elsewhere. He had a long face, and would probably have been a pleasant-looking man when he smiled. He wasn't smiling now.

"Who are you?" he asked sharply.

The nurse rolled her eyes in sympathy and went over to tend to the man in the other bed.

"Reverend Hollingsworth retired. I've taken his place," Clarissa explained. "I'm Pastor Clarissa Abbot, his replacement." She walked closer and held out her hand, but he just glared at it as if it might hold a concealed hypodermic. She sighed to herself and returned her hand to her side. Some older men responded positively to a female minister, others didn't. She'd learned to roll with the punches.

"Hollingsworth is gone? I'm in the hospital for a week and he runs off." David Ames stared at her for a long moment. "Maybe there *is* something you can do for me. There's something I need to talk about."

"I'm a good listener."

"I'm not going to tell you," he snapped.

"I saw Father Molloy down the hall," Clarissa suggested. "I'm sure you could talk to him."

"I don't need a priest. I'm not about to confess to anything . . . at least, not exactly." Ames looked away.

"I'm sure you could just have a chat with Father Malloy. It wouldn't have to be anything more formal than that," Clarissa said gently. Father Malloy was well into his seventies, probably around the same age as the man in front of her. She knew some men found it easier to talk with other men of their generation.

"Forget it."

"Is there someone you *do* know that I could arrange to have come see you?" she asked patiently.

David Ames stared across the room while Clarissa listened to his labored breathing. The rumor at church was that he was in the last stages of congestive heart failure. She'd been doing the job long enough by now to be aware of how people faced death differently, and she hoped that he would find some comfort in his faith.

"Have Jack Spurlock come to see me," he finally said.

"The sacristan," Clarissa replied with a nod.

Ames gave her a blank look. "I mean the church maintenance man," he said. "A guy about my age."

Clarissa fought back a smile, knowing it was useless to try to explain that "sacristan" was the proper term for Jack Spurlock's position. "I know him," she said. "I'll arrange for him to come."

Ames took in a particularly long breath and shuddered. "Tell him not to wait too long."

"I'll see that he comes as soon as he can. Now, would you like us to pray together?" she offered, reaching out to touch his hand.

He pulled his hand away and shook his head vehemently. "Just get Spurlock here."

Chapter Two

Clarissa drove the mile from the hospital to the Victorian house that served as the parsonage. Shore Side was a small city situated along the southern coast of New Jersey that survived mostly on the income generated during the four months out of the year when tourists swarmed to the beach. The entire neighborhood around the parsonage was composed of homes from the Victorian era or even earlier. The parsonage itself was a large, colorfully decorated structure right next to the church, so Clarissa could easily walk out the back door of the kitchen and across a short path to her office, which was sandwiched between the sanctuary and the fellowship hall.

Since it was lunchtime, she parked her car in the driveway and headed into the kitchen. As she walked in the door, Mrs. Gunn, the housekeeper and cook, greeted her: "Ah, it's good you're back already, you can have a timely lunch. I made a tuna sandwich on rye and a small salad. Will that be okay?"

"That sounds wonderful!" Clarissa replied, with perhaps a little too much enthusiasm. She still wasn't accustomed to being waited on and knew she tended to over-respond.

At her welcome luncheon last Sunday, she had spoken privately to Ramona Russell, the woman who currently chaired the church board, and explained that she really didn't need a housekeeper and cook. She could easily close off the parts of the parsonage she didn't need, and clean those she used herself. As for cooking, she was no chef, but she could do well enough to provide for herself. There was no reason, she concluded, for the church to spend more money than necessary on her care and upkeep.

Mrs. Russell had taken Clarissa some distance away from the crowd, and spoken to her quietly. "I appreciate your interest in saving the church money, but we employ Mrs. Gunn more as . . . I guess what you would call a social service project," she explained. "Barbara was widowed several years ago after looking after her husband, a virtual invalid, for many years. She had very little money, and was well into her sixties when he passed. Reverend Hollingsworth had just arrived and, unlike you, he was at sixes and sevens when it came to taking care of himself, so naturally we decided that bringing the two of them together would be ideal for both. She doesn't get paid a great deal, but it supplements her social security nicely and gets her out of the house for part of the day, which helps her stay active."

"I see," Clarissa had responded. "Well, that puts things in an entirely different light. I'll be happy to have her services."

Mrs. Russell smiled. "She'll probably treat you like a daughter, or even a granddaughter, and fuss over you. But she'll also show you the proper respect a minister deserves. That was one thing your predecessor demanded."

"I'm sure we'll get along fine. I'm not one for standing on ceremony."

"That will make a nice change," the other woman said with a thin smile. "Reverend Hollingsworth was a bit old-school. He could get up on his high horse at times, and tended to listen primarily to the men. Some of the women in the congregation thought he should have paid more attention to what we have to say, since *we* do most of the work."

Clarissa smiled. "It's not the first time I've heard that complaint," she said. "I hope you'll find that I listen to everyone equally."

Mrs. Russell put a hand on her arm. "You'll never satisfy everyone, but I'm sure you'll do your best."

In the six days since that conversation, Clarissa had already come to be thankful for Mrs. Gunn's help. She didn't know how she would have kept the parsonage clean and still have time to perform her pastoral duties, even if she *had* closed off most of the rooms. Like the majority of over-furnished and excessively decorated Victorians, the parsonage seemed to generate an inordinate amount of dust. Every time you turned around, new clumps of dust had appeared along the edges of the beautiful hardwood floor, just waiting to pounce on the rugs. Only Mrs. Gunn's strenuous efforts kept the house presentable as the public face of the church.

Mrs. Gunn had also proven to be a fine cook of what Clarissa thought of as church food: casseroles, pasta salads, and the like. During the day, Mrs. Gunn always prepared something that Clarissa could easily heat up for dinner. Even better were the cakes and pies she baked. Out of concern for her waistline, Clarissa insisted Mrs. Gunn take home a sizable portion of what she prepared, and she seemed happy to do so. It was, Clarissa thought, a bit like having a mother, without the emotional angst—although Mrs. Gunn wasn't above giving advice or acting on her own initiative.

"It got so warm this morning," Mrs. Gunn began as Clarissa bit into a sandwich large enough for two, "that I went over to your office and switched on the air conditioning to cool it down. That place gets so stuffy. I figured you'd be working in there this afternoon preparing your sermon, like the Reverend always did."

Although Clarissa had already prepared her weekly sermon, she saw no need to sound more efficient than her predecessor. "Thanks, Mrs. Gunn, I will be in there this afternoon," she said. "Mrs. Williams's niece, Ashley, is coming in to apply for the office manager's job."

Mrs. Gunn gave Clarissa a sideways glance. "You certainly do need a secretary what with Mrs. Dalrymple up and quitting like that. I know she was upset when the Reverend left without giving her warning, but still she should have stayed a few weeks until you got settled."

"But she was sick," Clarissa pointed out.

Mrs. Gunn humphed. "She's always been sick."

"It *would* have been nice if she'd stayed a bit longer," Clarissa agreed, keeping her expression neutral. Even from her limited experience as an assistant pastor, she'd learned to never say anything negative about one member of the congregation to another. Everyone was interrelated by blood, friendship, or enmity, and you never knew whom you might be indirectly insulting.

"But Mrs. Williams' niece . . ." Mrs. Gunn shook her head.

"You know her?" Clarissa asked.

"Of course. She lived here with her mom and dad until about six or seven years ago. She went to high school at the county school. A bright thing, I'll give her credit for that."

Clarissa put down her sandwich and gave the housekeeper a level look. "So what's wrong with her?"

Mrs. Gunn pressed her lips together and shook her head. "I never say anything bad about someone I haven't seen in a while. They could have changed."

Not thinking that sounded particularly encouraging, Clarissa slowly ate the rest of her sandwich, uncertain whether to pursue the matter further or not. Her curiosity was certainly aroused, but she didn't want to be prejudiced against a job applicant by what might be an irrelevant juvenile past.

"Let's say," Mrs. Gunn continued, just when Clarissa thought the topic was dead and buried, "you'll know right away if Ashley's the same as she was when she lived here before. One thing you can say for the girl, she was never one to hide her light under a bushel." For some reason, Mrs. Gunn chuckled at her last remark, as if it had been remarkably witty.

Slightly annoyed by the vagueness, Clarissa finished her sandwich. She thanked Mrs. Gunn once again for lunch and went across the way to her office. A blast of cool air greeted her as she went inside, reminding her that, whatever her quirks, Mrs. Gunn was a real treasure.

She went through the outer office and its small waiting room, and into the space designated for the pastor. She sat down behind the large, ornate mahogany desk and looked at the rich, wood-paneled walls. Ramona Russell had told her that Reverend Hollingsworth, when he first arrived, had strongly requested that money from the general fund be used to update his office so that it would have the "proper prestige." Not without some grumbling, the church board had agreed, and the result—apparently designed by the Reverend himself—looked to Clarissa like a room from some London gentlemen's club. According to Ramona, the Reverend had studied at Oxford in his earlier years, and developed a love of all things British—even affecting an English accent sometimes. In Clarissa's opinion, he had certainly surpassed himself here.

Although the room seemed oppressively stuffy, she wasn't about to suggest another renovation to the church board. Anyway, Clarissa thought, having such a pompously masculine office might help offset her age and gender. Glaring at the computer for which she still did not have the password, she gave a sigh of relief that the Reverend had been old-school enough to keep a rolodex with all his important phone numbers. She looked up Jack Spurlock's name and dialed his number.

"Something need fixing?" he asked immediately after answering, showing that he had caller ID.

"Probably in a place this old, but nothing that I'm aware of at the moment," Clarissa joked.

Jack laughed. "How are you doing, Pastor?"

"Just fine. I went to the hospital today to see David Ames."

"Yeah, I heard he wasn't doing well. I guess it's his heart."

"That's what I've heard. He would like to see you," she told him. "I was wondering if you had some time this afternoon to come with me to the hospital during visiting hours."

"Dave wants to see me?" Jack asked, the surprise evident in his voice. "Why?"

"Apparently there's something from the past he wants to talk about, but he doesn't want to tell me what it is," Clarissa said. "Are you good friends?"

"I wouldn't have thought so," Jack replied. "We went to school together and we've both lived in Shore Side all our lives, but we haven't had much to do with each other since we were kids. I'd nod to him when I saw him at church, but that's about all."

"Did he normally attend church?" asked Clarissa.

Jack laughed. "Dave didn't normally do anything except work on a fishing boat, smoke, and drink. He never married and lived kind of a rough life."

"Do you have any idea what he would want to tell you about?"

There was a slight pause. "No clue," he said. "I have the grandkids staying with me right now for an overnight. Their parents are at a wedding. Let me talk it over with Marcie. Maybe I can get away in the morning, and we can go see Dave then."

Clarissa dredged up from her memory that Marcie was Jack's wife. "Dave sounded kind of urgent," she said doubtfully.

"Sorry, Pastor, that's the best I can do. I have to help Marcie get the kids bathed and into bed right after supper," said Jack.

"Okay. Why don't you let me know first thing in the morning if you can go, and we'll meet at the hospital around ten?" she suggested.

"Sounds good."

After she hung up, Clarissa sat and stared again at the dark wood walls of her study. She wasn't very surprised at Jack's reluctance to see David Ames. Lots of people disliked going to the hospital on general principle, and others studiously avoided visiting people they knew when their condition was seriously diminished. All the same, something about Jack's hesitance struck her as odd. She had been a bit surprised when Jack said he'd gone to school with David, since Jack looked to be in his early sixties, while David appeared to be well into his seventies. *Maybe Jack was proof that leading a healthy life will keep you looking young,* she thought.

She heard a low thumping sound coming from the next room. It took her a moment to realize that someone was knocking on the outside door. Checking her watch, she saw that it was time for her meeting with Ashley. Apparently the "Come On In" sign she had hung on the office door when she took over last Monday didn't convince everyone that they should do just that.

Clarissa walked through the outer office just as there was another series of thumps on the door. She pulled it open—and was startled by the girl standing on the porch.

She was dressed completely in black: a black dress, black tights, and black shoes, topped off by a large black shawl. She had obviously dyed black hair and wore dark lipstick that gave her lips a purple, bruised look. She stood there giving Clarissa an expressionless stare.

Clarissa wondered if the local Wiccan group had sent her as a representative to welcome the new minister to the community. Not impossible, but surprising.

Nevertheless, Clarissa smiled. "Hello, how can I help you?" she asked.

"I have an appointment," said the young woman in a clear and composed voice that made her sound much older than her appearance. Clarissa decided she was probably only a couple of years younger than herself. "I'm Ashley Reynolds, Mona Williams' niece."

"Of course," Clarissa said, rallying her wits. "Please come in."

Clarissa now realized the cause of Mrs. Gunn's laugh. Ashley certainly wasn't hiding any light under any bushel, only shades of black.

Ashley glanced into the office suspiciously, as if expecting to be attacked by a horde of churchwomen. When she was assured that everything seemed safe, she stepped inside. Clarissa directed her into the pastor's office and pulled around her chair so she would be sitting in front of the younger woman rather than across the desk.

Clarissa smiled and thanked her for coming in, but got only her patented blank expression in return.

"So, what kind of a job did you have last?" Clarissa quickly asked.

"I worked in IT for an insurance company up in Newark," Ashley answered. "I've been there since I got my degree in computer science from Rutgers."

Clarissa's heart quickened. Surely here was somebody who could fathom the mysteries of the church computer. She herself was hopeless with technology. "Why did you leave?" she asked.

"Personal reasons," Ashley replied, not volunteering anything further.

"I see."

"Look, it had nothing to do with work," Ashley said. "I can give you a letter of recommendation from my former employer saying I did a great job, if you need it."

Clarissa nodded, not yet sure how detailed to get in vetting Mrs. Williams' niece, who, given her aunt's position in the church, was probably a lock for the job. "You do realize that the position is for twenty-five hours a week, so it's really only part-time," she explained.

Ashley shrugged. "I have plenty of money saved, and I'm living with my aunt, who doesn't charge me rent."

"So why do you want a job?" asked Clarissa, more out of curiosity than anything else.

"I don't, but my aunt said that I can only stay with her if I get a job." Ashley shrugged again. "I guess it's a character-building kind of thing. And this is the job she really wants me to take. It doesn't matter what it pays."

Clarissa told her the salary, and the other woman nodded.

"I didn't expect much more than that," she said.

Clarissa gave her a smile. "Well, then, why don't we try things out for a couple of weeks and see how it goes."

Ashley paused and glanced around the room. "The only problem is that I don't believe in all of this stuff," she said with a casual wave of her hand.

"What stuff?" For a moment Clarissa thought she was opposed to wood paneling.

"This religion stuff," Ashley said.

Clarissa nodded again, deciding it wasn't time for a theological discussion. "I see. Can you be polite to people who do?" she asked.

Ashley paused, then smiled. It was a surprisingly cheerful smile for such a somber face. "Sure, I guess I can do that," she answered.

"Then you're hired," Clarissa declared. "I know tomorrow is a Saturday, and normally the job is Monday through Friday, but could you be here tomorrow at nine? Your first project is to see if you can get this computer online, and I desperately need it done."

The young woman gave her a slightly superior smile. "I should be able to handle that." They stood up and shook hands. Ashley turned to Clarissa as they walked into the outer office. "What do I call you . . . Reverend Abbot?"

"That sounds like I should be running a monastery. Just call me Clarissa, or Pastor Clarissa if other people are around."

Clarissa thought she saw a small smile flit across Ashley's purple lips, and then it was gone. "How about I just call you 'Boss' when we're alone?"

"If you like."

Ashley nodded and, in a flurry of black, was gone.

Clarissa returned to her office and sat behind her huge desk, thinking about her conversation with

Ashley. The young woman seemed capable enough, and her demeanor gave Clarissa confidence that she would be a skilled computer operator and an organized office administrator. Her offbeat appearance and probably equally eccentric ideas might require some attitudinal adjustment on the part of the members of the congregation, but Clarissa believed that lifestyle diversity could be a good thing. She also knew that a lot of potential issues between her office manager and the congregation would be overlooked because Ashley was the niece of Mona Williams, an influential member of the church.

The phone rang; it was Jack Spurlock on the line.

"Hey, Reverend," he said, "I think I can make it tonight after all, if you're still available. Marcie says she can take care of putting the kids to bed." He chuckled. "She actually said that I'm more of a disruption than a help, and I'd be of more use at the hospital."

"That would be great, Jack," Clarissa replied.

"Yeah, Dave and I were never close, but I guess I can at least see what he wants. What time should we meet?"

"Visiting hours start again at seven. Let's meet in the lobby of the hospital right on the hour."

"Sounds good."

Clarissa hung up. Marcie had obviously been the catalyst in getting Jack to visit Dave. Clarissa wondered again if his reluctance was based on more than the fact that they weren't close friends. She also couldn't understand, if they weren't really friends, why David had chosen him as the person to confide in about this apparently important matter.

Maybe after the meeting tonight, she'd know more about this increasingly intriguing matter.

Chapter Three

It was seven o'clock. Clarissa was already standing in the small lobby of the hospital when Jack walked into the building.

A bantam rooster of a man, he was short and trim with a full head of white hair and a rolling gait, as if he had spent years at sea. When Clarissa first met him at the church, she'd asked if he had worked as a fisherman. He'd laughed and said that that life was too hard for him, but he did occasionally take people out on fishing excursions.

"Well, let's get this over with," Jack said grimly, coming up to Clarissa.

She nodded and they walked toward the elevator. "Are you sure you have no idea what he wants to tell you?" she asked.

"No clue," Jack said with a tight-lipped smile that didn't encourage any further conversation.

They went up to Ames' room, but when they went inside, his bed been stripped.

"I guess he's been moved," Jack said.

Clarissa went out to the nurses' station, Jack following close behind. The same nurse whom she had met in the afternoon was sitting behind one of the computers there.

"Still here, Wanda?" Clarissa asked.

"I'm working a double shift today," she answered automatically. Then she glanced up and recognized Clarissa. Her face filled with consternation. "I hope you're not here to see Mr. Ames again."

"Why not?"

"He passed away this afternoon about four hours after you left," said Wanda.

Clarissa took a step backwards in shock and felt Jack put a hand on her shoulder to support her. "He was old and sick, so it isn't very surprising," he said softly.

The nurse nodded, as if she agreed with that line of thought.

"I suppose that's true," Clarissa admitted.

"Well, I guess that's that," Jack said quickly, rubbing his hands together. He turned to Clarissa. "I'll be by tomorrow morning to fix that window latch in the sanctuary. Would you like me to walk you out to your car?"

She shook her head. "Aren't you frustrated not to know what he wanted to tell you?" she asked.

He smiled. "Probably something from the old days, and I already know everything he got into from back then. Are you sure you don't want me to wait for you?"

"No, that's okay." Clarissa really wanted to ask Wanda some questions, preferably without Jack being present. "Thanks anyway, Jack. I think maybe I'll stop off in the chapel for a few minutes to pray."

The man nodded nervously, perhaps slightly embarrassed at the thought of private prayer, and hurried down the hall to the elevator. Clarissa turned back to the nurse.

"Was he really that sick?" she asked.

"Well, he *did* die," Wanda answered.

"I know, but he didn't seem *that* sick this afternoon when I was here. He was fully conscious and knew what was going on," Clarissa protested.

Wanda shrugged and shook her head sadly. "You can't always tell. Some folks fade away gradually; others seem to be going along just fine, then suddenly quit."

Clarissa didn't buy it. Something was wrong here. "Did he have any other visitors after I left?" she asked.

The nurse lowered her eyes and hesitated. "Not during visiting hours."

"Someone came later?"

"I'm not certain," she said. "Early visiting hours are over at three-thirty because we have to get ready to feed the patients dinner. But I thought I saw someone come out of his room around four. I only saw a figure out of the corner of my eye, and I'm not even really sure they came out of Mr. Ames' room."

"Was it a man or a woman?"

"Don't know. Whoever it was wore a hooded sweatshirt. It could have been anybody. I didn't think anything of it." Wanda looked concerned.

"It's a little warm out for a sweatshirt," Clarissa commented.

"But it gets cold in here," Wanda pointed out.

Clarissa thought that the sweatshirt was also a convenient disguise. "Yes, I guess that's true. When did you discover that David had died?"

"When I went in to feed him at around five."

"Was he hooked up to some sort of alarm that would have warned you if he was in distress?"

Wanda blushed and nodded. "But Mr. Ames liked to get up to use the bathroom by himself, so he would disconnect the monitor and wheel his IV across the room to the john," she said. "A lot of men do that because they don't want a nurse standing outside the toilet waiting for them to finish. Mr. Ames didn't always bother to plug it back in. I warned him not to do that, but he was rather stubborn."

"So the monitor was unplugged?"

"Yes," Wanda admitted. She leaned forward. "Look, Pastor, I could get in trouble over this. Could we keep it between us?"

"I'll do my best," Clarissa promised. "Was there anything else strange that happened this afternoon? Did David say anything to you after I left?"

Wanda paused and stared at the computer screen. "He asked me to get his cell phone and charger out of his locker. He wanted me to plug it in for him."

"Did he make a call?" Clarissa asked.

"Not while I was there." She stopped and gave the minister a level stare. "Where is all this going?"

Clarissa smiled. It was a fair question. But she was curious; David Ames was one of the few members of the congregation that she'd gotten to talk to one-on-one, and now he was just . . . gone. Something didn't feel right about that.

"Probably nowhere," she replied. "I'm just surprised that he died so suddenly."

"It happens every day," Wanda sighed.

"Yes, I guess you're right. Where is his body now?"

"Down in the hospital morgue. Someone on staff is getting in touch with his family to let them know so they can make the funeral arrangements."

"Good. Well, thank you very much," Clarissa said.

Wanda nodded, but as Clarissa turned to walk away, she could see that the nurse was frowning, probably regretting that she had said something that she probably wasn't supposed to.

Once back out in front of the hospital, Clarissa stood for a moment, simply enjoying the cool air that was blowing up the street from the ocean. It was a beautiful May evening, and what she wanted to do most was take a quiet walk around town, getting to know her new community. But she couldn't seem to put from her mind the gnawing feeling that David Ames' death had not been completely normal.

She didn't know which bothered her most: the fact that Ames had desperately wanted to confess something, the appearance of an unidentified intruder in his room, the unplugging of his monitor, his desire to make a phone call, or simply the fact that a man who had seemed at some distance from death's door was so suddenly pulled through. But when you put them all together, there clearly was something distinctly odd about his death.

Of course, she could be making something big out of very little, and the thought of explaining her concerns to a hard-faced desk sergeant down at the police station had little appeal. She could easily imagine herself, minister or not, being given a patronizing pat on the head and being told to be a good girl, go home, and have a soothing glass of warm milk. If only she had a personal contact on the force, things might go differently.

Suddenly she recalled a man standing in front of her at last Sunday's welcoming luncheon. He was a couple of inches taller than she, about six feet tall, and was in his early fifties, with thinning hair and a slightly thickening waist. Clarissa had a good mind for physical details, but her ability to recall names was weaker. She thought hard for a moment, certain that he had introduced himself and said that he was a detective with the local police. He even told her that he was currently working the early evening shift and couldn't wait for it to end in a few days because he found it hard to adjust his sleep cycle. She closed her eyes and tried to recreate the conversation.

Slowly, it came to her. His name had something to do with food. No, she corrected herself, something to do with food preparation. Was his name Cook? Not quite; the image of a rich dessert appeared before her mind. Baker, that was it, Joshua Baker. Feeling a sense of triumph, she laughed softly to herself.

"Are you all right, Miss?"

Clarissa turned and saw a hospital security guard staring at her with concern. She nodded and smiled at him before hurrying to her car. *I'd better get out of her before I end up in the psych ward*, she thought.

Chapter Four

Shore Side's police station was located in the same stately brick building as the city hall. Clarissa pulled into the parking lot and slipped into one of the spaces designated for visitors. She walked up the steps to the front door and, once inside, turned left, opening the door with "Police Department" etched on the glass in ornate script that looked like it went back to the nineteenth century.

A counter, much like the one she remembered from the principal's office at her high school, divided the room, and a man in uniform came forward to greet her. But instead of a hard-faced sergeant, he was a fresh-faced young man, probably a couple of years younger than herself. He gave her a delighted smile, as if having a pretty young woman come to him for help had substantially brightened his evening. His name tag said Rudinski.

"How may I help you?" he asked smoothly, as if he were the concierge in a fine hotel.

"I'd like to see Detective Baker, if he's available," Clarissa replied.

"Do you have an appointment?"

"No, I'm afraid I don't."

The young man's face dipped into almost a parody of disappointment. "I'm sorry, but usually folks make an appointment to see a detective, unless, of course, they've been asked to come in. Maybe I could help you make an appointment?"

Clarissa decided to cut to the chase. "Could you tell him that Reverend Abbot would like to see him briefly, if he isn't too busy?"

"Reverend?" the officer stuttered. Then he blushed, as if whatever he'd been thinking was definitely sending him on the fast track to the wrong place in the afterlife. "Just a moment please, I'll check."

He went down a hall toward the back of the room. A minute later, he reappeared and opened a door in the counter for her to come through.

He pointed down the hall. "Third door on your right, ma'am."

Clarissa flinched at suddenly being converted into her mother—another drawback to being in the ministry. When she turned into the third doorway, Detective Josh Baker was on his feet, smiling. He indicated she should take the chair next to his desk.

"Not often that the pastor comes by to make sure that I'm earning my money and keeping the community safe," he cracked.

Clarissa grinned and took a seat. "I have no doubt you more than earn your money. But I'm afraid that I am here to add to your burdens."

His face turned serious. "How's that?"

After taking a moment to organize her thoughts, Clarissa clearly and concisely put forward her reasons for being concerned about the nature of David Ames' death. When she was finished, she was surprised to realize that her heart was beating quickly, as if she had walked up several flights of stairs. She wondered if it was due to being in the police department, or whether she very much wanted to have her suspicions, however valid they were, taken seriously.

Detective Baker stared at the top of his desk for a long minute. "You said that this David Ames was a member of the congregation?" he said eventually.

She nodded. "But from what Jack Spurlock told me, he didn't attend church much at all."

"That's probably why I don't know him. But he picked Jack to tell his story to?"

Clarissa nodded.

"And it had something to do with the past. How far in the past?"

"He didn't say, but Jack suggested that he and Dave had been friends back in high school. Since they're both in their seventies, that could be well over fifty years."

The detective nodded. "Let me just check on the computer." He dug around on the computer for about five minutes, then shook his head. "There's nothing here about a David Ames, or Jack either, for that matter—but the computerized records are pretty spotty before the seventies. I could check the original files down in the basement, but that's a slow, dirty job, and I think I've got a better idea." He picked up his phone and punched in a number. "I'll call my old partner, Arty Winslow. He's retired now, but he was on the job back in the sixties. He may be old, but his memory is better than any computer."

When Artie answered, they shared news about each other's wives, kids, and grandchildren, until Detective Baker finally asked Artie whether he'd ever heard of David Ames. Whatever Artie said, Clarissa could tell by the expression on the detective's face and his surprised grunts that the news was significant, perhaps even disturbing. When he finally hung up with a promise to get together with Artie for coffee in the near future, Clarissa was on tenterhooks wondering what he had learned.

Detective Baker gave her a level look and sighed. "Artie remembered that David Ames had something to do with the murder of Royce Llewellyn," he said, as if the name should mean something to her.

"Who was he?" asked Clarissa. "Was his murder particularly significant?"

"Most folks who have lived in Shore Side for a while have heard about this murder. Royce was the owner of a large hotel and restaurant down on the beachfront called The Surf Side. He was murdered in the summer of 1968. I was only a small child then, but those were bad times with the race riots up in Newark and anti-war protests everywhere. There was a lot of anger around, and no one wanted it to come to Shore Side."

"Are you saying his murder was hushed up?"

"I wouldn't say that exactly, but according to Artie, it wasn't pursued as vigorously as it might have been," the detective explained. "Apparently Llewellyn wasn't exactly a popular guy. He treated his workers like dirt, and had an even more racist attitude than was common at the time. Even the Chamber of Commerce didn't like him. He was an all-around confrontational guy."

"But David Ames was white, so there couldn't have been a racial motive," Clarissa pointed out.

"Yeah, that theory was discounted pretty quickly," he said. "Anyway, one night in June of '68, there was a knock on the door of Llewellyn's house. He lived in a big old place up on Washington. According to his wife, he went to answer the door at eleven o'clock. She heard a shot and rushed to the front of the house. When she got there, he was lying in the foyer with a bullet in his chest."

"Did she see his attacker?"

"She said she didn't. That's not surprising, really; she was probably focused on her husband. He died in the ambulance on the way to the hospital."

"That must have been horrible for her," Clarissa said.

Detective Baker shrugged. "According to Artie, they didn't really get along well. I guess he was as much of a tyrant at home as he was at work."

"Did he physically abuse her?"

"I wouldn't be surprised, but we didn't get involved in that sort of thing as much back then. Different times and all," he said, a shade apologetically.

"So how was David Ames involved?" Clarissa asked.

"He worked as a bartender in Llewellyn's restaurant," Baker answered. "He had a fight with him the day before his death. When Llewellyn fired him, Ames was heard threatening to kill the guy."

"So he must have been the prime suspect."

"Yeah, except that he had a solid alibi for the time of the murder."

Clarissa raised a questioning eyebrow.

"He was drinking with a couple of friends at the Lobster Claw Bar, at the other end of the beach from Llewellyn's house," the detective explained.

"Are a couple of friends really a solid alibi?" she asked. "Did anyone else see him there?"

"It was a Friday night in June and the place was busy. A couple of guys swore that Ames was there sometime during the evening, but they weren't sure he was still around at eleven."

"But his two friends said he was?"

"According to Artie, we couldn't shake them, and there was no way to prove they were lying. Do you want to know who his two buddies were?" Detective Baker asked.

Clarissa nodded.

"Jack Spurlock and Owen Chandler."

Clarissa paused and took a deep breath. She did some calculations in her head. "In '68, David and Jack would have been in their early twenties," she said slowly. "So Jack lied to me. He *did* stay friends with Ames after their time in school together."

Baker nodded. "Looks that way. One of the things you get used to in this job is that people lie to you all the time, even folks you think you know."

"Who is the other friend, Owen Chandler?" Clarissa asked.

"His parents owned The Admiral's Rest, a bed and breakfast down on Lincoln. They died about ten years ago and Owen was their only child, so he inherited. He runs it now. He's kind of a quiet guy who keeps to himself. I've never heard anything bad about him."

Clarissa sat back in her chair and thought things over. What had begun as an inquiry into the death of a member of her congregation had rapidly expanded into a journey through the history of Shore Side.

"What happens next?" she asked Baker.

"I'll have to take it upstairs to the chief because it's a cold case, but I'm pretty sure he'll say that, under the circumstances, Ames' death should be considered suspicious," he confirmed. "At least suspicious enough to have the county medical examiner check over the body before it's released to the family."

"What if it turns out that he was murdered?" Clarissa asked in almost a whisper.

"Then we dig into it, and reopen the Llewellyn case as well. Not that the two are necessarily connected," said the detective. "In either case, we're not going to publicize that we're looking into Ames' death, so I'd appreciate it if you kept this conversation between us."

Clarissa nodded. "Did David Ames have a lot of enemies?"

Baker shrugged. "Hard to say. He wasn't a natural diplomat, and when he was a younger man, Artie said he got into the occasional bar room brawl. He was never arrested that I know about. But later on, when I joined the force, rumor had it that he wasn't above running up to the edge of the law, and I suspect he put a toe over a few times. A guy like that usually has a few enemies in his past who might not be shy about using violence."

Clarissa thought for a moment. "It just seems too coincidental to me that he dies the same day he's getting ready to talk about some event from years ago," she said. "That says to me that this had something to do with the Llewellyn murder."

"You could be right." Detective Baker smiled. "But the first thing you learn as a detective is not to let speculation get too far ahead of the evidence."

Clarissa grinned. "That's a good reminder."

He stood up. "Well, thanks for coming in with this information, Pastor. It may turn out to be very helpful."

"You're welcome."

Suddenly he stared at her with a hard gaze, and she realized he was probably a very different man when dealing with criminals. "And, Pastor, I probably don't need to tell you, but this wouldn't be something that you'd want to get involved in investigating on your own," he warned. "If your suspicions are correct, there might be a murderer out there, and it's not safe for a civilian to be poking around in this matter."

"I wouldn't dream of it," Clarissa said with a smile. "I've got enough to do just keeping the church on an even keel."

He nodded. "See you on Sunday."

"Thanks for your help."

"That's what I'm here to do."

As Clarissa exited through the outer office, the young officer she'd met on the way in called out, "Have a good evening, ma'am."

"You have a good one, too," she responded, resisting the desire to call him "sonny."

Clarissa drove the mile back to the parsonage. After making sure all the doors were locked, she went upstairs to her study in the front of the house and sat by the window, looking out at the desultory traffic on the street below as twilight fell. She found her mind drifting to the past and all the generations of folks who had looked out on the Victorian streets of Shore Side, lost in their own little worlds: worlds that they were the center of and that now no longer existed.

Clarissa had meant it when she'd told Detective Baker that she had no intention of interfering in a police investigation. She truly did have enough things to worry about with getting up to speed with her job. But it deeply bothered her that Jack Spurlock, someone she had instinctively trusted and who she had hoped in time would become a friend, had lied to her.

She promised herself that when he came to the church tomorrow morning to fix the broken latch, she would make a point of talking to him about his relationship with David Ames. Surely she could pursue that matter without getting involved in the investigation of Ames's death. If Jack was going to systematically lie to her, or if he was involved in something shady, it was questionable whether he should continue on as the church's sacristan.

Although tomorrow was a Saturday and she had been working flat out all week, she planned to treat it as a normal workday. Ashley was going to be there, and Clarissa wanted to set a good example by being in the office, as well. There was certainly plenty to do, even without access to the computer. The file cabinets in Clarissa's office were filled with old bulletins, in-house memorabilia, and directives from other church organizations arranged in an order known only to Reverend Hollingsworth, who apparently hadn't been much of an administrator. The files in the outer office weren't any better, since apparently Mrs. Dalrymple had complemented the Reverend's packrat tendencies. Perhaps they actually *were* made for each other.

Clarissa sighed and stood up. There was no sense anticipating tomorrow's problems tonight. Her father had always warned her that thinking about possible difficulties only magnified them, making them seem insurmountable. Prayer and a bit of quiet time before sleep was the best remedy. Tomorrow would take care of itself.

Chapter Five

Clarissa felt rested when she awoke in her bedroom on the second floor at the back of the parsonage. She climbed out of bed and gazed out her window. Being on a corner, she could look down a row of backyards on the street behind her. She found it amusing that many of these Victorians, beautiful and stately on the street side, had gardens in the back that were a hodgepodge of dilapidated sheds, dying plants, and bizarre gazebos. She wondered if this was symbolic of the Victorian view that public appearances were what counted, and private lives could be allowed to be messy, as long as they remained hidden.

She quickly showered and got dressed in a pair of a denim slacks and a chambray shirt, more casual since she didn't have any meetings or appointments today. She planned to start the day by cleaning the office. She didn't want to impose on Mrs. Gunn by having her do that space, as well; plus, there were likely to be some confidential papers lying around that she'd rather keep to herself. She made a mental note to warn Ashley about that. Discretion was essential for a church office manager.

As she went down the stairs, the smell of coffee wafted up, letting her know that Mrs. Gunn was already on the job.

"How about some bacon and eggs this morning?" Mrs. Gunn greeted her as she entered the large kitchen.

Although Clarissa usually had cereal for breakfast, Mrs. Gunn had tried every morning so far to convince her to eat more. "A skinny girl like you needs a good breakfast to get through the day," was her refrain every morning.

Since she was planning to clean this morning, Clarissa agreed to a couple of eggs over easy with whole grain toast, but refused the bacon.

"A little fat never hurt anyone," Mrs. Gunn sniffed, but Clarissa could tell that she was pleased to have at least convinced her to have eggs.

One of the changes Clarissa had made when she began the job was that, instead of eating in lonely splendor as Reverend Hollingsworth had done in the ornate dining room that would seat fifteen comfortably, she ate at the table in the kitchen and chatted with Mrs. Gunn as she worked. For the first couple of days, the cook had been a bit nervous, as if this were some sort of devious ploy by Clarissa to check up on her work, but by now she had settled down, and seemed to enjoy having the young minister to talk with.

Clarissa opened the daily paper, which Mrs. Gunn had brought in from the front walk, and glanced over the headlines. The obituaries on the back reminded her of last night's events.

"David Ames died last night at the hospital," she said softly, putting the paper aside.

"Dave. I remember him from school," Mrs. Gunn mused. "He was a couple of grades ahead of me and always getting into trouble."

"He was a member of the church, but I gather he didn't come much."

"Maybe on the occasional Christmas."

"How did he happen to join in the first place?" Clarissa asked.

"His mother was a member, and she used to bring him along when he was a boy," Mrs. Gunn told her. "After he grew up, he pretty much disappeared. In the last few years, though, he would hang out with some of the guys in the congregation who played golf. He even got to be pretty good friends with the Reverend that way. Not that it ever brought him to Sunday services."

"Have you ever heard of Royce Llewellyn?" Clarissa asked, trying to sound casual.

"Glory, I haven't heard that name in a lot of years," the other woman exclaimed. "How did you come to hear about him?"

"Somebody mentioned the name to me at the hospital," Clarissa replied nonchalantly. "He said something about a murder."

Mrs. Gunn stared across the kitchen with a vague expression on her face, as if she were remembering a distant time and place. "I was still in high school when it happened. It was just before the end of my junior year. Everybody was talking about it. As you can imagine, we don't get many murders in Shore Side."

"I'd imagine not."

"I can see why it might have come up last night; some folks thought that Dave Ames was involved in the murder," Mrs. Gunn said matter-of-factly.

"Did *you* think he had something to do with it?" Clarissa asked.

"No idea. Like I said, he was inclined to get into trouble, but it's a long way from boyhood shenanigans to murder."

"It must have been terrible for Royce Llewellyn's wife to see him die like that," Clarissa remarked.

Mrs. Gunn lowered her voice, even though there was no one else in the room. "Well, I'm sure it was a shock for her, it would be for anyone. But I don't know how upset she truly was. He'd never been exactly faithful, if you know what I mean."

"Oh?"

"From what I overheard my parents saying at the time, he had lots of girlfriends over the years, even when he was married," Mrs. Gunn said, shaking her head. "His last girlfriend was a waitress in his own restaurant, and he'd set her up in a nice apartment right along the beach. Maggie Preston, I think her name was."

"I wonder what his wife thought about all that?"

Mrs. Gunn laughed. "Not much good, I'd imagine. But you could ask her."

"She isn't dead?" Clarissa asked.

"Doris was fifteen years or so younger than Royce. Kind of a trophy wife, I guess you'd call her today. She's up in her late eighties by now, I suppose, but the last I heard, she still lived in that big house up on Washington where he was killed. It's right across from the Blue Heron Restaurant."

"It would be interesting to hear what she has to say," Clarissa agreed—with such alacrity that Mrs. Gunn gave her a look, but said nothing.

Not telling Mrs. Gunn what she was planning to do out of fear of objections, Clarissa went over to the office after breakfast and began cleaning. She began by dusting all the surfaces in her office, then started in with a mop she had found in the back of the office closet. Clarissa was willing to bet that, although Mrs. Dalrymple might have used the mop, Reverend Hollingsworth had probably remained oblivious to its existence.

As she worked, she frequently glanced out her office window to the parking lot, ready to run out in case Jack Spurlock arrived. She wanted to tell him about what she had learned last night about David Ames and Royce Llewellyn, and question him about his involvement.

Eventually she moved on to the outer office, and had just finished there when the door opened and Ashley walked in. She had exchanged yesterday's black dress for a pair of black slacks and a black button-down shirt, which Clarissa speculated must be business casual Goth.

Ashley stared at the mop. "You've been cleaning," she said accusingly. "Couldn't you find someone to do that?"

Clarissa gave her an appraising look.

"Not me," Ashley said quickly, "I meant a cleaning lady or someone."

"I enjoy getting my hands dirty, and simple jobs help me clear my mind," Clarissa said.

Casting her a skeptical look, Ashley took a seat behind her desk. "You said that you need to find the password for this computer?"

"And the one in my office. I imagine Reverend Hollingsworth had a different password for his own computer."

Ashley nodded. "Yeah, he wouldn't have wanted Mrs. Dalrymple spreading his personal information all over town. From what I've heard from my aunt, she was quite the gossip."

"I'm sure the passwords are in a file on the computer," Clarissa said, "but I can't get into the computer to access the files."

"The solution may be simple. Do you have a key to this desk?" Ashley asked.

Clarissa took a small key off her key ring and handed it over. "You may as well keep this. It's your desk now."

Ashley put the key in the lock of the center drawer and opened it. She pulled the drawer all the way out and began feeling around under it. A few seconds later, with a look of triumph on her face, she withdrew a slip of paper and stared at it.

"This was taped under there," she said, waving it in the air. "In my experience, seventy-five percent of people write down their password and hide it somewhere on the desk. Under the center drawer is the most common spot."

She held the paper out to Clarissa, who read the word "affectionate." An interesting choice of password; she never would have guessed that.

"Now the only question left is what the password is to the Reverend's computer," said Ashley.

"Let me check under his drawer," Clarissa said. She rushed into her office and poked around under all the desk drawers, but came up with nothing.

She looked over the top of the desk, which was clear except for the rolodex. On a whim, she leafed through the names until she came to Hollingsworth.

"I'll bet 'handicap' is the key to the Reverend's," she called to Ashley. "It's written in his rolodex next to his name."

"Did Hollingsworth have a handicap?" came the reply.

"As far as I know, only at golf."

Ashley came into the inner office and grinned. "And we know that Mrs. Dalrymple thought she was being 'affectionate' to the Reverend."

Clarissa didn't comment. She was all ready to unlock the mysteries of her computer when she glanced out the window and saw Jack unloading a ladder from his truck.

She walked swiftly through the outer office and headed out the door, leaving Ashley to get settled.

"Hello, Jack," she called out as she reached the parking lot.

He looked over his shoulder from where he was releasing the ladder from the truck and gave her a small smile. "Hey, Pastor," he greeted her. "Are you okay after the shock of last night?"

"I'm better. I wanted to talk to you for a minute."

Jack kept smiling, but she sensed some reluctance in his manner. He slowly pulled the ladder from the truck and turned to face her.

"I wanted you to know that I went to see Detective Josh Baker last night about David's death," she said.

Jack let the ladder slip and it hit the truck, leaving a nasty scratch. "Why did you do that?" he asked, his voice suddenly rough.

Taking a step back and trying to remain calm, Clarissa told him about her conversation with the nurse about what had happened before David's death.

Jack shook his head. "That doesn't amount to anything—certainly not enough to be bothering the police about," he said.

"Detective Baker thought it might be relevant to the Llewellyn murder. You must remember that."

"You should have stayed out of this," Jack said, suddenly angry. "You don't know what you're doing."

"And you shouldn't have lied to me about not being good friends with David Ames," Clarissa shot back. "In fact, you were one of the people who alibied him for the night of the murder. Don't bother to deny it. I heard it directly from Detective Baker."

Jack turned pale. He opened his mouth several times as if about to speak, but no words came out. Grabbing his ladder, he walked across the lot to the church and propped it up against the wall. Clarissa stood for a moment watching him, thinking he might return to continue the conversation. When he ascended the ladder with tools in hand, she decided waiting was fruitless and returned inside to the office.

"I'm going through everything to see what Mrs. Dalrymple had on here," Ashley announced when Clarissa walked back into the outer office.

"Good," Clarissa said, and headed back toward her office.

Ashley gave her a long look. "Is everything all right?"

"Fine," Clarissa sighed, pausing in the doorway. "Sometimes all the church repairs get me down. Let me know if you find a list of the members of the congregation and their addresses. I'd like to compare it to the newsletter mailing list, if we can find it. We should be getting in touch with every member of the congregation at least once a month."

"If we had everyone's e-mail address, we could send the newsletter out that way," Ashley pointed out. "It would save tons in postage."

Clarissa nodded. "Good idea. But first we'll have to find out how many members have e-mail. Some of the older ones may not."

"We could always snail-mail it just to them."

"Agreed. Let's look into it."

Clarissa left Ashley to it and began going through the files on Reverend Hollingsworth's computer. She found a file that contained his past sermons and read through a few; they tended to be a bit dry and scholarly, enlivened only by the occasional golf joke. She also found the minutes to the past year's meetings of the church board. Although it took some reading between the lines, Clarissa got the clear impression that several members of the board wanted the church to reach out more to the wider community, while Reverend Hollingsworth resisted the idea in whatever specific form it took.

When she finally glanced up from the computer screen, Clarissa realized that it was almost noon. She looked out the back window into the parking lot and saw that Jack's truck was gone. A bit disappointed that he hadn't come inside to resume their conversation about Ames' death, she determined that when they next met, she would apologize to him for her harsh words and for pursuing a matter that obviously made him uncomfortable. It was the right thing to do.

She went back into the outer office. "How are you doing?" she asked Ashley.

Her office manager shrugged. "Fathoming the mind of Mrs. Dalrymple is a real mystery ride," she said. "But I should have the basics figured out in a few more hours."

"Well, you can pick that up again on Monday," Clarissa told her. "Let's knock it off for today. After all, it *is* Saturday, and a beautiful day at that. Keep a timesheet of your hours worked so you don't go over twenty-five in a week. We'll count today toward next week, okay?"

"Okay." Ashley stood up to leave.

"See you on Monday at nine," Clarissa said, then paused. "Or will you be in church tomorrow?"

Ashley frowned her dismay. "I'll be there."

"But I thought you didn't . . ."

". . . believe in that sort of thing," Ashley finished for her. "I don't. But my aunt made it a condition of my staying with her. She has more rules than a convent." She rolled her eyes.

Clarissa smiled. "Just keep telling yourself that it's free room and board."

"That's my personal mantra."

Chapter Six

After having lunch, Clarissa told Mrs. Gunn that she was going out for a walk around town to familiarize herself with the layout of the small community. She grabbed a map from the drawer in her study and searched out Washington Street; it was close to the pedestrian mall that ran through the former business center of town. Clarissa planned a walk that would begin at the north end of Washington and go south. Once she saw the Blue Huron Restaurant, she'd know the Llewellyn house was right across the street. What could she say? She was curious to see where it had all gone down those many years ago.

She walked along in no particular hurry. Many of the houses boasted very pretty gardens with spring flowers in full bloom. The sun filtering through the tall trees, the warm air, and the captivating scents made it a very pleasant stroll. Clarissa found herself thinking how lucky she was to have such a beautiful community for her first full-time assignment.

She'd almost turned down the job when it was first offered to her because she'd always pictured herself working in a place where the need was greater: a gritty urban neighborhood or an impoverished rural area. When the job offer had come through, she'd called her friend Pat Orwell, an older woman who was also a minister and someone Clarissa thought of as a mentor, and expressed her reservations about accepting the position.

"Your dedication is admirable," Pat had said, "but you have to realize that there is a need for ministry everywhere. Sometimes the places that look the most serene are the ones most in need."

Clarissa had taken her words to heart. And as she walked along, she realized that it was up to her to make this job into something that was of real service to the community's spiritual and physical needs.

Clarissa was so engrossed in making plans for what she would do as a minister that it barely registered with her when she was in front of the Blue Huron. Only the life-sized statue of the bird on the front lawn caught her attention.

She paused and looked across the street at the large, turreted Victorian that occupied the corner lot. Painted a bright yellow with blue trim, it looked to be in fine condition, as if the owner took loving care of it. Clarissa walked across the street and stood in front of it for a moment, staring up at the three floors of windows.

"Quite a pile, isn't it?" a voice chirped from the front porch.

Looking carefully, Clarissa could see a woman sitting in a rocker, studying her. Clarissa laughed in response. "It's certainly grand," she said. "I live in one like it myself, but it's not up to this level."

"You live in town?" the woman asked.

"I'm the new minister at the Shore Side Community Church."

"Been a Baptist my whole life, but a woman minister is a good idea. Why don't you come up on the porch and sit a while, if you've got the time? You can always just tell me if I get too boring like old people tend to do."

Clarissa opened the gate in the wrought iron fence that ran across the front of the property, and went up onto the porch. A thin older woman wearing nicely tailored slacks and a pretty blue blouse was seated in one of the rockers.

She reached out her hand as Clarissa drew near. "I'm Doris Llewellyn," she said, holding out her hand.

Clarissa gently shook the papery hand. "Clarissa Abbot."

"Have a seat," Doris said, nodding to the chair next to her own. "Nothing's better than having a chat on the front porch and watching the world go by."

Clarissa sat down in the other rocker. "Seems to be a quiet street," she commented.

"Trust me, if you wait long enough, everyone in Shore Side eventually walks by. Where do you come from?"

"Northern New Jersey."

"Bet you find things a bit slower down here."

"Yes. Much more relaxed."

"So how does the minister of the Shore Side Community Church, one I don't happen to go to, end up standing in front of my house?" Doris asked.

Clarissa considered saying something bland—she was out for a walk and just happened to notice the house—but something about the woman's shrewd brown eyes told her that wouldn't fly. Clarissa also didn't like to lie, considering this the first step to a lot of worse behaviors.

"I have to admit that I purposely walked past because I heard the story about your husband's murder," she admitted honestly.

Doris nodded. "I figured. That's about the only reason folks stop in front of my house. Not that it happens very much anymore, although I still get the occasional fan of unsolved mysteries. So how did you happen to hear about Royce's murder? Some gossipy woman at a church social?"

"No," Clarissa replied. "David Ames was a member of my congregation. He died last night, and your late husband's name came up."

Doris Llewellyn stared across the street, as if trying to see something on the other side. "A lot of people at the time thought that he killed Royce," she said musingly.

"Did you?"

"I was never sure. There were so many candidates. Royce was a difficult man." She sighed. "Oh, don't get me wrong, he could be fun, and certainly exciting, but it was always a roller coaster ride. And when he got angry about something—which happened a lot—well, you'd better keep away, a long way away."

"I heard that your husband had a fight with Ames shortly before he was killed," Clarissa said slowly.

"That's what I heard, too. And it wouldn't surprise me. Royce was always getting in fights with the men at work." Doris smiled. "We'd say today that my husband had anger issues. In those days, we just said he had a bad temper. Anyway, maybe Dave Ames *did* kill him. I didn't know him, but from what I've heard, he had something of a temper, as well. But like I said, there were lots of other possibilities. Those were pretty violent times around here."

"There were a lot of angry men around."

"And, of course, it could have been an angry woman."

Clarissa maintained a neutral expression.

Doris smiled. "You're too polite to say it, but I'm sure you've heard that my husband liked the ladies a little too much." She paused and her lips trembled.

"That must have been hard," Clarissa said softly.

"I'll admit when I first found out about it, I was hurt and furious," Doris said. "I wanted to take my daughter and go right home to my parents."

"But you didn't?"

"No. Partly because of Elise, my daughter," she said. "Despite his shortcomings, Royce was a good father, and she worshipped the ground he walked on. I didn't want to take that away from her. I kept telling myself that once she turned eighteen, I'd tell her the truth and let the chips fall where they may. So I waited and tried to pretend that I didn't care about all the other women."

"How old was Elise when her father was killed?" Clarissa asked.

"Fifteen. And then everything came out about Royce and all his philandering. It was the talk of her school. Finally, she just refused to go to class. I thought it would kill her, so I sent her away to a private school to avoid all the gossip. But by then, most of the damage had been done."

That must have been awful, Clarissa thought. Her heart went out to Elise. "You said that your daughter was only part of the reason you stayed with him?" she said gently.

Doris smiled sadly. "I loved the louse. I knew my life would never be the same without him. And it hasn't been." She paused and sniffed. "Funny how fifty years can disappear in the blink of an eye."

Clarissa gave her a sympathetic smile. "Was there anyone other than David Ames that you thought might have shot your husband?" she asked.

"Like I said, I always thought it might have been a woman."

"Any particular woman?" Clarissa pressed.

"The last one, Maggie Preston," Doris answered. "The one who worked at the hotel and that he set up in an apartment in town. I can tell you, I threw her out of there as soon as I could. I always figured that she might have snapped when Royce dropped her."

"Did he drop her?"

She smiled grimly. "He always dropped them—in time. But I have to hand it to Maggie, she didn't let herself be shamed out of town. She still lives here, even has a little business called Maggie's Luncheonette down by the beach."

Clarissa made a mental note of the diner. "It must have been very hard being here alone that night when your husband was shot," she said.

"Well . . ."

Doris stopped speaking as a woman opened the gate and came up the walk. She was carrying a supermarket bag in each hand. She put her foot on the first step of the porch very carefully, as if it might disappear from beneath her. When she looked up and saw Clarissa, she paused and gave Doris a quizzical look.

"This is my daughter, Elise," Doris said. "Elise, this is Clarissa Abbot, the new minister at Shore Side Community Church. She happened to walk by, and I invited her to stop by and chat for a while."

Elise smiled. She put down her shopping bags and took Clarissa's outstretched hand. She was tall like her mother, but more sturdily built. She gave Clarissa's hand a trembling shake.

"I was just filling Clarissa in on all the good restaurants in Shore Side—not that I get out to them much anymore," Doris continued.

Clarissa wondered if Doris had some kind of memory problem, since they certainly hadn't been discussing restaurants. But when she glanced at Doris, trying to keep the surprise from her face, the older woman gave her a look that warned her to keep quiet.

"Nice to meet you," Elise said. "I'm afraid Mother doesn't get many people who are just visiting."

Clarissa nodded, trying not to look guilty.

"How did you happen to drop by?" Elise asked. "Neither one of us has ever attended your church."

"I was taking a walk around the neighborhood and stopped to admire the architecture. Your mother kindly invited me to sit with her a while," Clarissa said.

"I see. Mother can be very friendly. She loves to meet new people. Well, I'd better get this stuff in the refrigerator," Elise said, reaching down to pick up her bags. "I hope to see you again sometime, Reverend Abbot."

Neither Clarissa nor Doris spoke for a minute or so after Elsie went inside.

"She doesn't like it when I talk to people about the past," Doris whispered. "She thinks everyone who comes to see me is either a reporter or a gossipmonger. That might have been true in the first few years, but now, it's usually just folks who are curious about the history of Shore Side."

"I suppose it's because your daughter is still sensitive about what happened back then," Clarissa mused.

"Yes. She hates thinking about those days." Doris gave her a small smile. "But that's the time I remember best. Some days I can't remember yesterday, but fifty years ago is clear as a bell."

Clarissa stood up and put out her hand again. "Well, I'd better be going now," she said. "It was wonderful talking with you."

Doris put her frail hand in Clarissa's. "I enjoyed it, as well. Stop by again some time. If I'm not out on the porch, just ring the doorbell. I'm usually around, unless I have a doctor's appointment. That's usually the highlight of my week nowadays." She chuckled good-naturedly.

Clarissa waved when she reached the sidewalk and got a cheerful wave from Doris in return. As she walked back toward the parsonage, she thought over what she had learned. Royce Llewellyn had certainly been a philanderer and a short-tempered bully. But he had also been a man of some charm—he'd managed to attract an intelligent woman like Doris, after all—and he had been a caring father. But with his long list of enemies, it wasn't any surprise that the police had found the case hard to solve fifty years ago. It would be even harder today when many of the principals were probably dead. But if David Ames had indeed been murdered, that had happened only yesterday, and Clarissa had a suspicion that solving his murder would lead back to Royce Llewellyn's killer.

But, she warned herself, as Detective Baker had made clear, this wasn't any of her business. So why was she so interested? Deep down, she knew that it was because David Ames had needed her help. He was the first person who had come to her for assistance in her new church, and she had failed him. If she had been more convincing as a pastor, maybe he would have told her his secret, and he'd possibly still be alive.

She couldn't make it up to David, but at least she could do what she could to find out what had happened to him. She'd just have to be careful, that's all.

Chapter Seven

The next morning, Clarissa stood at the door at the end of the church service, shaking hands with people as they left. She felt pretty pleased; she thought her sermon on how self-centeredness prevents us from relating to others and to our community had gone well. Also, it was another beautiful day, and as she stood in the doorway, she could smell all the wonderful scents of spring.

Clarissa was also happy to find that she recognized a fair number of the people filing past her, and could even recall many of them by name. She made a careful point of saying each of their names, and listening attentively to any corrections. Those who hadn't been in attendance last Sunday stopped to introduce themselves and welcome her to the area. So, all things considered, the line moved rather slowly.

"How are you doing, Pastor?" Detective Josh Baker asked her with an appraising glance when his turn arrived.

"Just fine," she replied, shaking his hand.

"No bad effects from the other night?"

Clarissa shook her head, feeling guilty that she had already gotten more involved in the Ames case than he would have wanted.

"Good," Baker said, giving her hand a pat. "I'll let you know if we find out anything new about what happened to Ames. I should have something by tomorrow afternoon."

"Thank you," she said as he left, glad the police were keeping her in the loop.

Finally, Clarissa could see the end of the line. In last place was a rather handsome man in his early thirties whom she had never met. When he reached her and extended his right hand, she glanced down at his left and saw that he wasn't wearing a wedding ring.

"That was a wonderful sermon. There's a lesson that I really have to take to heart," he said after they'd shaken hands.

"Are you particularly self-centered?" Clarissa asked without thinking.

He blushed slightly and smiled. "Probably not more than most. But we all get too caught up in being at the center of our own little universes."

"You're right about that. I know that I do." She paused. "I don't think we've met. I'm Clarissa Abbot." She felt a little silly extending her hand again in introduction, but committed to the gesture.

"I'm Andrew Corrigan," he said as he shook her hand once more. He didn't seem at all perturbed. "Actually, I was wondering if I could stop by and see you some time," he added.

Clarissa wondered for a moment if he was asking for a date. It was certainly a unique setting in which to make the approach.

Her confusion must have shown on her face because the man quickly said, "On business! . . . I need to see you on a business matter."

"What kind of business?" Clarissa asked, somewhat suspiciously.

Andrew shook his head and smiled. "I'm doing this pretty badly. Let me start at the beginning," he said. "The law firm I work for, Corrigan and Bailey, represents the Shore Side Community Church, and there's a legal matter that I'd like to discuss with you. We'd been talking to Reverend Hollingsworth for several months, urging him to get the church to make a decision, but he kept putting us off. This is a time-sensitive matter, and I'd really like to discuss it with you."

"I can't make any business decisions for the church—the church board has to do that—but I can certainly meet with you, get the information, and convey the matter to the board," Clarissa offered. "I'm free tomorrow. How about ten o'clock?"

"That will be fine," Andrew said with a relived smile. "You're much easier to deal with than Reverend Hollingsworth."

"Good," she said. "Well, I look forward to having a very cordial relationship with your firm."

"I'm sure we'll get along famously. And I really did enjoy the sermon."

Clarissa blushed. "Sorry I teased you about it."

He grinned. "The first step in being less self-centered is being able to take a little teasing."

Clarissa smiled and shook his hand one final time. "Until tomorrow."

When she'd made certain that no one remained in the church, Clarissa walked down the steps to the front walk. A number of congregation members were standing around in small groups, conversing. Not wanting to intrude on any of them, she stood there for a moment alone.

"Who's the hunky guy?" Ashley asked, sidling up to her. She was dressed in a severe black suit, which made her look like a funeral director on Halloween.

"The church lawyer," Clarissa replied easily.

"Too bad. I thought maybe it was more personal." Suddenly Ashley looked stricken. "Sorry, I guess you're not supposed to be interested in that sort of thing."

"I'm a minister, not a nun."

"Oh, okay. So . . ."

"Most ministers get married."

"But they're guys."

"So?"

Ashley smiled. "I get your point. What's sauce for the goose is sauce for the gander, as my aunt would say."

"Precisely."

"Well, maybe you'll get lucky, and there will be a lot of church legal business to discuss," Ashley said with a wink.

"As a matter of fact, he's got an appointment with me for tomorrow at ten," Clarissa said.

Ashley grinned. "You do work fast."

"It's purely business!" Clarissa protested.

"That's what they all say. Oops, there's my aunt waving to me. Time for me to drive her home so we can enjoy a giant roast with lots of artery-clogging gravy."

"That sounds good."

"Only if you don't plan on having a long future." Ashley snorted. "I was a vegetarian before I moved in with my aunt."

"Couldn't you still prepare your own food?" Clarissa asked.

Ashley rolled her eyes. "The kitchen is off-limits to everyone but my aunt. Plus she insists that I need to be fattened up, or I'll never find a man. Like I care."

"Don't you?"

"Maybe," Ashley said with a grin. "But any guy interested in me will have to get over a lot more than my being a few pounds underweight."

Clarissa smiled. "You'd be surprised what people can get over when the chemistry is there."

"You might be right about that."

After Ashley walked away, Clarissa headed back to the empty parsonage. She had insisted that Mrs. Gunn take Sundays off to be with her friends and family.

After some wrangling, the woman had finally agreed, but only if the meal she prepared for Saturday night was large enough to double for Sunday's dinner.

Clarissa went up to her bedroom and changed out of her robe and clerical garb before heading back downstairs. She knew there was a large casserole in the fridge that she had barely put a dent in last night, but she had other plans. Her conversation with Doris Llewellyn had given her an idea, and she decided to go to lunch at Maggie's Luncheonette in the hopes that she might get to meet Royce Llewellyn's old girlfriend.

Clarissa had a pretty good idea of where the luncheonette was located, so she cut across town toward the ocean and hopped up on the boardwalk to head downtown. The sun was warm and bright, with the temperature in the mid-seventies, so it was the perfect day for a stroll. There was a gentle breeze off the ocean, and she saw that a number of people had already set up on the beach. The ocean was probably still cold, but it would be a nice day to wade in the waves and sunbathe.

Although her fair skin was inclined to burn if she got too much exposure, Clarissa enjoyed lying on the beach under an umbrella. But the thought of doing it by herself made her feel lonely. Aside from Ashley, she had no acquaintances in town her own age, and she somehow didn't see Ashley as the beach bunny type. But, she reassured herself, she'd only been in town a week or so. Surely she'd quickly make friends.

Clarissa knew that she was really missing Tyler. Both of them had been studying to be ministers, and they'd dated steadily during their last two years of seminary, eventually considering themselves engaged. Then, about three months ago, right after they'd gotten their position assignments—the breakup.

Still too painful to think about, Clarissa pushed it out of her mind, and concentrated instead on the beautiful day.

About a quarter of a mile along the boardwalk, she noticed a sign across the road announcing that she'd arrived at Maggie's Luncheonette. She left the boardwalk, crossed the street, and headed into the restaurant.

There, she took a table for two. When the waitress finally came along—she was quite busy with tourists having late breakfasts—Clarissa ordered a tuna on rye and a cup of tea.

She glanced around the small eatery and saw a woman in her seventies, who looked vigorous and fit, busy seating people and helping the two waitresses clear the tables. She heard one of the customers at the counter refer to her as 'Maggie.'

When the people at the table next to Clarissa paid their bill and left, Maggie came over to clean their table.

Clarissa cleared her throat and the woman looked at her. "An old acquaintance of yours died just the other day: David Ames," she said. It was a bold move, but how else would she get the information she was looking for? She owed it to David.

Maggie paused and stared hard at Clarissa. "Now there's a name I haven't heard in a long time. And who are you?" she demanded.

"The pastor at the Shore Side Community Church," was Clarissa's reply. "I went to see David in the hospital because he was a member of the congregation. He died shortly after I talked with him."

The older woman sat down across from Clarissa. "Who would have thought Dave was a churchgoer?" she said. "Well, none of us is getting any younger, and folks like Dave and I are kind of getting up there. And from what I've heard, Dave never treated his body like a temple." She frowned. "So you just thought you'd stop by and fill me in on his death?"

Clarissa ignored the touch of sarcasm. "You knew him pretty well from when you worked at the hotel, didn't you?" she pressed.

"Oh, sure, he was one of the bartenders. He could be a real funny guy when he wanted to be, but he had quite the temper if you rubbed him the wrong way." Maggie gave Clarissa a shrewd glance. "But you probably know all about his fight with Royce, and I'm sure the good folks at church had told you about Royce's murder."

"I'm sure his death must have been very upsetting to you."

Maggie stared across the room. "I know that most people thought that I was just his little piece of fluff on the side." She gave a humorless laugh. "Hard to imagine me that way now. But I was quite a looker in my time, and Royce really cared for me. It wasn't the same as it had been with all the ones that came before me. If he hadn't been murdered, we'd have ended up together."

Clarissa nodded, wondering how much of that was self-deception. "David told me that he had some information he wanted to pass on," she said. "He didn't say what it was about, and as far as I know, he died without telling anyone."

"And you're wondering whether it had anything to do with Royce's murder because a lot of people suspected Dave of being involved." Maggie leaned back in her chair. "Well, I never believed that, and I told him so the first time I saw him after the killing. But Dave always acted a little shifty, so it could be that he knew more about it than he was willing to admit."

"But he never hinted to you about what he knew?"

She shook her head.

"If you didn't think David killed Royce, who did you think was responsible?" Clarissa asked.

Maggie frowned and twisted the cloth in her hands. "Why are you asking all of these questions? What's it to you? You weren't even born when all of this happened."

"I feel bad that David never got to tell anyone what he obviously wanted to get off his chest. He wanted the truth to come out and so do I," Clarissa explained.

"Sometimes knowing the truth doesn't help anyone, honey. But for what it's worth, I always figured that his wife, Doris, killed Royce because she knew the day was coming fast when he'd be leaving her for me."

"She thinks *you* did it because Royce was going to drop you like he did all the others."

Maggie's lips formed a tight line, and she quickly got to her feet. She grabbed the arm of a passing waitress. "This one will be taking her meal to go," Maggie said, nodding at Clarissa.

"I'm sorry if I offended you," Clarissa said.

"I'm not offended. I know what I know. And I think this is something you should keep out of." Without saying another word, Maggie walked to a door in the back of the restaurant and headed into the kitchen.

The waitress quickly brought Clarissa her sandwich in a plastic box and her tea in a cardboard cup. After paying, Clarissa walked across the street to the boardwalk and sat down on a bench to eat her lunch and watch the ocean.

The sandwich was good, but her thoughts were unsettled. Nevertheless, she was determined to get to the bottom of this. For David's sake.

Chapter Eight

Monday morning, Clarissa was already in her office working on next Sunday's sermon when Ashley walked into the outer office and stood in her doorway.

"Morning, Boss," she said in greeting.

"Good morning," Clarissa replied. "How was your roast beef dinner?"

"Okay, I guess. At least the EMTs didn't have to come with a defibrillator to revive me." Ashley gave her a long look, picking over the young minister's outfit. "A dark red silk blouse, huh? We're a bit more stylish than usual today. That should impress the legal beagle."

Clarissa smiled. "I just felt like dressing up more this morning."

"I know, I know. There was no special reason."

Clarissa quickly changed the subject before Ashley could tease her further. "Have you found a file on Mrs. Dalrymple's computer marked 'legal?'" she asked, but Ashley shook her head. Clarissa sighed. "I was hoping to get a little background on what this matter might be about before the meeting."

"Well, there could be a whole set of legal files buried under some other title. Mrs. Dalrymple's way of doing things was a bit eccentric. I'll take a look," Ashley offered, and disappeared around the corner to do just that.

Clarissa sat back in her plush leather chair, courtesy of Reverend Hollingsworth, and thought about the Ames case. She wasn't sure what to do next, and thought that she might benefit from bouncing ideas off of someone else. But it was hard to know whom to talk to. Detective Baker had told her not to tell anyone that David Ames had possibly been murdered. Still, without talking to someone, she didn't know what her next step should be.

She heard the keyboard clacking in the outer office, and it occurred to her that, although she had only known her a couple of days, Ashley was the person she knew best who probably had no connection with the town back in the time of the Llewellyn murder.

Clarissa got out of her chair and walked into the outer office. She paused in the doorway to talk to Ashley, who looked up from her computer.

"Do you remember when you took this job, I told you that there would be some things that had to be kept confidential? Things that you can't even tell your aunt?" Clarissa asked.

"I remember," Ashley said, her eyes widening.

Clarissa pulled over a waiting room chair and sat down. "What I'm going to tell you now is one of those things."

Clarissa then proceeded to tell her everything she had learned so far about the Ames case.

"Wow!" Ashley said when Clarissa was done. "You're really not afraid to get into things. You're a regular Agatha Whosis."

"Christie?"

"Right. But, you know, maybe the cops are on to something," Ashley said thoughtfully. "If somebody *did* murder this Ames guy, then there's a killer out there, and he may not like you poking into things."

"All I'm doing is asking a few questions."

"There's nothing in this life that will get you into more trouble faster."

"I'll be careful," Clarissa promised. "I'm just trying to decide who to talk to next."

Ashley rolled her eyes. "You're on the stubborn side, aren't you?"

"Let's call it 'persistent.' So whom shall I see next?" Clarissa asked.

Ashley thought for a moment. "How about having another chat with Jack Spurlock?" she suggested.

"He was pretty hostile two days ago," Clarissa said doubtfully. "I'm not sure he'll tell me anything."

"He's had some time to calm down by now. Heck, he's the church handyman; he should be willing to answer your questions. You're sort of his boss," Ashley pointed out.

"Good idea. I'll have a talk with him."

"By the way, I notice that you've got a pretty fashionable pair of slacks on, as well. Another special effort for Andrew the lawyer?" Ashley winked.

Clarissa grinned. "Just projecting a businesslike image."

"Hmm. I'd say the image is a bit warmer than that."

Clarissa was about to respond when Andrew Corrigan walked into the room. He paused for a second at the sight of Ashley, who was wearing a black dress that reached almost to the floor, but then he smiled and gave her a friendly nod.

He looked longer and more appreciatively at Clarissa, who reached out and shook his hand before introducing him to Ashley. She then led him into her office.

"This isn't exactly what I would have expected," he said, marveling at the wood-paneled walls.

"It was decorated to Reverend Hollingsworth's taste," Clarissa explained.

"Of course."

"You've never been in this office before?" Clarissa asked, surprised.

"Well, I just started working for my father's law firm. He's the Corrigan in Corrigan and Bailey. He handled all of the legal business for the church," Andrew said, turning around to take in all of the office.

"Has he retired?" Clarissa asked.

"Cut back on his workload is more like it," he said. "I used to be with a large firm in Manhattan, but when I got tired of the rat race a few months ago, Dad offered to take me in as a junior partner so he could ease into retirement."

Clarissa sat down behind her desk and motioned for Andrew to take the chair opposite. "Did you grow up here in Shore Side?" she asked.

"That's right," he replied, taking a seat. "I lived here until I graduated from high school. I went away to college and law school, although I came back for summers and holidays. And then I was living in New York City."

"How do you like being back home?"

Andrew smiled. "It took me a few weeks to get accustomed to the slower pace, but now I love it. I think I'll live a lot longer working a normal week instead of the fourteen-hour days I had to put in up in the city. I'll have some time to really live my life now."

"I know what you mean. I've only been here a little over a week, and I can already feel myself slowing down to really appreciate every moment of the day." Clarissa would have enjoyed spending more time getting to know Andrew, but she realized this wasn't a social call. "So, what's this legal issue you wanted to discuss?" she asked, getting down to business.

"Well, as you may know, the church owns ten acres of land down on the southern border of Shore Side," Andrew said. "The church has owned it for over a hundred years. It's my understanding that a member of the congregation deeded it to the church in her will. It's mostly marsh and meadowlands, but it's very popular with birders and is quite a wildlife habitat."

"I wasn't aware of that," Clarissa said.

Andrew raised an eyebrow. "I'm surprised Reverend Hollingsworth didn't mention it to you before he left."

"He left rather quickly. We didn't have much time to talk." Clarissa was starting to wonder if the Reverend had intentionally kept her in the dark.

"He never seemed to have much time to talk to my dad, either," Andrew said. "The problem is that the land has no designated environmental status, so it has no state or federal protection. Since the land is swampy and not really suitable for building, that was never an issue up until now."

"What's happened?" she asked.

"Someone has offered to purchase the land from the church."

"And what does this person want it for?"

"His plan is to put up a high-rise condominium. There's a real shortage of condos for sale in Shore Side, so he'd probably have no trouble selling them at a good price."

"Would the town be willing to give him permission to put up something like that?" she wondered. "It seems rather out of character with the Victorian flavor of the place."

"The man who wants to buy the land is Kenneth Rogers," Andrew informed her. "He owns KR Construction. They've put up a number of high-rise condominiums up and down the Jersey shore. He's a powerful man, and apparently managed to convince a majority of the town council to go along with his proposal."

"How did he convince them?"

Andrew shrugged. "I wouldn't care to say. But to take the high-minded approach, it is possible that the members of the council are looking improve the town's tax base."

Clarissa nodded. "Did you ever get to speak with Reverend Hollingsworth about this?"

"My dad did. Hollingsworth seemed to be in favor of the sale. Dad warned him that various environmental groups might seek to block construction, but the Reverend seemed to feel that as long as the sale went through, the lawsuits would be a problem for the construction company, not the church."

"It wouldn't be good publicity for Shore Side Community Church to be seen as more concerned with money than with the environment," Clarissa noted.

"We did point that out to him, but he seemed to feel that the church could really use the money."

She hadn't heard anything about the church being in dire financial straits, but perhaps the church board was waiting until the next official meeting to break the bad news to her. "How much money are we talking about?" she asked.

"My father was party to the early negotiations. For the ten acres, the amount being offered was five million," Andrew said. "But that was only a preliminary figure. It would likely have gone up."

Clarissa's jaw dropped. Five million, if invested wisely, would certainly insure the future of the church, and allow for programs that would assist the needs of the community. "I can see why Reverend Hollingsworth found it tempting," she said.

"He was also friends with Rogers. Apparently they played golf together."

"Yes, I gather the Reverend did a lot of that."

"My impression from what Hollingsworth told us is that the church board is divided down the middle on the issue," Andrew said. "Some of the board are strong environmentalists and preservationists, while others want to take the money."

"Well, the decision isn't mine, thank goodness," Clarissa said. "In fact, it's not even the church board's decision to make. The board can vote to recommend a course of action, but if I understand the church governance structure correctly, on an issue as important as this one, the entire congregation would have to vote."

Andrew smiled. "Democracy in action—that's refreshing in a religious institution. So there's no way to tell how things will turn out?"

"Not really," she replied. "I'm sure if the board were unanimous on something, the congregation would probably go along, but if the board is split, it could go either way. But let me get in touch with Ramona Russell, the chair of the church board. Maybe she can give me an idea of how far along this matter has gotten and when it might be coming up for a vote. I'll give you a call back as soon as I know something."

Andrew reached across the desk and handed her a card. "This has both my office number and my cell. Give me a call anytime." He paused and smiled. "I know you've just gotten into town and most likely don't know many people here, and I realize how that feels. Most of my friends from school left Shore Side years ago. So, since we're two lonely souls, I wondered if you'd like to have dinner with me. That is, if you don't have a boyfriend or significant other."

Clarissa returned his smile. The image of Tyler flashed through her mind, but she pushed it away. That was the past and in an old place; Andrew was the present in a new place.

"No, I'm on my own, and I'd like that," she replied.

"Saturday night?" Andrew asked.

"Could we make it Friday?" she asked. "I like to rest up on Saturday night. Sunday is kind of my big day of the week."

He laughed. "Friday it is."

Once Andrew had left, Ashley came into the office and smiled at Clarissa. "So, was he really here about legal business, or just funny business?"

Clarissa ignored her quip. "What do you know about the marshland to the south of town?" she asked.

"Dismal swamp, you mean," Ashley snorted. "A lot of people tromp around out there looking at birds. And when I was in high school, the more adventurous couples would use it as a kind of lovers' lane. I guess it's okay if you don't mind mosquito bites in sensitive places."

"Well, apparently Shore Side Community Church owns it, and someone wants to buy it," Clarissa said.

Ashley paused. "Hmm, hard call. Do you protect the creatures or the pocketbook?"

"Exactly."

"Was that all you talked about?"

Clarissa hesitated.

"Did he ask you out?" Ashley demanded.

Clarissa blushed slightly. "As a matter of fact, we're going out to dinner on Friday."

"So there *was* a little funny business mixed in," Ashley said with a note of triumph in her voice.

Clarissa grinned. "Maybe you could say that."

Ashley gave her a double thumbs-up. "I like the way you work, Boss. I like the way you work."

Chapter Nine

Clarissa was sitting in the kitchen, eating her lunch and half-listening to Mrs. Gunn talk about the price of eggs at the local grocery store. Her mind had drifted away to the Ames case, and she was giving serious consideration to contacting Jack Spurlock again.

"What would you like me to make for your dinner tonight?" Mrs. Gunn suddenly asked.

Clarissa's mind snapped back to the present. "There's still plenty of that casserole left over from Sunday. I could just have some more of that."

Mrs. Gunn shook her head firmly. "That's why you're so thin, you don't care enough about food! You need more variety."

"Okay," Clarissa said. She had learned to pick her battles with the housekeeper. "Then why don't you take the casserole home with you for dinner tonight?"

"If you're sure . . ."

"Of course, we wouldn't want good food to go to waste."

Mrs. Gunn paused. "Then how about a nice pork chop for tonight?"

"Sounds great."

"I can write down the directions for how to do it. I'm sure you could follow them."

Clarissa had baked and broiled a number of pork chops in her life, but she didn't want to disabuse Mrs. Gunn of her view that she was a complete novice in the kitchen. The older woman seemed to enjoy providing for her.

"That would be very nice," Clarissa said. "I'm sure I could follow your directions."

"And I'll fix a nice salad and some mashed potatoes before I go. I'll leave you directions on how to heat up the potatoes in the microwave."

"Great."

Mrs. Gunn nodded with a satisfied smile on her face as she pulled a bag of potatoes out of the pantry.

"I had a chat with Jack Spurlock the other day when he was working on the church window," Clarissa mentioned. "What do you know about him?"

Mrs. Gunn got the thoughtful expression on her face that she usually had when remembering the past. "He's a few years older than me, so I didn't really know him in school," she said. "He was a bit wild as a boy, and used to hang out with Dave Ames and Owen Chandler. They were together so much folks used to call them the 'Three Musketeers.' I imagine they got into their share of trouble. Nothing serious, mind, but the kind of pranks that young guys get up to."

"Jack doesn't seem particularly wild now," Clarissa observed. "He *is* the church maintenance man, after all."

"He changed like night and day once he met Marcie Green. After they got married, she brought him to our church. In a few years, they had three children and were all settled down," Mrs. Gunn explained. "Marcie is a lovely woman and living proof that a good woman can civilize a man."

"What did Jack do for a living originally?"

"He worked for a contractor that restores Victorian homes around town. Still works part-time, as far as I know. He's a fine carpenter. We're lucky to have him."

"I'm sure."

Clarissa's phone rang, and she saw that it was Detective Baker calling. She excused herself and went into the front room to answer.

"You were right," Baker said as soon as she picked up. "I just got the preliminary report on the cause of death for David Ames. He didn't die of heart failure, as was first thought. He was smothered."

Clarissa gasped; her suspicions had been confirmed. "How can they tell?" she asked.

"He had bloodshot eyes, a high level of carbon dioxide in his blood, and some fibers from the pillow in his nose and mouth. I'm sure they'll know more once they've examined him further, but there doesn't seem to be any doubt. Somebody put a pillow over his face and pressed down hard."

Clarissa thought back to the frail man she had seen in the bed. He would have struggled, but anyone vigorous and determined could have held him down. "So what happens next?" she asked.

"We declare it a homicide and start investigating," Baker replied. "I'm going over to the hospital this afternoon to talk to everyone who was working on the floor that night, to see if I can get a better description of that hooded figure seen leaving Ames' room."

"What about connecting it to the Llewellyn case?"

"We don't know there *is* a connection at this time," Baker said.

"But David was going to tell Jack Spurlock something right before he was killed," Clarissa protested.

"Sure, Pastor, but remember what I said about getting ahead of the evidence," the detective cautioned. "First of all, we don't know that Ames was murdered because of what he was going to tell Jack. Dave may have had lots of enemies here in town. He lived here his whole life, and he wasn't exactly as pure as the driven snow. And even if he *was* killed because of what he was going to tell Jack, we don't know that it had anything to do with the Llewellyn murder."

"Doesn't it stand to reason?" Clarissa said, hearing a note of stubbornness in her voice.

There was a long pause on the other end. "All I'll grant you is that it's a possibility," he said. "And we'll consider it."

"Well, at least talk to Jack and try to find out what he thinks David wanted to talk to him about."

"That's definitely on our list. And, by the way, we're not putting out the fact that Ames was murdered as public information, so keep it under your hat," Detective Baker told her.

"Sure. Thanks for calling and filling me in."

"My pleasure, and remember, this isn't something that a civilian should get involved in, especially now that we're certain it's a homicide," he warned.

"I'll definitely keep that in mind." With that, she hung up.

After ending her call to the detective, she immediately called Jack Spurlock.

"Hello, Jack. I need to see you," she told him as soon as he answered.

"I'm on a job right now, Pastor, I can't just pick up and leave," he protested.

"We need to talk more about David Ames. I can come to wherever you are."

There was a loud exhalation of breath, and when Jack spoke again, his voice was more subdued. "I'm working on a white Victorian at 51 Marshal Street. I'll be around back, so come and find me."

Clarissa agreed and quickly hung up. She said goodbye to Mrs. Gunn, who was seated at the kitchen table, carefully writing down the directions for baking a pork chop. She looked unhappy when Clarissa wrapped up the uneaten half of her sandwich and put it in the refrigerator.

"How am I ever going to put some weight on you if you don't eat?" she grumbled.

"I'm sure it will happen over time, but I have to go out now," Clarissa told her.

"Church business?"

"Sort of," Clarissa answered as she went out the door.

She walked over to the office and told Ashley she'd be out for a little while, then hurried to the parking lot and got into her car. Not knowing where Marshal Street was, she programmed her G.P.S. and followed its directions there.

In a little over five minutes, she was parked in front of a large Victorian that had clearly seen better days. Repairs had recently been made to the gingerbread along the roofline, and as she stood there, Clarissa could hear the sound of hammering coming from behind the house. She went up the walk, then left the sidewalk and started around the side of the house.

She had just started to walk toward the back when she heard a chilling scream. She broke into a run, and as she came around to the back of the house, Clarissa saw a figure dressed in dark clothes running between the tall bushes at the back of the property. To her left, she saw a ladder on the ground near the back of the house, and an inert body lying next to it.

She rushed up to the fallen figure. It was Jack Spurlock. Clarissa spoke his name softly, but his eyes didn't open. Then she noticed that his neck was at an odd angle. Turning away and ordering herself to remain calm, Clarissa dialed 9-1-1 on her cell phone.

The first officer on the scene was Officer Rudinski, the young man she had seen working at the desk in the station the other night. She stammered out the series of events as she understood them, from the time of her arrival in front of the house to finding the body. He walked over to look at Jack, and came back looking rather pale himself.

"Let's wait in front of the house," he said, putting a comforting arm around her and directing her around to the front, where they sat next to each other on the dilapidated porch, neither one saying anything for a good few minutes.

"I thought you were working evenings," Clarissa eventually mumbled.

"Detective Baker and I switched to days at the start of this week," he said.

A few minutes later, an unmarked car pulled up and Detective Baker got out. Following him was another squad car with two more officers. An ambulance arrived a moment later. The EMTs immediately got out and ran around the side of the house.

Baker stood by the curb and crooked his finger at the officer sitting next to Clarissa. "Rudinski," he said.

The young man jumped to his feet and jogged over to stand in front of the detective. Clarissa couldn't quite make out what was being said, but she guessed that Detective Baker was asking for a report of what had happened. When Officer Rudinski stopped talking, the two men walked around to the back of the house.

As she pictured them standing over Jack Spurlock, the image of what she had seen flashed before her eyes. Clarissa now knew what people meant when they said there were some things that you couldn't un-see. This was something she'd remember for the rest of her life. She shivered slightly even though the day was warm, and she wrapped her arms around herself.

"Do you feel up to answering some questions?" Detective Baker said, taking a seat next to her on the step and looking at her with concern. She hadn't even noticed he was back around on this side of the house. "You don't have to do it now. I can have an officer take you home, and we can put all of this off until tomorrow."

"I'm okay," Clarissa replied. "We may as well do it now."

"I know you've already told Officer Rudinski, but could you tell me what happened from the time you arrived here?"

She repeated what she had seen.

"Can you tell me any more about this dark figure you saw going through the bushes?" Detective Baker asked. "What he was wearing or how tall he was?"

"He was dressed in dark colors, black or blue. But it could have been a man or a woman. From a distance, I couldn't be sure. They were maybe around my height, five-nine or so. Like I said, they were moving fast, and I only caught a glimpse before I saw Jack." She swallowed. "About Jack, is he . . ?"

"Dead. I'm afraid so." Detective Baker sighed deeply. "From the angle of his head, I'd say he broke his neck when he hit the ground. The medical examiner is on his way. Maybe he can tell us more. The forensics people will be here in a little while, as well."

They sat for a moment looking out toward the street, each of them lost in their own thoughts.

Finally, the detective cleared his throat. "What were you doing here, Clarissa?" he asked.

"I wanted to talk to Jack."

"Why?"

Clarissa was momentarily tempted to make up some story about church business that she urgently needed to discuss with Jack, but she really didn't want to lie. "When I spoke to Jack the other day about David Ames' death being suspicious," she said slowly, "he got belligerent, as if there were something he really didn't want to tell me. I called him right after I spoke to you and said that I wanted to talk to him about it further. He told me to meet him here."

The detective sighed. "Even after I told you to stay out of this, Clarissa, you had to go talk to Spurlock."

"I need to know why David Ames died," she protested. "If I'd been better at my job, he would have told me his story, and maybe he wouldn't have been killed." She could feel tears welling up in her eyes and fought to hold them back. This wasn't a time to cry. "I owe it to David to find out who killed him."

"No, that's my job, not yours," the detective said sternly. "You are just going to foul up our investigation, and maybe end up the same way as Ames and Spurlock."

"I'm not fouling up your investigation. If I hadn't been here, you would never have known that someone pushed that ladder over. You'd have thought it was just a tragic accident," Clarissa retorted.

Baker stared down at his hands. "Maybe you're right about that, but you're still putting your life in danger. I can't arrest you or put you in protective custody, but I can ask you as a friend not to take risks."

Clarissa gave him a small smile. "And as a friend, I appreciate that. I can promise you that I will be careful."

"Do you need a ride home?" he asked.

"I'm fine to drive."

"Okay. For now, we're going to be putting out that Jack's death was an accident. As I told you, we haven't publicized that Ames was murdered, so we'll keep both of these deaths under wraps. There's no sense creating a panic at the start of tourist season."

"Okay. I won't tell anyone," she promised, standing up.

She nodded to Detective Baker and waved to Officer Rudinski. Then she got in her car, pulled out from the curb, and headed back the way she had come.

Before she reached the end of the block, though, she could feel her hands shaking on the wheel. They continued to do so all the way back to the parsonage.

She had never been so sorry to have been right.

Chapter Ten

Clarissa returned to the parsonage, washed her face, and put on different clothes. For some reason, she felt better after she had changed, as if putting on a new outfit helped the image of Jack's death fade a little from her memory. She sat for a while and prayed for Jack, then read her daily meditation.

When she was done, she went down to the kitchen. Fortunately, Mrs. Gunn had left for the day, so Clarissa didn't have to answer any questions. She was certain that the woman would have known something was wrong simply by looking at her. She smiled to herself when she saw the directions for the pork chops printed on a yellow pad. They were written in large block letters, as if Mrs. Gunn were giving guidance to a young child, not a twenty-seven-year-old.

Clarissa took the path across to the office and unlocked the door, which was locked because Ashley had also left. Just as well—Clarissa really didn't want to talk to anyone right now.

She sat in her office, stunned by the events of the early afternoon. The dark, paneled walls felt consoling, like a wooden cocoon—or a coffin?—and she gently closed her eyes.

Although she had sounded defiant when speaking to Detective Baker about the case, she was very uncertain whether to continue her investigation. With both David Ames and Jack Spurlock murdered, she had double the reason to want to find out the identity of the killer, but she also felt that she had no viable suspects.

Doris Llewellyn might have murdered her husband fifty years ago because of his philandering, but she was in her late eighties and hardly strong enough to suffocate even a weakened David Ames, let alone be capable of pushing over a heavy ladder with Jack Spurlock on it and running off through the bushes.

Even though Maggie Preston was in her seventies, she was vigorous and strong enough to have killed the two men, but did she really shoot Royce Llewellyn because he was going to drop her? It seemed to Clarissa that even after fifty years, she still spoke of Royce with love and affection, convinced that he would have left his wife for her if only he had lived. She could be lying, but Clarissa didn't think so.

With Doris Llewellyn incapable of the recent murders and Maggie Preston with no motive, neither of them was a likely suspect for the deaths of Ames and Spurlock.

Then who, Clarissa asked herself, was out there killing people?

Her cell phone rang. She answered and was greeted by the voice of Pat Orwell, her professor from seminary who was now a close personal friend. Pat had been a pastor for many years before becoming a professor, and her course on women in the ministry had been formative for Clarissa.

"How's it going in your new ministry?" Pat asked after a few moments of small talk.

"Oh, you know, adjusting to a new place is always difficult," Clarissa replied.

"Of course, and it takes a while to get accustomed to all the new personalities, as well."

"That it does."

"The reason I called is that I'm coming down to Rutgers University to give a talk the day after tomorrow," Pat said. "It's a sudden thing. Their original speaker canceled. I know it's short notice, but I wondered if we could get together. I know you'll have almost a two-hour trip to get up here, but I thought we could meet at a halfway point for lunch—maybe that fish restaurant we went to once in Belmar. I know it's the last minute, so if you can't make it, I'll understand."

"Don't worry, I'll fit it into my schedule. I need to talk to you," Clarissa admitted.

"You do sound stressed."

"There have been some strange things happening here. But I'll explain when I see you."

After setting a time to meet and hanging up, Clarissa called Ramona Russell to tell her about her meeting with Andrew Corrigan concerning the sale of the church property.

"I was going to call you later this week to set up a time to talk about that," Ramona said after Clarissa had described her conversation with Andrew. "This is a pretty contentious issue. Reverend Hollingsworth was a golf buddy of Kenneth Rogers, the developer who wants to purchase the land, and some members of the board implied rather strongly to him that he had a conflict of interest in suggesting the church vote for the sale. In fact, several members strongly suggested to the Reverend that it might be time for him to retire before he was ousted by a church vote."

"And I thought he was running away from Mrs. Dalrymple," Clarissa remarked.

Ramona laughed. "There was that, too. It's hard to tell which one influenced him more. How about we get together tomorrow at nine-thirty? Does that work for you?"

"Fine," Clarissa agreed. "By the way, Jack Spurlock died today." She figured it was best that Ramona know as soon as possible, being head of the church board.

"Oh, my! How did that happen?" Ramona gasped.

"Apparently a fall from a ladder at a house he was working on," Clarissa said, remembering what Detective Baker told her about not spilling the beans. "I got there right after he fell."

"How horrible! Are you okay?"

"A little shaken up, but I'll be fine."

"Marcie will be devastated," said Ramona. "I'll give her a call. If she wants, I'll gather together a couple of other women and go visit her later on this evening."

"I'm sure she'll appreciate that," Clarissa said. "And I'll see you tomorrow morning. Is there anything I should read to get up to speed on this swamp matter?"

"No. I'll fill you in on all the details," Ramona promised.

They then said goodbye and hung up.

After sitting in silence for a few moments to compose her thoughts, Clarissa went back to the parsonage. In the quiet of her study, she prayed for Jack Spurlock and his wife. Then she also prayed for herself—that she'd do the right thing.

Chapter Eleven

The next morning, Clarissa went down to breakfast after a restless night. She'd had trouble getting to sleep and had awakened at four, only to fall asleep again and oversleep. By the time she got downstairs, Mrs. Gunn had already started cleaning the dining room.

"I almost went upstairs to see if you were all right. It's not like you to sleep past eight," she commented.

"I had a restless night."

"Did you hear about Jack Spurlock?"

Clarissa nodded.

"A terrible thing," Mrs. Gunn said. "You don't always think about it, but construction can be a dangerous line of work."

"I suppose so."

"Would you like me to scramble a couple of eggs for you?"

"No, thanks. I think I'll just have some cereal and coffee."

"It's no trouble," Mrs. Gunn insisted.

"That's okay, I'm fine," Clarissa said with a wan smile. "I guess I'll call Marcie Spurlock later this morning and set up a visit. We can talk about the funeral arrangements."

"She'll have the wake at Zeloniks," Mrs. Gunn said. "That's really the only place in town. But I'm sure you'll want to find out the special details about Jack's life that she'd like you to mention in your eulogy."

Clarissa nodded and went into the kitchen. She felt even worse about Jack's death today than she had yesterday. If only she had found out what David Ames was keeping secret, Jack might still be alive. Even though she knew it wasn't completely rational, Clarissa still felt responsible for the way things had turned out.

Under Mrs. Gunn's disapproving eye, she threw most of her cereal away and drank half a cup of coffee before going across to her office to work on her sermon for Sunday. She had decided to make it a sermon about coping with loss.

Right at nine o'clock, Ashley came bursting in with the news about Jack.

"I've already heard about it. In fact, I was the one who found the body," Clarissa told her.

Ashley's eyes widened. "The first thing I thought when I heard about it is that the killer had struck again."

"You didn't say anything about Ames being murdered, did you?"

"Of course not. So you never got a chance to talk to Jack before he died?" Ashley asked.

Clarissa shook her head. "He'd already fallen from the ladder when I got there."

She spent a moment debating whether to tell Ashley what had happened, given her promise to Detective Baker, but since she'd already told her about Ames' death, she thought she might as well keep her informed. She needed a discreet confidant. Clarissa once again swore Ashley to secrecy, and then told her everything she knew about Jack Spurlock's death.

"You saw someone running away who could have been the same person who was at the hospital?" Ashley asked after she was finished.

"The clothing was similar to what Wanda Bascom, the nurse, saw the intruder wearing."

"Do you think the killer saw you?"

Clarissa paused. She hadn't thought about that. "I don't know," she answered. "If he ran off right away, then probably not. But if he hid somewhere and watched me, of course he would know who I am."

"Aren't you worried about being the next victim?"

Clarissa shook her head. "Whoever is doing this is trying to prevent David Ames' secret from getting out. The killer must realize that if I knew, I'd already have told the police, so I think I'm safe."

"Not if you keep poking around," Ashley pointed out.

"I'll just have to be careful."

"So the killer must have thought that Jack Spurlock knew the secret?"

"Or knew enough to figure it out."

"How are you going to find out this secret now that Ames and Spurlock are both gone?" Ashley asked.

"Whom does a man tell his deepest secrets to?" Clarissa replied.

"A bartender?"

Clarissa smiled. "I suppose that's true, but I was thinking more of his wife. When I speak with Marcie Spurlock it will be primarily to comfort her, but I'm also going to try to find out if Jack mentioned anything about David Ames' secret."

With that, Clarissa went into her office and called Marcie Spurlock. One of her grown daughters answered and said she couldn't come to the phone right now, but that she was sure her mother would be happy to see the pastor around two in the afternoon. The daughter explained that she and her sister were taking turns being with their mother. They lived in the area and fortunately had flexible work schedules.

When Clarissa hung up, she heard Ashley greeting Ramona Russell in the outer office, and went out to join them.

Ramona was smiling at Ashley, who was wearing a black jumper that was actually quite mainstream, given her normal wardrobe. Ramona, a woman in her fifties, was perfectly made up as usual: her brown hair had just the right blond highlights and her fit body was complemented by a dark red sundress. She looked every inch a fashionable lady of the beach—very unlike the stereotypical image of the dowdy churchwoman.

Clarissa brought Ramona into the office, closed the door, and pulled her chair around the desk so they could sit directly across from each other.

"I can't get over the terrible news about Jack," Ramona sighed.

"Yes, I'm going to visit Marcie this afternoon," Clarissa said.

"After all his years in construction, it's hard to imagine something like this happening, but I suppose accidents do occur. One moment of inattention can be fatal." Ramona paused. "I know this sounds rather cold-blooded, but we really should give some thought to replacing him as sacristan."

"Is it really that urgent?" Clarissa asked.

"When things go wrong in the church or the parsonage during tourist season, it can be almost impossible to get a handyman because they're all busy working on rental properties," Ramona explained. "And we start our Friday night dinners for the public in another two weeks, which means we need someone to set up and take down the tables. That was another of Jack's jobs, in addition to cleaning the church. Yes, we definitely need someone right away."

"Do you have anyone in mind?"

Ramona looked off into space. "I recommended someone to Reverend Hollingsworth five years ago when we hired Jack, but the Reverend wasn't interested in hiring a woman for the job."

"Is she qualified?" Clarissa asked.

"She graduated from the local vocational school where she studied construction, and she's worked with several different contractors around town. She markets herself as a handyperson in the local newspaper, and does all sorts of jobs, large and small. Older women in town who need something done rely on her."

"Is she a member of the congregation?"

"No, but most of the folks in the church know her because she's also got a fine voice, and we've occasionally hired her for solo parts at Christmas and Easter. She's also a veteran. She was in Afghanistan, I believe," Ramona said.

"What's her name?"

"Samantha Jones."

"Can we hire her without a vote of the board?" Clarissa asked.

"We can bring her on for a probationary period of six weeks, pending a full board vote," Ramona replied.

"If you think she can do the job, let's hire her," Clarissa decided. "As you say, things do need to be done. Now that you mention it, Mrs. Gunn was just saying the other day that the sink in the kitchen is getting slow to drain."

"That's the downside of these old Victorian homes. They need constant care. I'll have Samantha give you a call and set up a meeting. You should meet with her before deciding on whether to give her a try."

"Sounds good. Now, what's the status on this land deal?" Clarissa asked.

Ramona sat back and sighed. "We've had the land for years, and it's never been a problem," she said. "The taxes on it were almost nonexistent because it was undeveloped, and birders and other wildlife enthusiasts were the only ones who wandered out there. We had it posted as 'no trespassing' for insurance purposes, but never enforced it."

"But now someone wants to buy it and put up a high-rise condo."

"And they managed to get the city council to go along with it."

"Does the church need the money?" Clarissa asked.

Ramona laughed. "Who couldn't use five million? But actually, the church is pretty secure financially. From what we take in on Sundays and our investments, we can easily meet our expenses. Our Friday dinners during the tourist season are pretty successful, and we get a nice rent for the use of the church hall for lectures during the off-season."

"So there's no pressing need for the money?"

"No," said Ramona. "Of course, it *would* enable us to do more for outreach to the growing immigrant population in the county and to help school children living in poverty."

"But it would also outrage environmentalists and the folks who want Shore Side to remain the way it is," Clarissa pointed out.

"A big high-rise condo would be the first of its kind in Shore Side, and many people think that it would create a slippery slope, leading to more and more of them being built until the nature of the town is changed forever," Ramona said.

"What's your opinion?"

"I've lived in Shore Side all my life, and I like it the way it is. It's a unique and special place. I'd hate to see it change for the sake of allowing a developer to make a killing." Ramona shook her head.

"Sounds like a project to stay away from to me," Clarissa said.

"I agree, but not everyone sees it that way. The church board is pretty evenly split. Most old-timers are against it, while the more recent residents tend to favor it. Your influence may be decisive."

Clarissa frowned. "I'm not sure I have much influence. People hardly know me."

"The pastor's opinion is always important. It comes with the position." Ramona grinned. "Some people think you speak for God."

Clarissa grinned back. "I wish I had that kind of confidence in my opinions."

"Just as well you don't, or you'd be insufferable like Reverend Hollingsworth."

"He was that bad?"

"Worse," Ramona said. "At any rate, I'm trying to get the board together for a special meeting on the land issue. Does Thursday evening work for you?"

"I'll be there."

"Maybe we can get this settled once and for all, now that Reverend Hollingsworth is gone. He kept delaying the vote by claiming that we needed more information, but I think he was just playing for time in the hopes of swaying more board members to the side of taking the money."

"Won't we still need the entire congregation's vote on a matter of this importance?" Clarissa asked.

"Yes," but the board's recommendation is usually accepted," Ramona said.

They stood and Clarissa escorted Ramona to the door. Then she turned back to where Ashley was studying the computer screen.

"I'd like you to use your computer skills to find out all you can about Kenneth Rogers," she told the younger woman.

"The old country singer?" Ashley asked, raising an eyebrow.

"I think he went by Kenny," Clarissa remarked. "No, this guy is a property developer, particularly active along the Jersey shore."

"I'm on it, Boss."

Clarissa smiled and returned to her office. She worked on her sermon for the rest of the morning. She had frequently been told by more experienced ministers that, upon arriving in a new placement, you'd be quickly judged based on how nice you were and how well you preached. So she spent a great deal of time polishing what she wanted to say about the important issue of personal loss.

When she returned to the parsonage for lunch, Clarissa found Mrs. Gunn staring dolefully into the sink.

"It get slower every day," the woman said. "Now that Jack's gone, do you think we should call a plumber?"

"Ramona suggested that we give Samantha Jones a try as sacristan," Clarissa said.

Mrs. Gunn sniffed. "She's got a beautiful singing voice, and I've heard she can fix things. But this seems to me like a job for a man."

Clarissa smiled to herself, wondering what it was about a clogged sink that required a Y chromosome. "Is it hopelessly stopped up?" she asked.

Mrs. Gunn shook her head. "Just very slow."

"Well, let's see if Samantha gets back to me by tomorrow. If she does, I'll have her take a look at it before paying a plumber."

Grudgingly, Mrs. Gunn agreed.

After lunch, Clarissa went up to her bedroom and changed into her formal attire of a dark blouse and slacks along with a navy jacket.

"You look like you're going to a funeral," Ashley said when Clarissa returned to the office.

"Not quite, but I *am* going to console a widow."

"Sorry, I forgot," Ashley said with a blush. She was eating salad out of a blue plastic container while simultaneously moving the mouse cursor across her computer screen.

"You can go out for lunch if you want; just put the answering machine on," Clarissa said, gesturing to her setup.

Ashley shook her head. "I'd rather eat here. I've started bringing my own lunch. At least that way I get one healthy meal a day. It's okay that I use the fridge to store stuff in, isn't it?" she asked, nodding toward the dorm-sized refrigerator in the corner of the room.

"Of course."

"I've also found out something about this guy Kenneth Rogers, along with learning more about country music than I ever wanted to know." She rolled her eyes.

"What have you got?" Clarissa asked.

"Rogers spends a lot of time in court. He's currently got cases pending where individuals or towns have sued him for a variety of reasons, from shoddy construction work to ignoring town zoning ordinances. But more importantly, he's also under investigation by the state for violating environmental regulations. Unless he's very lucky, this guy could end up in a whole lot of trouble."

"Would you print out copies of everything you've found, so I can take them with me to the church board meeting on Thursday?" Clarissa asked.

"Sure thing, Boss," Ashley replied.

"Well, I'm on my way to see Marcie Spurlock," Clarissa said, heading for the door.

"I don't envy you that job."

"But it's an important one. If a person's faith doesn't comfort them in times like this, I don't see much point in it. Do you?"

"I guess not," Ashley admitted with a thoughtful expression.

***

The woman who opened the door when Clarissa knocked appeared to be in her mid-forties and introduced herself as Tammy McGuire, Marcie and Jack's younger daughter. She said her mother was in the living room, and guided Clarissa down the hall and into a room in the front of the bungalow.

Clarissa introduced herself to Marcie while Tammy went off to make tea. Marcie was a plump woman with a pleasant, open face that Clarissa thought probably smiled a lot, but wasn't smiling now.

She expressed her condolences, and said that although she hadn't known Jack for long, he had seemed like a good man.

Marcie's eyes filled with tears. "He was a wonderful husband, and a good father."

"How many children did you have?" Clarissa asked, pulling out her notebook to take down some notes for the eulogy.

"Three. Two daughters, Tammy and Melissa, and one son, Jerry. We also have six grandchildren."

"Perhaps you could tell me about Jack's life?" Clarissa asked.

Marcie looked confused. "I wouldn't know where to begin."

"Why don't we start with how you met?"

Tammy came into the room with tea and cookies. She poured the tea, and then discreetly left the room.

As suggested, Marcie began with how she and Jack met, and before long, she was caught up in the story of their life together. Clarissa thought they sounded like a happy couple that had survived the normal ups and downs of life with love and companionship. Every time Clarissa heard people recount this kind of life, she thought how much she wished for something similar for herself: a long-term loving relationship with someone who was both lover and best friend.

When Marcie was done, Clarissa said, "It sounds like Jack had a very fulfilling life."

The woman sighed. "But too short. He should have lived longer."

"Yes, a sudden death is always shocking."

"But I think you're right, he did have a good life." She smiled. "Jack always said that marrying me had saved him from a wasted life."

"Why did he say that?"

Marcie sighed and sipped her tea. "When he was younger, Jack made some bad choices in friends. He was close friends with David Ames, as you know, and I'm sure that man would have gotten him in trouble if they'd stayed friends."

"He was also friends with Owen Chandler, wasn't he?" Clarissa asked.

"Yes, the three of them were thick as thieves," Marcie said, then looked slightly horrified at what she'd said. "Not that I think they ever committed any crimes."

"I don't know Owen Chandler," Clarissa remarked.

"He was a worthless layabout," Marcie said. "His parents gave him everything when he was growing up. He was spoiled silly, and never did a lick of work. I'm sure he'd be destitute now if they hadn't left him The Admiral's Rest B&B. But it's still in business, so maybe he's more industrious now than he used to be— although I find that hard to believe. Jack was well rid of the both of them. I'm afraid I insisted that he stop going out drinking with them once we were married. I also got him started going to church and hanging around with a better class of people."

Clarissa nodded. "As you know, David Ames wanted to tell Jack something the other night, but he died before we could find out what it was," she said.

"Do you think Jack had any idea what David wanted to tell him?"

Marcie shook her head. "Not that he ever told me," she said. "Jack didn't even want to go see him when you called. But I insisted. I said to him that Dave might not be your friend now, but he once was. Now he's dying, and you can't just ignore him. Not that I really wanted him to ever see the man again."

"Did Jack seem upset at all in the last couple of days?" Clarissa asked.

Marcie thought for a moment. "When he came back from doing some work on the church the other day, he was very quiet. I asked him if anything was wrong, but he said he was just tired."

Clarissa paused, uncertain how hard to push. "Did Jack ever mention anything to you about David Ames and the Royce Llewellyn murder?"

"I grew up in Shore Side, so I heard the rumors at the time Llewellyn was killed that he'd had a fight with Dave," Marcie said. "I didn't put much store in them, but it was just another reason why I didn't want Jack associating with the man. Jack did tell me that he and Owen were Dave's alibi, and if not for them, he might have been in a lot of trouble."

"I only ask because Jack seemed so uncomfortable about seeing David again," Clarissa clarified.

"Jack didn't like to talk about those times. All he ever said to me about Dave is that it was always a mystery where he got the money from to live as well as he did."

Clarissa thought that might be a good piece of information to keep in mind.

"How did you happen to be there when Jack fell?" Marcie asked, setting down her teacup.

"I had called him a little while before, and said I had a couple of things to discuss with him. He invited me to meet him on the job. But I got there only seconds before he fell."

Marcie reached over and touched Clarissa on the arm. "I'm glad you were the one who found him. If he was aware of his surroundings at all, I'm sure he found your being there a great comfort."

Clarissa smiled, patted Marcie's hand, and hoped that was true.

Marcie cleared her throat. "We'll be in touch when we find out when the funeral will be," she said. "We've called Zelonik's, of course, but they said that the medical examiner hasn't released the body yet. I gather they're talking about doing an autopsy. I hate to think about them doing that to Jack. Why would they go to all that trouble over an accident?"

"Maybe in the case of an accident they have to establish the cause of death," Clarissa suggested.

Marcie shrugged. "I'd just like to have it all over with, and that can't happen until Jack's at rest."

Clarissa nodded. But she knew that wouldn't happen until his killer was caught.

Chapter Twelve

The next morning, Clarissa went over to her office right after breakfast. Ashley was already there, and she asked how the conversation with Marcie Spurlock had gone.

"Naturally, she was upset, and we talked most of the time about Jack's life," Clarissa informed her. "I got plenty of information for my service at the wake."

"Nothing helpful on the Ames' murder?" asked Ashley.

"Apparently, Jack didn't talk a lot about that period of his life because Marcie didn't really approve of his being friends with David Ames and Owen Chandler. The only interesting thing I learned is that David apparently had some secret source of income."

"Maybe he was dealing drugs, or something like that."

"I suppose anything is possible," Clarissa said. "According to Detective Baker, David wasn't above cutting legal corners. But if he *had* been dealing drugs for all those years, I'd be surprised if the police weren't aware of it. Shore Side is a pretty small place. I think a local drug dealer would at least be known by reputation."

"So you think it was something more secret?" Ashley asked.

"That's my guess," Clarissa replied. "Look, I'm going to be away most of the day today. I'm going to visit an old friend up in the Asbury area. I don't think anyone should be wandering in looking for me, so maybe you could devote some time to seeing if you can find anything about the Llewellyn murder, David Ames, Jack Spurlock, or Owen Chandler."

"Sure thing, Boss. You know, I think I've heard of Owen Chandler," Ashley remarked. "Doesn't he own a B&B in town?"

"That's the guy," Clarissa said, heading for the door. "Print out whatever you can find and put it on my desk. I'll take a look at it tonight when I get back."

"Drive safe," Ashley called out as Clarissa left.

After turning her car out of the church parking lot, Clarissa headed north out of town. She crossed the bridge that separated Shore Side from the mainland and got on the Garden State Parkway heading north. The traffic was usually pretty sparse at the southern end, and wouldn't thicken until she was closer to Toms River, so Clarissa had lot of time to think about what had been happening so far.

David Ames obviously knew something significant about the death of Royce Llewellyn, even if he wasn't the actual murderer. Perhaps he knew the identity of the killer and had been blackmailing that individual for the last fifty years. But what had motivated the murderer to suddenly stop paying and start killing?

Clarissa went over the events of David's last day in her mind. He had talked to her and asked to speak with Jack Spurlock. After she left, he had possibly called someone from his hospital room. What if Ames had called the person he was blackmailing, and said that he was going to pass on his secret to someone else? To Jack Spurlock? That would certainly explain why the killer had murdered Ames and then Spurlock. They must have been driven frantic at the idea that the blackmail would never stop.

Did that mean the killing would stop now that Jack was dead? Clarissa wondered. Or would the killer suspect that Jack had passed his secret on to someone else? And who would that someone else be? The only name that came to her mind was Owen Chandler, the other member of the Three Musketeers. He would definitely be the next person she talked to.

As she went further north, Clarissa began to think about her parents, who lived in northern New Jersey. She had stayed with them for a couple of weeks after her graduation from seminary and before taking up her post in Shore Side. There had even been the opportunity for a get-together with her two older brothers, one of whom was a physician and the other doing something in finance in the city. It was nice being together as a family again, even if only for an afternoon.

After Clarissa had told her parents that she and Tyler would not be getting married as planned, they had tactfully avoided the issue for the rest of her visit. Even though the breakup consumed many of her waking hours, she had no desire to talk it over with anyone. Her feelings were still too raw. Also, her parents had always liked Tyler, and she wasn't sure whose side they would take once they learned the cause of the breakup. She was sure they would profess to support her, but deep down in their hearts, they might be sympathetic to his point of view. Clarissa didn't feel she could deal with people taking sides on the issue, even now.

She got off the Parkway at the exit for Belmar and headed east. Twenty minutes later, she turned down Belmar's main street, hoping that she could remember the location of the restaurant she and Pat had eaten at several years before.

Fortunately, it still looked much as it had and was easy to find. When she went inside, Pat was already seated at a table near the window. She stood up and gave Clarissa a firm hug, then stood back and gave her a lingering look.

"Aside from appearing a bit tired, I'd say that your new position agrees with you," she announced. "The sunshine has definitely put a bit a color in your cheeks; they had gotten way too pale from all those hours spent in the library."

"And you look good, as always," Clarissa said. Pat was a slender woman who always dressed fashionably, and kept her gray hair cut stylishly short.

Pat smiled. "My continuing battle against age. I've come to accept that I'm getting older, but I refuse to allow it to limit me any more than absolutely necessary."

They sat and both ordered glasses of white wine when the waitress stopped at their table.

"How did your talk go?" Clarissa asked after the waitress left.

"It was mercifully early in the morning, at nine, so I made my presentation, answered a few questions, and immediately headed out," Pat replied. "I find that my patience with academic conferences has lessened over the years. The only reason I go now is to speak with women who are active in the ministry and feel they need guidance."

"What was the topic of your talk?"

"Being a Woman Minister: Its Effects on Marriage."

Clarissa winced at the title.

Pat reached over and grasped her wrist. "Sorry, I know that must cut close to the bone." She paused. "I saw Tyler on campus a few weeks ago. The church he's assistant at is only about half an hour away from campus. He asked me how you were doing. I told him that I hadn't seen you in six weeks, but the last we'd talked, you were enthused about your new job."

"Does he like *his* new job?" asked Clarissa.

Pat shrugged. "I'm sure he'd prefer to have a church of his own, but apparently the pastor is willing to give him lots of responsibility, particularly with the church youth."

"Good."

"But he didn't seem happy," Pat said. "When he asked me for information about you, it was like a man in the middle of the desert begging for a drink of water."

"I miss him too, but it just didn't work out," Clarissa said.

"Tell me to mind my own business if you want, but what happened?" Pat asked. "I thought the two of you were ideally suited and really planned to make a go of it."

Clarissa sighed. "I haven't really told people what happened, but I think you may understand better than anyone else," she prefaced. "We knew when we met in seminary that the time would come when we would be assigned to different churches, and we'd either have to live apart, or one person would have to give up his or her dream of being a minister. We promised each other that whoever got the better job would be the minister and the other would come along as the spouse. But when I got my own church and he got a job as an assistant pastor, he balked at the idea of giving up his career and following me. And I refused to be a pastor's wife."

Pat nodded. "The job of being a pastor's spouse used to be a thankless one. You ended up doing almost as much work for the church as your mate did, but had none of the authority or respect. Plus, you had the responsibility for the bulk of the childcare on top of everything else. In the old days, the role of minister's wife was taken for granted because the congregation thought they were hiring a couple rather than just one person."

"Do you blame me for not wanting to take on that role?" Clarissa asked.

"But things aren't that way anymore," Pat told her. "Even thirty years ago, when I started preaching, no one complained because my husband had a job teaching high school."

"That's because he was a man."

"That's true," Pat admitted. "But today, I don't think a congregation would object to the wife of the pastor having a job outside the home."

They paused in their conversation as the waitress came to the table with their wine and took their order. After she left, they continued again.

"Maybe you're right, but that isn't really the problem," Clarissa said. "I don't want to have just any job, I want to be a pastor. I just feel that it's the right job for me, and the one that allows me to make the most of my talents."

"And I'm sure Tyler feels the same way."

Clarissa nodded. "It was our shared goal that brought us together as a couple. We wanted the same thing. That's why we promised to follow the one with the better position. If Tyler had gotten to be pastor of a church and I hadn't, I'd have gone with him and made the most of it. I don't know what I would have done, but I would have found something worthwhile to do with my life. But when it went the other way, Tyler wasn't willing to do that for me. I think he must have felt all along that my promise was more binding than his, and his role in our relationship was more important and took precedence. *That's* why I broke up with him. I don't think he really took my wishes seriously. He just pretended to."

"You thought he was a more modern man than he turned out to be when push came to shove," Pat said.

"I guess you could put it like that."

"I understand why you feel the way you do, and you are certainly justified," she said. "But I doubt that Tyler meant to deceive you. He probably truly believed when he made that promise that if the time came when he had to give up the ministry to follow you, he would do so. But when the moment came, he couldn't do it. We often misjudge ourselves even more than we misjudge others."

"So what are you saying?" asked Clarissa.

"Only that you should forgive him and not hold a grudge," Pat answered. "He's disappointed himself even more than he's disappointed you."

"I'll work at doing that," Clarissa sighed. "But there still doesn't seem to be any way for us to be together, and I think we both have to move past that possibility."

Their food arrived, and they both ate in silence for several minutes.

"There is one thing I *do* know," Pat said, sipping her wine. "It is very difficult to be a pastor when you're all alone; it doesn't matter whether you're a man or a woman. When Marcus died, I felt a sense of loss even beyond the normal sadness of losing a spouse. It's hard to support others when there is no one to support you. Suddenly, there was no one in whom I could confide, no one who really understood me and with whom I could share my deepest feelings. That's part of the reason why I left the ministry and became a professor. I didn't have the strength to lead a congregation anymore. I still don't."

"Did you ever consider remarrying?" Clarissa asked.

Pat grinned. "All the time. But apparently a lot of men find me somewhat intimidating. However, I do have a boyfriend now—although 'boyfriend' is an odd term for someone over sixty. He's a professor who joined the faculty at the seminary last year, and we've taken a liking to each other."

"That's wonderful!" Clarissa exclaimed. "I look forward to meeting him."

"You will the next time you visit the university. I'll make a point of it."

Clarissa smiled. "And I have a date for this Friday with the church lawyer," she told her mentor.

"A real date? Not a business meeting?"

"The real thing."

"Well, I won't insult you with the usual lecture about being careful on the rebound," Pat said. "I know you'll think before you leap. If there is no practical way for you and Tyler to be together, then it's time for you to move on, and I wish you the best of luck."

Clarissa thanked her. "There is something else that I wanted to discuss with you, which sort of relates to the job," she said.

"How to deal with the church board?"

Clarissa smiled. "That will be for a future lunch, I'm sure," she said, and then went on to give Pat an abbreviated version of her investigation into the death of David Ames. When she finished, Pat's brow was wrinkled with concern.

"I can understand your feeling of responsibility," the professor said slowly, "but it really wasn't your fault that this man refused to confide in you. In my experience, people only tell you things when they are good and ready to do so. You shouldn't feel responsible for his death. Delving into what happened to him could be dangerous, and it would probably be best left to the police."

"On one level, I know all that, but I still think that I should somehow be trying to find out what David wanted to tell me," Clarissa insisted. "And I don't think the police are as motivated as I am."

Pat paused and spoke carefully. "When you start out as a minister, your enthusiasm often gets the better of you, and it's easy to get too involved in the life of the congregation," she said. "Every problem seems pressing, and you want to help solve each and every one. But quite quickly you learn that you have to keep some professional distance, or else you'll burn out. Also, people will begin to resent your involvement in their lives. They want the church to be there for them when they need it, but not to be intrusive."

"This is a one-time thing," Clarissa replied. "You have to admit that puzzles like this don't come along every day. I just have a burning need to solve it."

"You were one of my brightest students, but also one of my most stubborn." Pat chuckled and shook her head.

Clarissa smiled. "I suppose that's true."

Pat reached over and took her hand. "I won't even try to change your mind, but at least promise me that you'll be careful?"

"I promise you that I'll be as careful as I can possibly be."

And she meant it.

Chapter Thirteen

Clarissa was back in Shore Side by six o'clock. She and Pat had spent an hour after lunch talking about old times and the challenges Pat was confronting, both in the classroom and from the administration of the seminary. Clarissa came away happy that she was not part of such a large, bureaucratized institution. She was answerable to the church board, and ultimately to the congregation of the church, but at least she didn't have anyone whose paid job it was to oversee her activities.

Because she wasn't very hungry after having had a large lunch, she didn't bother heating up the spaghetti sauce Mrs. Gunn had prepared, and just had toast and tea for supper. Clarissa knew she would face a scolding in the morning from the woman, who would once again accuse her of being too skinny and not eating enough.

Neither one was true. She ate plenty, and had stayed slender because she had been an athlete in both high school and college. In fact, she warned herself, she had better get back to running soon, or else she'd pack on some unwanted pounds.

When she'd finished her light supper, she walked over to her office. Not bothering to put on a light in the outer office, she went directly to her desk. Ashley had left a message that the company that supplied fuel oil to the church had called with their new rates for next winter. Clarissa made a mental note to pass it along to the financial board of the church, which handled such things. There was also a message that Ramona Russell had called to say the church board meeting was definitely on for tomorrow night at eight in the church hall. Clarissa knew she had to put some time in tomorrow preparing for that.

In the middle of her desk was a pile of printouts Ashley had left for her. They were obviously the fruits of her research into the various subjects Clarissa had assigned to her. The largest stack concerned Kenneth Rogers' various real estate deals. Clarissa promised herself that she would study them in the morning and decide which ones to copy for the church board meeting.

The local newspaper printouts covering the Llewellyn murder yielded little that Clarissa hadn't already learned from her previous conversations with Detective Baker and Maggie Preston. Llewellyn had been shot in his front doorway. His wife found the body, and nobody saw the attacker. One of the articles mentioned that David Ames had been a person of interest, but his name disappeared from the later stories as the investigation had foundered.

On David Ames himself, all Ashley had discovered was a recent photograph of David at the opening of a new restaurant in town, standing next to a woman named Sharon Meissner. Since he had his arm around her waist, Clarissa thought they were probably more than mere acquaintances.

Ashley had found nothing about Jack Spurlock, and the information on Owen Chandler was limited to a picture from the newspaper showing him standing in front of a large gray Victorian, which was described as The Admiral's Rest, his newly renovated B&B. Clarissa paused to wonder where Owen, who had been described by Marcie Spurlock as a lazy hanger-on, had managed to get the money to renovate the inn. Perhaps his parents had left him a sizable chunk of cash along with the inn. Or perhaps he was getting his money from another source.

While she was brooding on that question, Clarissa heard a noise in the outer office. It had gotten dark while she was going through Ashley's research, and she had left the lights off in her office, as well, so turning on the lights as she went into the outer office left her momentarily blinded.

Before she could even see if anyone was there, a figure charged into her, giving her a forceful shove. Losing her balance, Clarissa fell backwards and landed hard on the linoleum floor.

"Forget about David Ames," a muffled voice demanded. Clarissa glanced up and saw a hooded figure in a ski mask standing over her.

Even though she'd taken harder hits playing lacrosse in college and touch football with her brothers on autumn afternoons, the unexpectedness of the attack left Clarissa momentarily stunned. By the time she climbed to her feet, her attacker had run out through the open door.

Clarissa went outside onto the path to the church, but the deepening twilight revealed no one nearby. Clarissa went back into the office, locked the door, and turned on all the lights. She knew this was locking the barn door after the horse had escaped, but psychologically, it made her feel better.

She sat behind her desk, feeling both frightened and angry. Her heart was beating rapidly, and it took her several moments to calm down.

What should she do next? Clarissa asked herself. Although tempted to simply go to bed and decide how to handle the whole thing in the morning, she recalled her conversation with Pat and her promise to be careful. She didn't think that leaving the attack unreported was in keeping with that promise. This had significantly raised the risk level of her investigation, and she really should notify the police promptly. She also knew that

Detective Baker would be less than pleased to discover that she hadn't heeded his advice to stay out of the matter, but she'd just have to take her medicine.

Clarissa called the police station. When she said the attack had something to do with the Ames case, her call was immediately put through to the detective's cell phone.

"Where are you right now?" he asked as soon as she had explained what had happened.

"In the church office," she answered.

"Keep the door locked until I arrive. Don't open it for anyone else," he said in a businesslike tone bordering on curt.

Clarissa agreed. She quickly cleared the printouts about the Ames case from her desk so Baker wouldn't see the full extent of her involvement in the matter. Then she sat down and thought how she could downplay her activities without lying.

A few minutes later, there was a loud rap on her door. She went back to the outer office and asked who it was.

Detective Baker identified himself. She let him inside and led him towards the back office, but he stopped her.

"This is where the attack took place?" he asked, surveying the room.

Clarissa said it was, and he carefully examined under the pieces of furniture and along the floor, clearly hoping to find something that the attacker had dropped. When he had completed his unsuccessful search, they went into her office.

Although tempted to retreat behind her desk, she pulled her chair out and sat directly across from him. Baker asked her to describe exactly what happened, and she did.

"You hadn't locked the door to the outside office?" he asked.

"No."

He raised a critical eyebrow. "A woman alone at night should keep the door locked."

"It *is* a church," Clarissa pointed out.

"Doesn't matter."

"Okay. I'll be more careful from now on," she promised.

"Can you describe your attacker for me?" Detective Baker asked, taking out a small spiral notebook.

"At least my height. Fairly strong. Whoever it was gave me a good solid shove."

"Man or woman?"

"I couldn't tell."

"What about the voice?" he asked.

"Too muffled. It could have been a man or a woman putting on a deep voice," she replied.

"Did you smell anything? Perfume? Aftershave?"

Clarissa shook her head.

Baker sighed. "Aside from going to see Jack Spurlock on the day he died, have you had any other involvement with the Ames investigation?"

Although she was tempted to say "none," Clarissa knew she had to tell the truth. So, somewhat hesitantly, she told Detective Baker about visiting Doris Llewellyn at home and talking with Maggie Preston at the restaurant. She didn't feel the need to tell him about her conversation with Marcie Spurlock, since that was part of the preparation for Jack's funeral.

When she was done, Baker smiled grimly and shook his head. "You really can't stay out of this, Pastor, can you?"

"I'm afraid not," she said. "I need to find out who murdered David Ames."

"Can't you leave that to the police?"

"And what have you found out so far?" Clarissa knew that came out a bit more sarcastic than she had intended.

Detective Baker wasn't fazed. "We interviewed everyone working on the hospital floor that night, and found that, aside from the one nurse, Wanda Bascomb, who thinks she saw a hooded figure leaving Ames' room, no one noticed anything unusual," he answered evenly. "We interviewed all of Ames' drinking buddies down at the Salt Horse, which was where he spent most nights. He hadn't said anything important to any of them, except that his heart was acting up."

"Did you talk to Maggie Preston?" Clarissa asked.

"No. Because she wasn't a friend of Ames."

"But she was a good friend of Royce Llewellyn."

"True," the detective conceded. "But we have no proof that the murders of David Ames and Royce Llewellyn are connected."

"Seems likely."

"That isn't proof."

"And where did David Ames get all his money from?" Clarissa asked.

"What money? As far as I know, he worked odd jobs around town for years before he went on Social Security."

"But he had lots more money than that."

"Who says so?" Baker asked sharply.

"Jack Spurlock."

"He told you that?"

Clarissa shook her head. "Not exactly. He told Marcie, and she told me."

"So you've been grilling the widow, as well."

Clarissa blushed. "It happened to come up in the context of talking about Jack's life."

Several emotions passed over Josh Baker's face, but finally he smiled. "You know, you're actually pretty good at this," he said. "Maybe you should have been a cop rather than a minister."

"No, thanks. This is a one-time experience for me."

"You might find it addictive," he warned.

"Being attacked in my own office isn't that appealing."

"But it *does* show that you're on to something." Baker sighed. "Look, just sit tight for a few days and be careful when you go out at night. And let's keep the story of this attack a secret. No sense in alarming the entire church. We'll go back and have a chat with Doris Llewellyn and Maggie Preston. Sometimes folks will tell a cop more than they'll tell a civilian."

And sometimes less, Clarissa thought.

***

When Clarissa got out of bed the next morning, her rear end was sore. It took her a moment of wondering before she remembered her fall last night during the attack. Linoleum floors didn't provide much of a cushion.

She took a moment to give thanks that it hadn't been worse. Who knew how far this person would go to frighten her off the Ames case? The sooner it was brought to a conclusion, the safer she would be.

A half hour later, down in the kitchen, Mrs. Gunn asked about her lunch with Pat, and Clarissa briefly told her that it had gone well. Mrs. Gunn then went on to complain because Clarissa hadn't eaten any of the spaghetti she had left. Clarissa explained that she had eaten a great deal at lunch and wasn't hungry. After making a few more forays at conversation, Mrs. Gunn gave up and left her alone. Clarissa smiled in relief; all that was on her mind right now was what to do about the murder she was trying to solve.

After breakfast, she went directly across to the office. She pored over the Kenneth Rogers materials

Ashley had left, and made copies of those she wished to hand out to the church board members; she wanted to make certain that any opinion she expressed would be backed up by substantial evidence.

A while later, Ashley came into her office and asked how the lunch with Pat had gone. Summarizing it briefly, Clarissa then went on to tell Ashley about last night's attack.

"This person actually knocked you down? Are you all right?" Ashley gasped. "Maybe you should go to the hospital to be checked out. You could have a broken bone or something. I hear the tailbone is pretty easy to break." Ashley was about to continue when Clarissa raised a hand for silence.

"I'm fine," she said. "I've been hit harder playing sports, and look, let's keep this between us. I don't want it getting around town."

"Right, Boss."

Ashley went over to her desk and fished around in her handbag. She pulled out her keys and took something off the key ring. She returned with a black canister, and handed it to Clarissa.

"Keep this with you at all times," she said. "It's pepper spray. It will hit someone up to ten feet away. Aim for the eyes."

"Is carrying this legal?" asked Clarissa, looking over the canister.

"If you're over eighteen and not a felon. I'm pretty sure you're of age," Ashley said. "Are you a felon?"

"Maybe I should be asking you," Clarissa said drily.

"Very funny. Practice taking it out of your bag until you can point it in the right direction without looking."

"Thanks, I appreciate this," Clarissa said. "But don't you need one, too? Or maybe I should ask why you carry pepper spray in the first place?"

"When you look different, you need protection," Ashley said shortly. "And don't worry. I've got another one at home in basic black to go with all my outfits."

Clarissa thanked Ashley once more, then went into her office and closed the door. She wanted peace and quiet to jot down her presentation to the church board tonight. She had just finished when there was a knock and Ashley poked her head in.

"Kenneth Rogers is here to see you," she said loudly. "He doesn't have an appointment, but he would *really* like to see you. I can reschedule some of your other appointments if you'd like." She grinned and rolled her eyes.

"Of course I'll see him," Clarissa responded. "Show him in."

The man who walked into her office then looked to be in his forties. He had wavy black hair and was wearing a casual knit shirt with a sport coat, as if to show that he was really a manual laborer who also happened to dabble in business.

"Sorry to barge in without an appointment," he said briskly, clearly not in the mood to waste any time in getting down to business. "I just wanted to have the opportunity to speak with you before the church board meeting tonight."

Clarissa smiled, wondering how he knew about the meeting; he must have an informant on the board.

"I knew Reverend Hollingsworth rather well," he continued. "We even played golf together several times, and now that you've taken his place, I thought it important that we meet. Are you familiar with my proposal for the church land on the south end of Shore Side?"

"I think I'm pretty much up to speed," Clarissa said. "You're offering five million for the land. Your plan is to put up a high-rise condominium building. Is that right?"

Rogers smiled and opened his hands as if he were the poster child for generosity. "I'm sure we could sweeten the deal for the land to something closer to six million—and the condo won't be that high, only fifteen floors."

"But high by Shore Side standards," Clarissa pointed out.

"I grant you that, but Shore Side needs to change with the times if it's going to remain popular with tourists. And we both know how important that is."

Clarissa smiled. "Some would say Shore Side's popularity is based on not changing."

Rogers' smile became slightly strained, and he shrugged. "New ideas are always open to different interpretations."

Clarissa gave a noncommittal nod.

The man glanced out the window. "I noticed an old Ford in the church parking lot as I was coming in. Is that yours?"

"Yes. It does have a few miles on it," Clarissa admitted. "I've had it since I started college."

"I'm sure that being able to visit the members of the congregation is important to a minister," Rogers said. "Perhaps you'd allow me to provide you with more reliable transportation."

Clarissa took a deep breath in order to control her temper. "Thanks for the offer," she said. "My old car may not be elegant, but it still gets me where I need to go. And it has sentimental value."

Rogers nodded. "Of course, I understand. But please keep my offer in mind." He gave her a joyless smile. "It seems to me that you are very familiar with the issue at hand, and I'm sure you can be trusted to do what is right for the church."

"I'll certainly do my best."

"I'm sure you will," the man said doubtfully. He shook her hand and left the office.

"What did he want?" Ashley asked a moment later after the front door had closed.

"Mainly to offer me a bribe," Clarissa said, somewhat disgusted.

"How much?" Ashley asked.

"A new car."

"What kind?"

Clarissa grinned. "We never got that far. Obviously I should have had *you* negotiating for me."

"I don't have any wheels right now. I could have used your old one," Ashley sighed.

"Too bad, I didn't know."

Ashley thought for a moment, and then shook her head. "Nah, you'd never take a bribe." she said.

"Because I'm a minister?"

The younger woman paused for a moment. "More because you're you."

Clarissa smiled at the compliment and walked back to her office, still thinking about the fact that someone had told Rogers about the board meeting scheduled for tonight—perhaps someone with a new car.

Whatever the case, she was sure that tonight's meeting would be interesting, to say the least.

Chapter Fourteen

Clarissa stood in front of the Admiral's Rest. It was aptly named, being a restful shade of gray and having two wings that stood out on either side from the main body of the Victorian, as if to embrace you in a comforting hug. She walked up the stairs to the large front porch that ran the length of the center part of the building, and walked in through the double doors.

She was determined to be more aggressive in her questioning than before. The attack last night had proven to her that she needed to come up with some answers fast, before things became even more dangerous.

The lobby of the inn was done in dark wood and filled with so many shadows that it took Clarissa's eyes a moment to adjust.

"I'd like to help you, but we're filled up right now," a disembodied voice to her left said.

She blinked and could make out a small check-in desk tucked in under the stairwell. Behind the counter stood a tall, thin man in his seventies wearing a T-shirt and shorts. He leered at her and grinned as if he regretted not having a room. This must be Owen Chandler.

"That's okay, I'm not looking for a place to stay," Clarissa said. "I'm here to talk about David Ames."

The grin disappeared, replaced by a frown. "Yeah, I heard that old Dave died—real shame. And a shame about Jack, too. Who ever thought a guy as experienced as him would ever fall?"

"I'm David's pastor, and I'm looking for some background on his early life that I can include in the service at his wake," Clarissa said.

"So you're out interviewing his old friends. You certainly are thorough," the man replied. "But, although I knew him in the old days, we really haven't kept in touch. I'd run into him on the street once in a while and say hello, but that's all. Or once in a while, we'd be in the same bar and pass the time of day."

"The way you would with Jack Spurlock?" Clarissa asked.

Owen Chandler's eyes narrowed suspiciously. "Yeah, although I saw even less of Jack. After he got married, his wife made him stay in at night. He had to walk the straight and narrow. I heard he was even working for a church. Is that the one you're at?"

She ignored the question. "So there were no more nights out together like the one when Roger Llewellyn got killed?" she demanded.

"Hey, what's this all about?" Chandler demanded. "Are you a minister or a cop?"

"A minister. But I can have Detective Baker come here very quickly and ask you the same questions if you don't want to answer them for me," she threatened.

Chandler rubbed his mouth and looked across the dark lobby.

Clarissa thought it was time to take a shot in the dark. "I know David Ames was paying you money. I'd like to know why."

"You can't know that," Chandler said, then backtracked. "It never happened."

"Okay. That's something else you can talk about with Detective Baker," Clarissa said.

"Aw, c'mon," Chandler said in a wheedling tone, "you've got me all wrong. I never did anything illegal."

"But you *did* know something that David was willing to pay you to keep quiet about."

"Look, all I know is that on the night Llewellyn got killed, Dave left us in the bar at ten o'clock," he said. "He was drunk and angry. He said that he was going to have it out with Llewellyn once and for all for firing him from the hotel."

"And did he?"

"How should I know?" Chandler grumbled. "Jack and I stayed in the bar. Forty minutes later Dave comes back, looking like he'd seen a ghost. He won't tell us anything about what happened, but he makes us promise to say that he was with us the whole night, if anyone asked."

"And that's what you told the police?" Clarissa asked.

"Sure. We were buddies back then. They called us the Three Musketeers."

"So I've heard. But that didn't stop you from blackmailing Ames, did it? Not exactly one for all, and all for one."

Chandler twisted his hands together. "Look, I was twenty-one and my parents had me working here at the inn for nothing more than room and board and a tiny allowance, like I was still a kid."

"You could have gotten work outside the inn."

"They told me if I did that, they'd change their wills and leave the place to my cousin Bernie. They always liked him better anyway." He scowled.

Clarissa paused for a moment. "Do you think David killed Llewellyn?" she asked.

"No. I'd never have covered up for him if I thought he was a killer," Chandler said. "He swore to the both of us that he didn't do it."

"And you believed him because he was your buddy?"

"Mostly I believed him because he was suddenly flush with money." Chandler grinned. "That's why I got the idea to put the touch on him in the first place."

"Who was giving him all this money?" Clarissa asked.

"No idea. I asked a few times, but Dave wasn't about to tell me. He was probably afraid that I'd go around him to the source. Not that I would have."

Clarissa guessed that David had his buddy Owen pretty well figured out.

He put on a sad face. "I was real sorry when I heard that Dave had died. We went back a long way."

"A long, lucrative way for you," Clarissa accused.

Chandler grinned again. "That's true, too." He sighed. "It'll be hard to get along without the extra income. Running an inn in a resort area isn't the license to print money that most people think it is."

"But why was this mysterious somebody paying David all this money?" Clarissa asked.

"I always figured because whoever it was had killed Llewellyn, and Dave saw him do it," Chandler replied. "That's the most likely explanation, isn't it?"

Clarissa was silent for a moment, considering what to say next. She had promised Detective Baker not to reveal the fact that Ames and Spurlock had been murdered. However, Owen Chandler seemed to her to be a likely third target. Could she, in good conscience, conceal the truth from him?

"Maybe you'd better be careful for a while," she advised.

"Is that a threat?" Chandler demanded.

"Not from me."

"What are you talking about, then?"

Cat's out of the bag now, she thought. "David Ames may not have died of natural causes, and it's possible that Jack didn't fall off that ladder by accident," Clarissa said in a low voice.

Chandler's eyes widened. "Are you saying someone killed them and might be planning to kill me?" he gasped.

"Let's just say you may have information that somebody doesn't want to get out," she said.

"I don't know anything about who killed Royce Llewellyn!"

"Neither did Jack, but he's still dead."

Chandler's eyes went wide and he rubbed his forehead. "What am I supposed to do? It's tourist season. I've got reservations. I can't just close up and leave town!"

"Maybe your cousin Bernie would take over for you," Clarissa said with a small smile.

"Fat chance," Chandler said, shaking his head. "He became a brain surgeon."

***

That evening, Clarissa got into her business attire and walked over to the church hall fifteen minutes before the board meeting was due to start. She felt rather nervous; she had little experience with church politics and doubted that it would be her strength. In many ways, it seemed diametrically opposed to her job as a pastor, which involved healing rather than taking sides.

More experienced ministers had frequently told her that it was the least pleasant part of the job and that politics could divide a congregation, leading to a church split. She also knew that it was going to be impossible for her to remain neutral on this controversial issue.

Fifteen minutes past the time the meeting was due to begin, the seven members of the board had finally gathered around the table. Ramona Russell, who was chairing the meeting, was careful to introduce Clarissa to each of the members, even to those she had already met. Aside from Ramona, there were four other women: three were senior citizens and one who looked to be in her thirties. There were also two men: a man in his twenties named Jackson Monroe and a middle-aged fellow named Harry Blanchard.

After a perfunctory reading and approval of the minutes of the last meeting, they moved on to the one item of old business: whether to sell the land to KR Construction.

As soon as Ramona introduced the subject, Harry, a short, bald, fireplug of a man in his fifties, said that he saw no reason for a prolonged discussion of the matter. "This is like found money," he said. "The church could certainly discover uses for it, and I'll bet we can easily get six million if we negotiate aggressively. I see no reason to bat this back and forth all night."

Clarissa studied him, wondering if he was already aware of Rogers' willingness to raise his offer to six million. Might he be the developer's man on the board? That would explain how Rogers had known they were having a meeting tonight on the issue. It might be worth checking whether Harry was driving a fancy new car.

Ramona brushed aside Harry's attempt to speed things along by insisting that each member say something on the matter. Two of the older women and the younger one deferred, saying they wanted to hear other peoples' opinions first. Clarissa guessed that, in the end, they would go whichever way the prevailing wind seemed to be blowing.

Jackson, who wore a denim shirt and jeans, diffidently raised his hand. "I think we have to consider the environmental impact that a high-rise will have on the Shore Side ecosystem," he said. "From what I've heard, the town council did a pretty sketchy impact study, so we don't really know what this will mean for the environment."

Harry snorted his disdain. "You can save a lot of trees and help a lot of people for six million. The only thing that land is good for now is mosquitos."

One of the older women, Marion Blesser—Clarissa remembered she was a retired high school history teacher—gave Harry a disapproving look. "I think that in addition to the environment, we have to consider how a high-rise would change the nature of Shore Side," she said. "One of our charms is that we haven't gone over to fast food restaurants and a beach lined with condo towers. Allowing one high-rise condo might soon lead to others, and before long, this wouldn't the Shore Side we love anymore."

"That's a question best left to the town council," Harry said. "And they've already approved the project. Why should we second-guess them?"

Marion straightened her shoulders and stared across the table at him like he was a fresh schoolboy. "Because sometimes, a church has to act as the conscience of a community and keep it from going astray," she said severely.

Harry simply smirked.

"Does anyone else have anything they'd like to say?" Ramona asked.

"I do," Clarissa said.

"She's only an *ex officio* member of the board and doesn't have the right to vote," Harry protested.

"But she certainly has the right to speak," Ramona said.

"I don't see why," Harry grumbled.

"Because that's what our bylaws say," Ramona responded. "And I don't remember you ever objecting when Reverend Hollingsworth spoke, often at great length."

Several of the women around the table rolled their eyes.

"Okay, okay, let her speak," Harry said with a wave of his pudgy hand.

Clarissa stood. "I'd like to pass around the results of some preliminary research that I've done into other projects developed by KR Construction up and down the shore," she said. She passed out the handouts and gave everyone a few moments to study them. "As you can see, KRC has become mired in a number of legal disputes on many of its projects due to their negative environmental impact and the shoddy quality of construction."

"Some of these issues haven't been resolved in court yet," Harry objected. "The charges could be false."

"But if you read the information carefully, some have already been decided against KRC. And I think there is a very real question as to whether the church should be involved with a company that has such a checkered history," Clarissa countered.

She looked around the table and saw a number of people nodding agreement.

"Every construction company has its problems. It comes with the territory." Harry shook his fist at everyone in general. "I can't believe you folks are going to be stupid enough to pass up six million."

"Nonetheless, the pastor raises a good point," Ramona said. "Does anyone have anything else to say before we put the matter to a vote?"

She was greeted with silence. Slips of paper were handed out to the board members, and after a few minutes, she collected the completed ballots.

"The vote is five to two against selling the property to KRC," she announced.

"Well, I guess that answers my question. You *are* stupid enough to pass up six million," Harry said, his face turning red. He stood up and stomped out of the room.

The board then moved on to new business, which consisted primarily of assigning responsibilities for an upcoming tag sale, and the meeting was swiftly concluded.

"You did well," Ramona said softly to Clarissa afterwards. The others were scattered in private conversations around the room. "Sometimes presenting facts does make a difference."

"It convinced everyone but two," Clarissa remarked.

Ramona nodded grimly. "Harry and Kenneth Rogers are thick as thieves, and the other vote was from Miranda," she said, subtly nodding toward one of the older women who had stayed silent throughout the meeting. "Harry is her cousin, and she always votes with him."

"So, we did a good thing?" asked Clarissa.

Ramona shrugged. "Harry is a big contributor to the church. You never know—if he gets angry enough, he may take his money and go elsewhere." Then she smiled. "I say good riddance. I think we did a very good thing."

"Let's hope the congregation goes along," Clarissa said.

"Most likely it will. We'll find out at the all-church meeting this Sunday after the service."

Clarissa nodded, but she felt proud nonetheless. She had done a good thing here, and the matter would turn out, one way or another. If only solving murders were this simple!

Chapter Fifteen

The next morning, Clarissa was sitting at the kitchen table, eating an egg and two large pieces of a substantial multigrain toast that Mrs. Gunn insisted she consume as part of her "putting meat on her bones" program.

"So I gather that the church board decided not to sell the land," Mrs. Gunn said. She was working at the sink and looked over her shoulder at Clarissa for confirmation.

"That's right. How did you know?" Clarissa asked between bites of toast.

"Marion Blesser gave me a call last night," Mrs. Gunn replied. "She was pretty happy about the way things went. She said you were the one who convinced people to vote against the sale."

"I just presented the facts about Kenneth Rogers' past projects. I didn't express an opinion."

Mrs. Gunn grunted doubtfully.

"What was *your* opinion on the sale?" asked Clarissa.

"I never trust easy money. If you didn't work for it, somehow you'll end up paying for it in the end," Mrs. Gunn said sagely. "Reverend Hollingsworth was always telling me how wonderful it would be for the church, but I was always suspicious. Any deal that sounds too good to be true usually is. Look at all those old folks who get scammed out of their savings because they're convinced they'll get something for nothing. Life doesn't work that way."

"That's a good attitude to have," Clarissa agreed.

Mrs. Gunn went back to her work and Clarissa began slowly chewing on her second slice of toast, wondering if there was any way she could dispose of it without being rude.

"Do you happen to know a Sharon Meissner?" she asked after swallowing. "She was a friend of David Ames, and I want to talk to her to get some information for the funeral, since David didn't have any family."

"I know Sharon, but I didn't realize she was a special friend of Dave's. She must be about twenty years younger than him—but she *is* a widow, so maybe she was just lonely," Mrs. Gunn mused. "From what I've heard around town, plenty of women thought that Dave was fun. I could never see it myself. Sure, he liked to kid around, but he never did more work that he had to do."

"Do you know anything more about Sharon?" Clarissa asked to get Mrs. Gunn back on point.

"I see her picture in the local paper a lot. She goes to all the social events around town, probably to make contacts for her job. She's a realtor, so she needs to know folks."

"Do you know which agency she's associated with?"

Mrs. Gunn shook her head. "There's so many around town, I never keep track of them."

Clarissa kept eating, wondering how she was going to get in touch with the woman. She suspected that if David had revealed the source of his mysterious income to anyone, it would be to a girlfriend.

Mrs. Gunn turned around and gave Clarissa a long look. "So, how are you getting along with Ashley?" she asked.

"Very well. She's smart, organized, and pleasant to work with," Clarissa replied.

Mrs. Gunn nodded her head. "Good. Poor Ashley hasn't always had it easy."

"Why's that?"

"Well, from what her aunt tells me, she was bullied a lot in school. She never fit in easily and was very bright. Some kids didn't like her for being different, and others were jealous of her for being so smart. You know how kids are; some of them are just natural bullies, and Shore Side can be a little closed-minded."

"I'm surprised she ever came back here once she had left," Clarissa said.

"Well, her parents died within a year of each other, both from cancer," Mrs. Gunn said. "That left her aunt all alone down here. So I think she moved back mostly to be with her. Her aunt's health isn't the best."

"I got the impression from Ashley that she lost her job and her aunt took her in."

Mrs. Gunn smiled. "That's just Ashley being Ashley. She always acts tough, and wouldn't want people to think that she was ever doing something for somebody else."

"Sometimes the best people are those who don't shine a light on their virtues," Clarissa observed.

"Agreed. I'm just happy that the two of you are getting along."

Clarissa nodded. She was more than glad she'd hired Ashley. "On another subject," she said, "you won't have to prepare anything for my dinner tonight. I'm going out."

"Oh?" Mrs. Gunn stared at her with a raised eyebrow.

Clarissa wished she were strong enough to ignore that silent query, but she knew she wasn't. "I'm having dinner with Andrew Corrigan, the church lawyer," she admitted.

"Discussing business?"

Clarissa blushed. "I'm sure business will come up."

Mrs. Gunn set her mouth in a firm line. "I know his father. He and Arthur Bailey have had a law firm in town for years. But . . . I've never heard anything bad about them," she admitted grudgingly.

"I'm sure that's why they're the church lawyers," Clarissa said.

"I heard the boy had come back to town. He was working up in New York, wasn't he?"

"That's what he told me."

"Well, of course your life is your own, but just remember that people in town have a tendency to gossip," Mrs. Gunn warned. "Your life will be an open book. And, being a minister and all, they'll gossip even more than usual."

"Don't worry," Clarissa said. "I'll observe all the proprieties."

Mrs. Gunn stared at her, as if wondering whether that was true.

After grudgingly finishing her second piece of toast under the housekeeper's watchful eye, Clarissa went over to the office. There, she sat behind her desk, thinking about the sermon she had planned for this Sunday. Normally she'd already have it done, but between preparing for the board meeting and keeping up her murder investigations, she'd gotten behind schedule.

She was in the process of jotting down some notes when Ashley popped her head in the doorway.

"So, how did things go last night?" the younger woman asked. "My aunt already told me the result of the vote, but I want the blow-by-blow."

"There's not much to tell," Clarissa said, leaning back in her chair. "I presented the evidence that you got for me—thanks again for that. And then the board was swayed to vote against KRC's offer. Harry Blanchard wasn't happy and walked out of the meeting."

"Harry was born unhappy. I went to school with his two sons. They were equally miserable human beings," Ashley said matter-of-factly.

"It's probably not easy having Harry for a father."

"I suppose not. Another reason why Harry wanted the sale to go through is that he's a commercial realtor, and he was probably hoping this was the beginning of the commercial development of Shore Side."

"He should have recused himself from the vote if he had a conflict of interest," Clarissa said with a frown.

Ashley gave a grim smile. "That would be expecting him to have some integrity."

"What's done is done," Clarissa said with a wave of her hand, and then changed the subject. "I was wondering if you could get me the phone number of a Sharon Meissner. She's a realtor here in Shore Side."

"Should be easy. All I have to do is check out the websites for the ten or so realtors in town until I find her number," Ashley said. "Planning to buy a house? I thought you got the parsonage for free."

Clarissa motioned for Ashley to come in the office and sit down. She then told her everything she had learned from her interview with Owen Chandler.

"Wow!" Ashley exclaimed. "You did make some progress. Now you know that Ames was blackmailing a killer."

"I don't exactly know it, but it seems like a reasonable suspicion," Clarissa said.

"Chandler's lucky to still be alive."

"I warned him of that."

"So now you're thinking that maybe Ames told his girlfriend who the killer is?" Ashley asked.

"Maybe," Clarissa replied. "David Ames wasn't a big talker, at least not when it came to things he wanted to keep secret. But everyone slips up once in a while. I'm wondering if maybe he dropped a hint."

"Pillow talk," Ashley said with a grin.

"Something like that."

"Speaking of which, isn't your date with Andrew the Hunk tonight?"

"Mrs. Gunn has already warned me that the entire town will be watching, so I have to be every inch the lady," Clarissa said primly.

"That's the trouble with Shore Side, it's filled with spies. Where are you going to dinner?" Ashley asked.

"I don't know. He's picking the place."

"Maybe you'll be lucky, and he'll take you somewhere fifty miles outside of town where you can kick up your heels. I'll look forward to hearing about it." Ashley smiled at the startled expression on Clarissa's face. "Of course, only the expurgated version. My ears are too young to hear all the steamy details." With a final laugh, she left the office and closed the door behind her.

An hour later, Clarissa was putting the finishing touches on her sermon when her phone rang. It was Ashley, who told her that she had a call from a Samantha Jones.

"Hello, Ms. Jones," Clarissa answered once Ashley had transferred the call.

"Hi, Reverend Abbot. I received a message from Ramona Russell saying you were looking for someone to replace Jack Spurlock as the church's maintenance person," a woman said in a deep, smooth voice. "It was certainly a shame about Jack. I worked with him on a couple of projects. He was a good man."

Clarissa agreed. "You came highly recommended by Ramona," she said, "so I thought we should get together and see if we can come to an arrangement."

"That sounds fine. I've got a small job I'm finishing up in your neighborhood. Could I come by and talk with you in about an hour?"

"Perfect," Clarissa responded.

After she'd hung up, she returned to working on her sermon, which was on spring and the rebirth of life. She'd gotten her church assignment too late for the Easter service this year, so she was going to visit a similar theme in a different context.

The phone rang again, and this time Ashley told her that Ramona Russell was on the line.

"Hi, Clarissa," Ramona said. "I'm calling because I've heard that Harry Blanchard and a couple of his friends have been calling members of the congregation, urging them to override the board decision and pass the land sale at our church meeting on Sunday."

"Can he do that?" Clarissa asked.

"He's within his rights to call others and express his opinion. All I can do is mount a phone campaign by the people on our side to vote against the sale."

"That sounds divisive."

"It is, but we can't have Harry overriding the board and getting his own way. Otherwise he'll keep doing it, and before long, he'll be running the church," Ramona said. "The next time, he might override the board on something even more important."

"Such as?"

"Such as you keeping your job. I'm sure that there's nothing Harry would like to do more than replace you with a clone of Reverend Hollingsworth." Ramona paused for a moment, and then went on in a softer voice. "But don't be concerned. I'm pretty sure he's not going to get his way."

Troubled by the conversation, Clarissa hung up the phone and stared at the mahogany walls. Only her third week on the job in her first church, and she was already mired in a bitter controversy. She knew that however this issue turned out there were going to be long-run implications. But maybe peace and serenity were too much to ask for when running any institution made up of flawed human beings.

Ashley popped her head in the doorway and announced that Samantha Jones had arrived. Clarissa pulled her chair out from behind the desk and rolled it around so she could sit directly across from her visitor. She was just done as the woman walked through the doorway.

Samantha Jones was African-American, around Clarissa's age, and an inch or so taller, and although she wore a loose-fitting work shirt and baggy jeans, they did little to conceal her shapely figure. Clarissa invited her in and they sat across from each other, having agreed to go by first names.

"Thanks for coming," Clarissa started off. "As I said on the phone, Ramona highly recommended you, so I wanted to explain the job to you to see if you'd be interested."

"Ramona's a wonderful person, and I'm honored that she should think of me," Samantha said.

After Clarissa explained in some detail the responsibilities of the position, Samantha sat for a moment without speaking.

"So essentially, I'd be a combination janitor and handyperson," she finally said.

"The official church title is sacristan, but your description is pretty accurate," Clarissa replied. "I realize that it *is* below your skill level. I'm sure it was below Jack's, as well. I suspect he only did it because he was a member of the church."

"And the salary?" asked Samantha.

Clarissa told her the salary, and Samantha smiled. "The title is clearly a substitute for money."

Clarissa smiled back. "Afraid so. I can promise that, over time, I will try to get you more."

Samantha shook her head. "Doesn't matter. I wouldn't take the job for the money. It'll be a good way to get my name out in the community—better than paid publicity. I'll be happy to take the job," she said.

"Great," Clarissa replied. "As I said, there will be a six-week probation period, and then the church board votes on making you sacristan. If you like us and we like you, we'll be all set. I'd be particularly pleased to have you on the job since you're a veteran."

Samantha smiled and nodded. "Since I have some time and my equipment with me, are there any jobs you'd like me to work on right now, Clarissa?"

"As a matter of fact, Mrs. Gunn the housekeeper says that the parsonage sink is draining slowly," Clarissa informed her. "She's over there right now and will be happy to tell you all about it."

"I'll go right over and take a look."

"And, whenever you get a chance, I'd appreciate it if you'd inspect the church from top to bottom to see if there are any problems that may have been deferred."

"Will do." Samantha put out a hand. "Thanks for the position."

Clarissa shook her hand. "I look forward to our working together."

As Samantha walked through the outer office, she and Ashley looked closely at each other, as if each recognized another person who might not fit into a simple social mold.

Once Samantha left, Ashley turned to Clarissa and said, "If she's as capable as she looks, she'll do fine." She handed Clarissa a slip of paper. "Here's Sharon Meissner's phone number. She works at Ocean Breeze Realty."

Clarissa thanked her and returned to her office to make the call. It was high time to resume her investigation.

Chapter Sixteen

Clarissa stood in front of Ocean Breeze Realty and tried to formulate an interview strategy. She had walked six blocks from the church to the pedestrian mall in the center of town where Ocean Breeze was located, nestled between an art gallery and a kitchen supply store. Crowds of spring tourists were strolling along through the mall, browsing in the shops and enjoying the pleasant weather.

When she had called Sharon Meissner to make the appointment, Clarissa had used her by now shopworn reason that she was gathering information for David Ames' eulogy. Sharon had immediately invited her to come over and had sounded anxious to help.

After some back-and-forth with herself, Clarissa had decided that it would be best to take a gentler approach than she had with Owen Chandler. Sharon was probably grieving over David's death and might yield more information if approached with sympathy rather than suspicion.

Clarissa went into the office and told the young receptionist staffing the front desk whom she was there to see. The girl nodded with a smile, and quickly made a phone call.

The woman who immediately came out of a back office was stylishly dressed, petite, and in her mid-fifties. Clarissa wondered what Sharon had seen in the emaciated man Clarissa had met in the hospital, but then she chided herself that no one looked his or her best when seriously ill.

"Hello, Reverend, nice to meet you," the woman said, putting out her hand and giving Clarissa a warm smile.

"Please, call me Clarissa," Clarissa said, shaking her hand.

"And I'm Sharon."

The realtor led her into a small office that was slightly claustrophobic due the one small window being half-concealed by shutters. A large computer monitor seemed to dominate the room.

"So how did you find out that I was a friend of Dave's?" Sharon asked, sitting down behind the desk.

Clarissa took the chair opposite Sharon. "I was doing a computer search on David and came across a newspaper picture of the two of you at the opening of a new bar in town," she said.

"Of course, I remember that night," said Sharon. "I was there because I'd helped the owner purchase the bar. I invited Dave along because they were going to put on quite a lavish private party. He enjoyed that sort of thing."

Clarissa smiled. "Did you know David very long?"

"We went out together for about two years. Of course, I'd sort of known him before that. I've lived in Shore Side for over twenty years, so I'd seen him around town a few times." Sharon's face darkened. "My husband died four years ago. It was very sudden. His heart. I didn't socialize for a couple of years after that, except for what I had to do as part of my work. Then I met Dave."

"What was he like?"

"Older than I was," she laughed. "It took me a while to get over the fact that he was almost old enough to be my father. We even used to joke about it."

"I can see where that might be a problem," Clarissa said.

"But it wasn't . . . not really," Sharon said. "Dave was the kind of guy who made that stuff seem unimportant. He was just a fun guy who never acted his age, at least not until near the end."

Clarissa decided to work around to what really interested her. "Did David ever talk about his past?" she asked.

"Bits and pieces. But he wasn't one of those guys always rambling on about the good old days. He'd talk about working on the fishing boats, and some of the restaurants he'd worked in when he was younger."

"Did he tell you about working for Royce Llewellyn?"

"He mentioned it once," Sharon said. "I'd read a newspaper story on the history of Shore Side that talked about the murder, and I asked him if he remembered it, since it was before my time. He said he'd worked for Llewellyn for a little while. But he didn't say any more than that."

"What sorts of things did the two of you like to do?" Clarissa asked to lighten the mood.

"Oh, the usual. We'd go out to dinner. Hit a movie. Walk on the beach. That sort of thing. We'd go to a bar occasionally, but not often. A lot of guys in bars would recognize Dave because he grew up here. They'd want to come over and join us, but I think he liked to keep me more to himself."

And away from people who might say too much, Clarissa thought.

"Probably the biggest thing we did was to go on a Mediterranean cruise together," Sharon mused.

Clarissa raised her eyebrows. "David must have had a good pension to afford that sort of thing."

Sharon shook her head. "From what he told me about his work history, it was mostly on fishing boats and pick-up construction jobs, so I doubt he had any pension," she said. "I asked him once where he got the money to take us around. I figured I was making more than he was, and I should at least pay my fair share. But he never let me pay. When I asked him, he just put a finger beside his nose, which I took to mean that it was a secret. But with Dave you could never tell. He was quite a kidder."

Clarissa smiled. "So he never gave you a hint?"

The realtor leaned back in her chair. "One time I got a little more insistent than usual because I was feeling particularly guilty about not paying my way. And he said that someone else was paying for both of us. I asked who that was. He just smiled and said that sometimes, the people who do things are the ones you would least suspect. He wouldn't tell me anything more than that." She shrugged.

"What you've told me will be very helpful for when I speak at his wake," Clarissa said. And very helpful for her investigation.

"Do you know when that will be? I'd like to attend, even though we hadn't been going out for the last couple of months," Sharon said.

"Why not?" Clarissa asked.

"When Dave found out that he was really sick, he told me it was over between us," Sharon said sadly. "He didn't want me hanging around watching him die. I tried to reason with him, but he wouldn't listen. I hadn't seen him in the two months before he passed away."

"Well, I haven't been told exactly when the wake will be," Clarissa said, avoiding any mention of police involvement. "But once I find out, I'll definitely let you know. Did David have any other good friends that I could talk to?"

Sharon paused. "I don't know that he had *any* close friends, which is kind of odd when you figure that he lived in town his whole life. There were some guys at church that he used to play golf with, but I never got the impression that they were close friends. Once he said to me that 'old friends were the best friends.'"

"What did he mean?" Clarissa asked.

"When I asked him, he said Jack Spurlock was his only old friend, and the only one left that he trusted, because Jack had been there for him when he needed him. He said that, when he died, he intended to pass something important on to Jack."

"Did you have any idea what he intended to pass on?"

"Maybe money." Sharon laughed. "He certainly didn't have any valuable stuff. His apartment was so bare that you would hardly think that anyone lived there."

Clarissa figured she knew what David planned to pass on to Jack—the identity of Llewellyn's murderer.

"I wonder if Dave left a will?" Sharon said.

Clarissa didn't know the answer to that. "Did he have any family?" she asked.

"Some cousins, but they weren't close. Who will settle his estate?"

"I imagine his lawyer, if he had one," Clarissa supplied.

"So Jack Spurlock will get whatever Dave left him."

Clarissa shook her head. "Jack died a couple of days after Dave."

Sharon shook her head and tears came to her eyes. "Maybe he died because of the death of his friend."

"Perhaps," Clarissa said, and thought, *but not in the way you think.*

Chapter Seventeen

Clarissa stood in the shower, enjoying a brief few minutes of relative relaxation. She was getting ready for her date with Andrew Corrigan, but her mind was focused more on David Ames and wondering whether she would ever find out who had killed him. She felt that she knew *why* he was killed, just not who had done it.

As the hot water sluiced over her body, she reviewed her suspects. Maggie Preston and Doris Llewellyn had accused each other of killing Royce Llewellyn, and both were likely suspects for that murder. But while Maggie was physically capable of smothering David Ames, Clarissa doubted that Doris was strong enough. So that gave Maggie the edge as the killer. But it was somewhat doubtful that Maggie had enough money to have paid blackmail to Ames for almost fifty years. Her luncheonette was doing well now, but it must have been a long struggle before she was financially secure. Doris, on the other hand, was probably well enough off to have paid Ames to keep quiet. Therefore, both women were flawed suspects.

Clarissa sighed. She got out of the shower and began to dry herself.

Then a thought came to her. She had been assuming that Royce had been murdered for a personal reason based on his philandering or his mistreatment of his employees, but what if someone had stood to gain financially from his death? She decided to talk to

Detective Baker after church on Sunday to ask about Llewellyn's business associates.

As she was drying her hair, her mind drifted to her other pressing problem: Kenneth Rogers and his sidekick, Harry Blanchard. If Harry was able to convince enough members of the congregation that the sale of the land was a good idea, he might get it approved. If that happened, Clarissa could imagine some members of the church board being forced to resign in protest of the result.

What if Harry got his cronies elected to a new board, and they did everything he wanted? Clarissa could easily see herself losing her position. She wondered with grim humor what the record was for the shortest tenure as a minister. Then she took a deep breath and told herself not to rush down that dark tunnel. Probably none of this would come to pass.

She slipped into her dress, applied some light makeup, and ten minutes later, was standing by the front door waiting for Andrew to arrive.

Why had she agreed to have Andrew pick her up at the parsonage? She should have said she would drive herself to wherever they were having dinner. What if things didn't go well? If she had her own transportation, she could just get up and leave because she wasn't dependent on him for a ride home. Although dramatic exits weren't exactly her thing, she always liked to leave her options open.

She shook her head; she was worrying too much about this. After all, it had been a while since she'd last been on a date.

The doorbell rang, and Andrew stood on the doorstep with a bouquet of spring flowers in his hand. He followed Clarissa into her kitchen, where she put the flowers in water.

"Where are we going to eat?" she asked, trying to sound casual as she arranged the flowers in their vase.

"The Stafford Inn, if that's okay with you?" Andrew replied.

"That's fine," she said, relieved that it was only half a mile from the parsonage, within easy walking distance—even in dress shoes. "I could have walked down there and met you."

Andrew smiled. "On a first date I like to observe all the proprieties."

She wondered if that made him a gentleman or a hidebound traditionalist. She was still wondering about that as she got in his car and they drove the few blocks to the restaurant.

Andrew turned his keys over to the valet, and they made their way to the hostess' station. She quickly led them to a nice table for two that looked out on the garden.

The waitress took their drink orders. Andrew asked for a martini, while Clarissa chose a glass of white wine.

Andrew looked across the table at her and smiled. "Well, let's get the most difficult question out of the way first. Why did you decide to become a minister?" he asked.

Clarissa sighed to herself. This was the question that every man asked her. Most ministers, male or female, found themselves frequently queried about this, but she thought it was more common for women to be asked, since female ministers were still a bit of a novelty.

Andrew must have detected her discomfort. "Sorry," he said. "Maybe I shouldn't have asked that."

"No, it's okay," Clarissa said. "It's just that people seem to expect some kind of dramatic answer, like there was a banner across the sky from God that told me to follow this profession."

Andrew smiled. "There wasn't?"

"Not exactly. It all started when I was a junior in college and got hurt just before our championship lacrosse game," Clarissa explained. "I was the captain of the team, and I was completely devastated. For me, winning that game was the most important thing in my life, and I wasn't even able to go on the field and help my team."

"Did your team lose?"

"Actually, they won easily." She gave a short laugh. "Somehow that made it even worse, because they won without me, their star player. That's when I began to realize that I wasn't as important as I thought I was, and that I had to start getting over myself. So I devoted a lot of my time during my senior year to doing volunteer work through a local church. The minister there was a great guy, and that's how I began to think about going into the seminary."

The waitress brought their drinks, and they were silent for a few moments before the conversation started up again.

"Did you ever go back to playing lacrosse after your injury?" Andrew asked.

"Yes, but I was never quite as good as before."

"Because of your injury."

Clarissa paused and looked across the room. "No, because I was less aggressive. I never cared quite as fiercely about winning after that."

"I get the feeling that you've never stopped caring about winning," Andrew said.

Clarissa smiled. "Maybe just not at any cost."

"And was it through volunteer work that you got involved in religion?" he asked.

"Through serving others, I found my way to God. I also found that all the studying I was called to do in the seminary somehow spoke to me and met some need that I had. I still can't fully explain it."

The waitress came by and took their dinner orders. As soon as she left the table, Clarissa said, "Enough about me. Time to turn the tables. Why did you become a lawyer?"

"The easy answer would be because my father is one," Andrew answered. "I've always admired him and felt that the job he did was definitely a service to others. But when I got my first job in Manhattan, I began to see that there are many different types of lawyers. I was spending all my time defending large corporations, often against suits brought by the little guy who had been wronged. I know someone has to protect the rights of businesses, but that wasn't what I wanted to spend my life doing. I was more interested in working on the individual level like my dad did, helping out friends and neighbors. The money certainly isn't as good, but the job satisfaction is greater."

"Your job isn't that different from mine, except you use different tools," Clarissa observed.

"And answer to the authority of the law rather than the authority of God."

Clarissa smiled. "The law might be easier to interpret than the will of God."

Andrew grinned. "Not always."

They sat and sipped their drinks, looking out at the garden, which was gradually becoming dappled with shadows. Their waitress brought their food and they began to eat.

"Speaking about winning, as we were earlier, I wanted to congratulate you on getting your way on the land deal," Andrew said.

"I wouldn't say I got my way," Clarissa said, maybe a shade sharply. "I just presented the facts and the board made a decision."

Andrew frowned. "But do you really think that decision was the best for the church? Couldn't it use the money?"

Clarissa put down her knife and fork. "What's going on here, Andrew?" she asked suspiciously. "The other day when we spoke, you were the one who emphasized the environmental concerns. Now all of a sudden it's about the money."

"I never said that," he retorted. "I just want you to look at it from all sides."

"And who encouraged you to do that?" she asked.

He blushed. "My father."

"And why does he suddenly care so much that I see all sides?"

Andrew looked uncomfortable.

"Who does he have as a client? Kenneth Rogers?" Clarissa demanded.

Andrew shook his head.

"Of course not; Rogers is too big to use a local firm. It must be Harry Blanchard."

Looking even more miserable, Andrew nodded. "They've worked together on a lot of commercial real estate deals in the past. They're sort of friends," he admitted.

Clarissa leaned across the table, her eyes fierce. "So your father told you to go out with me to soften me up, so I'd go along with Harry?"

"No, of course not," Andrew replied. "If that were the case, I would have gone out with you before the vote."

"So why bring all this up now? It's over."

"But it isn't," he said. "You know that Harry is out there campaigning to get people in the congregation to vote against it. If you could just say something neutral from the pulpit on Sunday, people might go along with him."

"And why would I want that?"

"I know Harry. He's not a nice man, and you don't want him for an enemy. If you remain neutral, he can't blame you if the vote *does* go against him," said Andrew.

"So you're suggesting all this for my sake—not because your father wants Harry's real estate deal to go through?" Clarissa could hear her voice becoming louder.

Andrew nodded. "I wouldn't have brought it up at all if I wasn't afraid of what might happen to you as a result of getting involved in this controversy."

"Would you like some coffee or dessert?" the waitress asked, eyeing them cautiously.

"Not for me," Clarissa said, not taking her eyes from Andrew, who was glancing about him nervously.

Andrew shook his head, as well.

"Then I'll get your bill," the waitress said, edging away from their table.

Clarissa got to her feet. She reached in her purse and threw three twenties on the table. "I hope that covers my share. It's all I've got with me."

"You don't have to . . . "

"I think I'll walk home," she snapped. "Thank you for a *partially* nice evening."

Without looking back and with her head held high, Clarissa strode out of the restaurant.

Chapter Eighteen

A ringing telephone woke Clarissa the next morning. She'd had trouble getting to sleep after she got home from her dinner with Andrew. She'd tried meditation, prayer, and warm milk, but was still so angry over his attempt to manipulate her that sleep wouldn't come. It wasn't until the early hours of the morning that she'd fallen soundly asleep. Now her cell phone was insistently ringing, even though her bedside clock said it was only six in the morning.

"Have you seen the newspaper this morning?" Ashley asked when Clarissa answered the phone.

"Is it even printed yet?" Clarissa mumbled, struggling to focus.

"Good one, Boss," Ashley said. "I know it's a little early, but I thought you'd want to know. The state attorney general has indicted Kenneth Rogers for bribery and fraud."

Clarissa awoke with a start. "Really?"

"Yep. There's a front-page story. I think our boy is in a world of hurt. Do you think that will influence the church vote?"

Clarissa smiled to herself. "I think it very well might."

"So how did your date go? Hey, I'm not interrupting anything am I?"

"Very funny. And don't ask."

"That bad?" Ashley said, the concern apparent in her voice. "I had high hopes for that guy. He's a real cutie."

"Yeah, well, looks aren't everything," Clarissa said, and she went on to give a summary of what had taken place.

There was a long silence on the other end of the phone. Finally, Ashley said, "Well, I can see why you were angry. He shouldn't have mixed business with pleasure."

"For him it was all business. He was just interested in getting me to support his father's client," Clarissa said, getting angry all over again.

"Sure, but, you know, it's hard for a boy to go against his father."

"Not if he's a grownup," Clarissa snapped.

"Okay, but he was, after all, *somewhat* concerned for your well being," Ashley pointed out. "Getting in wrong with Harry Blanchard could jeopardize your job. Andrew was really just suggesting that you remain out of it, so Harry would be less inclined to come after you."

"I see. Are you implying that I should be more understanding of Andrew's position?" asked Clarissa.

"I think he was sort of between a rock and a hard place, so maybe you should cut him a little slack."

Clarissa paused for a moment. Was it possible that she had been a little too hard on Andrew? Her initial anger when she realized that he had a hidden agenda had begun to dissipate, encouraged by Ashley's comments.

"I'll give some thought to what you've said," Clarissa replied. "See you in church tomorrow."

"Oh, that's guaranteed. It's all part of my contract with my aunt."

When Clarissa had washed up, she went down to the kitchen, where Mrs. Gunn was just starting to prepare breakfast.

"You're up early," she said with a note of concern in her voice. "How about a fried egg for breakfast with some bacon?"

"I'll have one egg, but not bacon."

Mrs. Gunn sighed.

"Ashley called me early this morning to tell me about Kenneth Rogers being indicted. Have you seen the paper?" Clarissa asked.

"Just before I left the house. I guess that puts an end to the plans to buy the church land. All for the best, I say," Mrs. Gunn said.

"Harry Blanchard won't be happy."

Mrs. Gunn grunted, as if to say that was all for the best as well. "How are you otherwise?" she asked, eyeing her carefully.

"Fine. Why do you ask?"

The woman stared at the egg in her hand as if unsure of what to do next. "Mrs. Dorman—you know her, she's the short woman in church with the large perm."

Clarissa nodded.

"Well, her daughter is a waitress at the Stafford Inn."

Clarissa felt her stomach sink, anticipating what was coming next.

"Anyway," Mrs. Gunn continued, "Mrs. Dorman called me to say that she heard from her daughter that you'd had a spat with a young man in the restaurant last night."

Clarissa shook her head sadly. "I guess nothing is private in town. I feel really terrible about having caused a scene."

"Having an argument isn't so bad. I had lots of them over the years with Mr. Gunn. The making up was actually quite nice," she said with a surprisingly mischievous twinkle in her eye.

"But I shouldn't have had a fight in public," Clarissa said. "I should have controlled myself more."

"Perhaps. However, it only goes to prove that you're human," Mrs. Gunn replied. "Some of the more strait-laced members of the congregation may not approve, but they probably didn't want a woman minister in the first place. Most will feel that it proves you're more aware of the problems that can come up in real life. You're not floating ten feet above the ground on a cloud like Reverend Hollingsworth was."

Clarissa tried to smile. "Thank you for that charitable interpretation of what I did."

Mrs. Gunn sat down across from her at the table, the egg still clutched in her hand. "Do you want to tell me what the tiff was about?"

Clarissa gave her a condensed version of the argument.

Mrs. Gunn clicked her tongue. "Andrew was wrong in the way he approached the whole thing," she said. "He should have been more open with you from the start about his father's involvement with Harry. But Ashley may be right; perhaps you did overreact a wee bit. After all, the boy was in an awkward spot with his father on one side and the woman he's interested in on the other. Maybe you should consider giving him a second chance."

"Perhaps you and Ashley are right," Clarissa conceded. "I'll certainly think about it."

"But wait for him to call you first."

"Really?"

Mrs. Gunn nodded firmly. "If he doesn't call to apologize, he isn't a keeper. Now, how about that breakfast? Sure I can't interest you in some bacon?"

After breakfast, Clarissa walked over to the office. Since it was Saturday and Ashley wouldn't be coming in today, Clarissa decided it would be a good time to sit, meditate, and pray.

But before she could settle in, the phone rang. It was Detective Baker.

"I'd like to stop by to see you, if you aren't too busy?" he said.

"When?" Clarissa asked.

"Right away," he said, with a note of asperity in his voice.

Sensing that perhaps she had been found doing something wrong, she quickly agreed.

Fifteen minutes later, Detective Baker was sitting across from Clarissa in her office, staring at the walls.

"You know, I've seen interrogation rooms that were less depressing than this," he commented.

"Reverend Hollingsworth designed it. I think he found it comforting."

"Figures." Baker got down to business. "Look, the reason I'm here is that we went to talk with Owen Chandler, but he appears to have flown the coop. He put some college girl who was assisting him in charge of the inn and then disappeared without leaving a forwarding address. The girl reports that he did this after meeting with a woman who, according to her description, looked a lot like you." The detective stopped speaking and sat there staring at her.

Clarissa wondered where the girl had been hiding during her conversation with Owen. She'd certainly thought their conversation was private. Since Detective Baker had a good description of her, there was no point in denying it—not that she would have lied anyway.

"I did go to see Chandler," she admitted.

"What did you say to him that made him run?" Detective Baker asked.

"I may have suggested that the deaths of Ames and Spurlock might have been murders."

Baker gave her a stern glance and his face turned slightly red. "I thought we had agreed to keep that a secret."

"We did. But I couldn't let Owen Chandler stay around without knowing that his life might be in danger," Clarissa insisted. "That would make me a virtual accessory to murder if he got killed."

"Not in the eyes of the law."

"Well, morally."

"Well, now I have no way of finding out what he knew about the Ames murder."

"I can help you with that," Clarissa said, and she told Detective Baker about Chandler's scheme to blackmail Ames.

"So, let me get this straight," Baker said when she was done. "Ames was blackmailing the killer of Royce Llewellyn, and Chandler was getting a cut of that money by blackmailing Ames, because he gave him a phony alibi."

"That's about the size of it."

"And when were you planning to share this information with me?" he asked.

"As soon as I could put together whom Ames might have been blackmailing," she responded. "I talked to his girlfriend, Sharon Meissner, but she didn't seem to have any idea."

"How did you find out about her?" asked Baker, suddenly sounding very tired.

"Ashley did a search on Ames and found a picture of him in *The Shore Side Courant* with Sharon at a bar opening."

Detective Baker sat back and shook his head. "Although I hate to admit it, you've done good work, certainly better than we have so far. But you've got to share information with me in a more timely way," he said. "We might have been able to interrogate Chandler before he disappeared, and could have found out more than you did."

"Probably not," Clarissa said. "I used the threat of having to talk to you to get him to tell me what he knew."

"Glad I could be of some service," Baker said sarcastically, but he was smiling, so Clarissa figured he wasn't too angry. "But what really worries me," he continued, "is that you're still poking around in this case when there's a killer out there trying to cover his trail."

"I'll be careful."

Clarissa wasn't sure when the last time was that she'd seen a grown man roll his eyes.

"Did you ever get the original file on Royce Llewellyn's murder up from the basement?" she asked.

"I did. Actually, Officer Rudinski did. He's still complaining about the noise of the rats in the walls. Personally, I think he's making it up," Baker commented.

"But still, you sent him down to do it, rather than getting the file yourself."

He smiled. "Rank has its privileges, and I hate rats. Why did you want to know about the files?"

"What I wanted to know was whether anyone other than David Ames was seriously considered as a suspect in the murder," Clarissa said.

Baker stopped and thought. "There was one fellow who worked as a cook in the kitchen; Llewellyn had fired him a couple of days before for coming in late to work. And there was a hostess in the bar that he accused of stealing from the till around the same time. They were both checked out and had solid alibis."

"As solid as the one Ames had?" asked Clarissa. The detective frowned at the implied criticism, and Clarissa gave an apologetic smile. "Sorry, that was out of line."

"Not really," he replied. "The case really wasn't handled very well at the time. But according to the files, the alibis on these other two suspects were pretty solid. The cook had gotten another job in Wildwood and was working that night. Somebody went up there, and it checked out; ten other people in the kitchen vouched for him. The woman got another job at a bar in town, and she was there at the time of the murder. Again, lots of people saw her. I guess she was quite pretty, so a number of the guys remembered her."

Clarissa stared at the mahogany walls and frowned. "I was just thinking, maybe we're wrong to assume that the killer was someone looking for revenge because Llewellyn had treated him or her badly," she said. "Instead, we should ask who stood to benefit financially from Royce Llewellyn's death."

"Good thinking," Baker said. "Sex and money are usually the two most common motives for murder. His wife inherited a pretty good chunk of change, especially after she sold the hotel, *and* he was cheating on her. So I guess by that standard, she'd be at the top of the list. Do you think she shot him, and then claimed it was some mysterious stranger?"

"She could have, I suppose, but the woman has got to be close to ninety," Clarissa said. "I doubt she's got the strength anymore to suffocate David Ames, even on his deathbed. It's even more unlikely that she knocked Jack off his ladder."

"Yeah, probably not," Baker agreed. "Although they do say that ninety is the new sixty."

Clarissa smiled and shook her head. "I've seen her, and she seems pretty frail. Did anyone else benefit from Llewellyn's death?"

"As I recall, Royce had a partner in the hotel who was quite a bit younger than he was," said Baker. "In fact, after the murder, I believe Llewellyn's wife sold her share of the hotel to him."

"Is he still alive?" Clarissa asked.

"Last I knew. His name is Ralph Blanchard. He's a member of our church, but he doesn't come out to services much anymore."

"Is he related to Harry Blanchard?"

Detective Baker nodded. "Harry is his grandson. His son was named George—that's Harry's father—but he died about ten years ago. I remember that Reverend Hollingsworth conducted the funeral service, right after he took over the church."

"Does Ralph still own the hotel?" asked Clarissa.

"I think he sold it in the early nineties, and it was torn down," Baker answered. "A new one was built on the site. The Sea Star, it's called, but as far as I know, Ralph never had anything to do with that."

"Do you think Ralph made a killing by buying out his former partner's half cheap?"

"You mean, do I think he had a motive for murder?"

Clarissa shrugged. "It's a thought."

"I don't know; that was all before my time. You could ask the widow or, of course, you could ask Ralph himself."

"So could you," Clarissa pointed out.

"Sure. I suppose I could. But Ralph, despite his age, is still pretty influential in town. I don't think I want to go questioning him without more evidence implicating him in a crime," Baker said.

Clarissa sat for a moment, staring across the room. "Maybe I could have a talk with him," she said. "If he's still in the church, he's probably the oldest member. It would only be right for the new minister to make a courtesy call."

Baker grinned. "You do have a devious side, Pastor. But there's no problem with that as far as I can see.

However, I still don't make him for our murderer. He's got to be almost as old as Royce's widow, so the same physical limitations apply. Unless he's stayed in phenomenal shape, I doubt that he killed Ames and Spurlock."

"Maybe he got his grandson to do it."

"Harry? Well, he's young enough, and has anger management problems. I know he can be a royal pain in the butt, but I'm not sure I see him as a murderer." The detective smiled. "If Harry were the one, it would be handy for you. You'd have the murder solved and get rid of a thorn in your side at the same time."

Clarissa sighed. "Life is rarely that cooperative, but talking to Ralph Blanchard might give me some new leads. I'd certainly come away with a new perspective by talking to someone who was there at the time and wasn't the wife or lover of the victim."

"I can't say that it's a bad idea, but be careful," Baker warned. "We've still got a killer out there. Whoever it is may be confident that they've eliminated all the loose ends, but if he or she becomes aware that you're asking questions, it could lead to trouble. You wouldn't want to be seen as the next loose end."

"Definitely not. I'll be careful not to make waves," Clarissa said.

Baker nodded. "By the way, I read about the Kenneth Rogers indictment this morning. That should be an end to this land deal controversy."

"What side did you take on that, if I may ask?" asked Clarissa.

"Absolutely against," he replied. "I've lived in Shore Side my whole life, and I don't want to see it change."

"Harry Blanchard's lived here his whole life, as well. That doesn't stop him from wanting change," she pointed out.

"Yeah. But he sees money to be made with more development. I just see more people to police. I don't have to arrest mosquitos."

"Even with the indictment, Harry may not give up," Clarissa cautioned.

"Maybe not, but I'd say his odds of winning over a majority of the congregation have been substantially reduced," Baker said.

"Let's hope so. I don't need controversy within the church right now."

After Detective Baker left, Clarissa spent the next hour closeted in her office, rehearsing her sermon for Sunday. She prided herself on making a good delivery, and had found that only practice guaranteed it.

She wondered if all this attention to her sermons would last once she became a more experienced minister. Maybe it would become easier as she relaxed into the job. She certainly hoped that time wouldn't make her indifferent to the spiritual and pastoral needs of her congregation.

She went back to the parsonage for lunch. She was eating a sandwich Mrs. Gunn had left for her (which was enough for three women) when the phone rang. It was Ramona Russell.

"I'm sure you've heard about the Rogers indictment by now," she said. "The whole town seems to know."

"Ashley delivered the message at dawn," Clarissa replied.

Ramona chuckled. "Well, at least it was some good news to start the day."

"But will it finally put an end to this? Or will Harry continue his campaign?" Clarissa asked. "He might still be able to get a lot of support for the sale."

"That's why I called to put your mind to rest," said Ramona. "Rogers took his offer off the table half an hour ago."

"He did?"

"I got a call from his lawyer saying that his client had reconsidered and wasn't interested in purchasing the land at this time."

"Why?"

"Don't know," Ramona said. "Lawyers never tell you any more than they have to. Maybe Rogers thought that the bad publicity would prevent him from getting the funding to build the condos. Or maybe he figured that he would need the money to fight the indictment in court."

"So it's all over with," Clarissa said with a note of relief.

"Yep. If you can give me a couple of minutes during the announcements section of the service tomorrow, I'll let everyone know that the full church meeting for tomorrow is canceled."

"Fine by me. You've got as much time as you need," Clarissa told her. "This is all a great relief, but I'm sure that Harry will be crushed."

"No doubt. I'd heard rumors that Rogers was going to throw some commercial real estate deals Harry's way if he could get the church to sell. Nothing bothers Harry more than losing money," Ramona said drily.

"By the way, what do you know about Harry's grandfather, Raymond?" Clarissa asked. She might as well use this chance to dig deeper into her investigation.

"I haven't heard anything about him recently," Ramona replied. "I know he still gives a substantial amount of money to the church. He was a real big deal on the church board until about ten years ago when his son died. Then he sort of retired from everything. I've heard that he still has some involvement in several business ventures around town, but he doesn't leave his house much."

"Is he like Harry?"

Ramona paused. "Only in that they both like making money from business ventures. But Raymond is known for being a decent, honest guy who did a lot to help the church and all sorts of charities around town. His son, George, was the same way."

"How did George die?" Clarissa asked.

"It was all very sudden. A heart attack, I think. Harry took over the commercial real estate business from his father. I'm afraid poor Harry has all the money-making instincts of his father and grandfather, but none of the charitable impulses. Unless he changes dramatically, he won't be remembered as fondly as they are."

"I was thinking of paying Raymond a visit. Is he still a member of the congregation?"

"You could check the official roll, but I'd certainly think so."

"I figured that I would visit everyone in the congregation over the next year, but I'd begin with the oldest first," Clarissa said.

"Sounds wonderful," Ramona said. "I suggested something similar to Reverend Hollingsworth years ago, but I guess he couldn't find the time. Visiting Raymond Blanchard would be very nice. As I said, he did a lot for the church. When you get to be that old, it means something to be remembered."

After she said goodbye to Ramona and hung up the phone, Clarissa went on the computer and checked the membership roll. Sure enough, Raymond was still listed as a member.

Feeling somewhat guilty due to her mixed motives for contacting Raymond—partly to stay in touch with a church member, and partly to find out what he remembered about a long ago murder—she dialed the number on the computer screen.

A woman with a brisk, efficient voice answered, identifying herself as Mrs. Rush, Raymond Blanchard's secretary. Clarissa told her that she was the pastor at Shore Side, and she'd like to visit Mr. Blanchard. Although she knew it was short notice, she wondered if he'd have any time available this afternoon. Mrs. Rush asked Clarissa to hold the line while she checked with her employer.

A few minutes later, she came back on the line and said that Mr. Blanchard would be pleased to see her at three o'clock. In fact, she said in a softer tone, he was looking forward to it. Clarissa ended the phone call happily.

Deciding that it was time to take a break from both church work and her investigations, she got into a T-shirt and shorts, and went out for a run. It was the first time in the three weeks since she'd taken over the church that she'd been able to exercise, and after a short spell of stiff awkwardness, her body loosened up and she felt herself relax into the rhythm of the run.

There was a sense in which running was a form of prayer for her, as her mind drifted away from her surroundings and she became more and more present to the moment. When Clarissa reached the promenade along the beach, she turned right to head down to the southern tip of Shore Side, not far from the vacant land owned by the church.

She was at the busiest part of the boardwalk where there were a variety of arcades, saltwater taffy shops, and rides for children, when she heard a man urgently call her name. He had to call twice before it fully registered with her.

She stopped and turned in the direction of the voice, and saw Andrew walking quickly towards her. He was wearing a pair of chino shorts and a polo shirt that accentuated his broad shoulders and narrow waist. Suddenly Clarissa was aware of standing there in a pair of washed-out shorts and a tattered T-shirt dripping with sweat, while Andrew, by contrast, appeared cool and crisp.

He came up and stood close to her. "I'm glad I ran into you today," he said. "I intended to phone you this morning, but I got called into work to get a will signed. I wanted to apologize for last night. The more I thought about it, the more I realized that I shouldn't have brought up the land deal when we were on a date. I should have kept the personal and the business separate."

Clarissa nodded. "That's true. However, I think I overreacted a bit as well," she admitted. "You were partly trying to give good advice to help me avoid getting mired in a nasty church controversy. Your intentions were good, but the timing was bad."

"Yeah, I let my father pressure me into doing that," he said. "I've just joined the firm, and I guess I didn't want to refuse to do something that was important to him. But I should have used better judgment."

Clarissa shivered slightly as a cool breeze came in from the ocean, chilling her sweating back. Andrew noticed her discomfort.

"Look, I don't want to delay you in the middle of your run, but I was wondering if you'd be willing to give me a second chance to make a first impression," he said with a smile.

Clarissa grinned. She remembered that both Ashley and Mrs. Gunn had urged her in that direction. She knew that she sometimes tended to judge men a bit harshly, especially since breaking up with Tyler. Maybe this was a time to go in a different direction.

"I guess I can do that," she said.

"Friends, then," he said, putting out his hand.

She took his hand in hers. "Friends."

"Are you free this Wednesday?" he asked. "I was thinking that on a Wednesday, there might be fewer locals to see us make a scene. I've already had a couple of people mention that I got into an argument with a beautiful woman in a restaurant last night."

"Flatterer," Clarissa said with a smile. "I was spotted by the daughter of a church member, so it's probably all around the congregation."

Andrew looked stricken. "I'm so sorry. Maybe this time we should go somewhere out of town."

"Are you expecting a repetition of last night?" she said, teasing.

"I certainly hope not. But a little privacy might not be a bad idea."

"Sounds good. Shall we say seven o'clock?"

"And I pick you up at the parsonage?"

Clarissa paused, then relented. "Okay. But don't bother to bring a gift. I've still got the flowers from last time."

"Sure. I'll see you then. Hope you haven't cooled down too much."

"I'll be fine."

They waved goodbye and Clarissa continued on her run. Although she tried to return her focus to the rhythm of the run and reestablish her meditative state, she found that the memory of Andrew filled her mind.

Clarissa tried to avoid being overly influenced by his good looks and charm. Although she had decided to forgive him after her conversations with Ashley and Mrs. Gunn, she didn't like people trying to manipulate her. She would go out with him again, but remain on her guard. She didn't want another Tyler situation on her hands.

Chapter Nineteen

The next morning at church, everything went smoothly. Ramona made the announcement about the offer for the land being withdrawn and the cancelation of the all-members meeting. Clarissa imagined that she heard a sigh of relief pass through the church, and was pretty sure she saw a number of people visibly relax. Harry Blanchard wasn't in church, so the one person who would probably have been infuriated by the outcome couldn't raise the stress level.

Clarissa's sermon also went well. Most people seemed attentive, laughing at the jokes and nodding when she made more serious points. Of course, there were a few who remained uninterested, but Clarissa figured there would always be some who would be bored even at the Second Coming.

After the service, she briefly spoke to Ramona; they again expressed their satisfaction that the controversy over the land deal had not led to what might have been a divisive vote.

Ashley sidled up to Clarissa as she stood outside the church later. "We dodged a bullet on that one," Ashley said.

"Indeed we did," Clarissa agreed.

Ashley bit her lip. "Look, I'm sorry I woke you up early yesterday morning with the news about the land deal falling through, and I certainly shouldn't have grilled you about your date."

Clarissa waved away her apology. "I was glad you let me know right away about Rogers, and your advice on Andrew was timely. I ran into him yesterday afternoon on the boardwalk."

"That's cute. Almost like one of those romantic comedies. So, did he grovel enough to get back in your good graces?"

Clarissa told her about his apology.

"Wow, that sounds great," Ashley remarked. "Maybe the guy really understands what he did wrong."

"And I understand what I did wrong as well."

"Sure. Although what he did was worse."

Clarissa smiled. "Spoken like a true friend."

Ashley grinned. "We girls have to stick together. So are you going out again?"

"On Wednesday. Probably somewhere out of town."

"Based on my vast experience with men," Ashley said with a smile, "I'd say you did the right thing by giving him another chance, and going out of town is a good idea, as well. No sense living your life in a fishbowl."

"I agree," Clarissa said. "This afternoon I'm also going to begin my long-term project of visiting every member in the congregation. I plan to start with Raymond Blanchard."

"Is he related to Harry?"

"His grandfather."

Ashley shook her head. "Why start with him?"

Clarissa explained that Raymond had been Royce Llewellyn's partner, and he had probably gained financially from his partner's death.

"Yeah, but he's got to be pushing ninety. He couldn't have killed Ames and Spurlock," Ashley objected.

"I don't suspect him of being the killer, but he might have some valuable information that would lead to a suspect."

Ashley looked thoughtful. "You know, maybe the killer feels safe now, and would be willing to just let things be if you would. If you start stirring the pot, who knows what might happen?"

"That might be true, but I can't let two deaths go unpunished."

"I suppose you're right, but stay alert. If there's anything I can help you with, let me know."

Clarissa reached over and squeezed her friend's hand. "Don't worry. I will."

***

After eating a small portion of the giant casserole that Mrs. Gunn had left for lunch, Clarissa drove the half-mile to Raymond Blanchard's house—more of a mansion, actually—set back from the street with a portico that made it look more Southern than Victorian. There was a parking area off to one side of the house, so Clarissa left her car there and went up on the grand porch.

The woman who answered the door was in her thirties; wearing a white blouse and a black pencil skirt, she gave the impression of a secretary more than a housekeeper.

"I'm Mrs. Rush," she said to Clarissa, guiding her inside and down a long hall. "Mr. Blanchard has been looking forward to meeting you."

"And I him."

The woman nodded, as if Clarissa was in for a pleasant experience. She knocked, then opened a door at the end of the hall.

At the far end of a long room, a tall, slender man was sitting in a wingback chair with a walker in front of him. He slowly stood as Mrs. Rush announced Clarissa and began to move in their direction.

Although Clarissa was tempted to hurry toward the man to cut down the distance he had to travel, something told her that he wouldn't appreciate having his infirmity demonstrated so blatantly. So Clarissa and Mrs. Rush stood where they were as Raymond Blanchard laboriously approached. When he finally got close enough, he put out his hand. Clarissa took it and found it to be warm and dry, his handshake surprisingly firm.

"Thank you for coming, Reverend Abbot," he said. "I appreciate that the church is taking an interest in its more senior members."

"Please, call me Clarissa, Mr. Blanchard," Clarissa said.

He raised an eyebrow. "Then you must call me Raymond."

"Very well. And I think the church will be the richer for being aware of all its members," she said.

"Shall I bring tea and some cakes?" asked Mrs. Rush.

"That would be nice," her employer said.

Once the woman had left the room, Raymond directed Clarissa to a couple of chairs in front of an ornate fireplace.

"I could see by the expression on your face that you were a bit surprised that Mrs. Rush took on the role of a servant," Raymond said as he seated himself. "She doesn't look the part because she isn't. She's actually a fully qualified nurse." He smiled. "Of course, she doesn't dress like a nurse, either, but that's due to my insistence that I don't want my house to look like an assisted living facility. She is also a highly qualified secretary and functions primarily as my assistant for business matters, when she isn't doling my pills out to me. I also have a cook and a housekeeper, so Mrs. Rush is generally free to handle office chores."

"So you remain active in business?" asked Clarissa.

"I've scaled back somewhat, but the mind is still sharp, even if the body is in decline. I need something to spend my time on, and business is what I know."

Mrs. Rush came in with a tray on which a tea set and a tray of assorted cakes were arranged. She poured the tea and placed it on the side tables next to each chair.

"I highly recommend the almond cake," said Raymond.

"That sounds splendid," Clarissa said.

Mrs. Rush put a piece on a plate and set it on the table next to her. After serving her employer, she quickly left the room.

Clarissa added some milk to her tea and took a sip, then she tasted the cake.

"Wonderful, isn't it?" the man asked, taking a piece of his own.

"Scrumptious."

He smiled. "I've always enjoyed eating, but with age, it's become one of the few pleasures that I haven't had to drastically curtail."

"I'm sure you've seen a lot of changes in the world during your lifetime."

"From when I began remembering things in the early thirties until today seems like several lifetimes in many ways; other times, it seems like the blink of an eye. Change, of course, often happens gradually, so it is only in looking back that you realize how different things are today than when you were a child," Raymond said.

"Do you have many regrets?" Clarissa asked, genuinely curious.

He chuckled. "Anyone my age would be lying if he said he didn't. The one thing I regret the most is that I didn't serve in World War II. I was a year or two too young. At the time, I admit, I felt lucky, but as time has gone by, I've come to regret not having taken part in the great adventure of my generation."

"But you might not have survived."

"There's always that," he said with a smile. "I suppose I should be grateful for the experiences I *have* had. And some of them have been quite delightful, like having beautiful women as ministers instead of stodgy men."

Clarissa blushed and smiled, thinking that this fellow was probably quite the charmer in his day. "Thank you," she said. "I hope my skills as a pastor also prove satisfactory."

"The fact that you've come to see me within a couple of weeks of taking up your duties demonstrates that will be the case," he complimented. "Coming to see the oldest first is probably wise, just in case." He winked. "You've already done far better than your predecessor, who visited once in ten years, and only came then to ask for money to get the church painted. I granted his request, but it was a bit galling."

"I think ministers today are being encouraged to get out more to meet their congregations," Clarissa said.

"They were sixty years ago, too. Perhaps the problem was with Hollingsworth rather than with ministerial training. Although he did play golf with my grandson, Harry, quite frequently. So perhaps I'm being too harsh."

"I gathered that was the Reverend's favorite sport. I also knew he was friends with Harry."

Raymond gave her a shrewd glance. "More than you are?"

Clarissa warned herself not to underestimate this man because of his age. His mind indeed was sharp, and his information was current. "Harry and I have had a recent disagreement over the sale of church land. Are you familiar with the issue?"

Raymond nodded. "I try to keep up-to-date on matters concerning Shore Side. I still have a number of friends from when I was more active who keep me well-informed," he said. "I knew that Rogers would eventually be exposed as a crook, and I warned Harry to have nothing to do with him, but I'm afraid my grandson has always been a bit too tempted by the allure of quick money."

"You prefer longer-term investments?"

"Harry likes to buy and sell commercial real estate; I prefer to run a business. Now, when I can't run them anymore personally, I invest in them. The profits are gradual, but more reliable."

"You were once partners with Royce Llewellyn, weren't you?" Clarissa asked.

Raymond smiled. "Ah, yes, those golden days of yesteryear. That really brings back memories. We owned The Harmony of the Sea Hotel together." He frowned. "Of course, not all of the memories are good. Royce was murdered."

"Yes, I know."

He gave her a sharp look. "How did you happen to find out about the murder so soon after arriving in town?"

"David Ames died a few days ago, and I've been preparing his funeral service," she explained.

Raymond tapped the arm of his chair, as if to stimulate his mind. "Of course, he was the prime suspect for a while because he'd had an argument with Royce, and was fired shortly before the murder. Royce was a friend and had a good head for business, but he had a tendency to be short-tempered with the staff. I'm sure the police found several suspects among our employees."

"After Royce was murdered, you bought the hotel from his widow, am I correct?" Clarissa asked.

"That's right. I did it more as a favor to Doris than as a wise business decision. The building was in need of extensive repairs, and even by the late sixties, people were losing interest in staying at traditional Victorian hotels. Modern was in," he said. "I was tempted to have us just sell it, but I thought it would be easier for her if I bought it and sold it later myself. Royce was really the one who enjoyed running the hotel."

"He liked the feeling of being in charge?"

"That was part of it. A side of him saw himself as the captain of a ship."

Clarissa took a deep breath and decided to risk a more controversial question. "Wasn't it also a way for him to form liaisons with women?"

Raymond smiled sadly. "By today's standards, Royce was a very politically incorrect employer, and by any standards, he was a less than faithful husband. I put up with it because he had good qualities, as well. In any event, after his death, I wanted to sell because it was not a big money maker. Oh, it made a profit, but there were lots of better places to put the money."

"If it was such a poor investment, why didn't you sell the hotel until 1980?" Clarissa asked.

"You are very well-informed," Raymond said with a shrewd glance at Clarissa. "Well, the answer is that my son George was a bit like Royce, and he loved being the boss of something. He had been Royce's assistant manager, so when I bought the hotel from Doris, I put it in his hands and told him he could run it as long as it made a profit. It did until 1980."

"That's why you sold it then—it stopped being a good investment?"

Raymond sighed. "Yes, at the time it was purely a business decision. At least that was the way I looked at it. But given what it did to my son, perhaps I should have thought about it differently."

"What happened?" Clarissa asked softly.

"Once George didn't have the hotel to manage, the heart went out of the boy. Oh, he carried on for another ten years dabbling at this and that. He started the commercial real estate company that Harry runs today, but his life was a misery. When the heart attack came in his late fifties, I'm sure that, for him, it was almost a relief."

"The hotel meant that much to him?"

"Indeed." Raymond nodded sadly. "Before Royce died, George was always urging me to buy him out. I made several offers just to appease George, but Royce was adamant that he wasn't going to sell. George was furious about it. He seemed to believe that Royce was doing it just to frustrate him. They got into several fierce arguments over it. Being an assistant manager wasn't enough for George. He wanted to be the captain of the ship, but so did Royce. And a ship can't have two captains."

"He must have been somewhat pleased when Royce was killed," Clarissa remarked.

Raymond gave her a troubled look. "I can tell you're thinking along the same lines that I did at the time. Is it possible my son killed Royce to get control of the hotel? I worried about that enough at the time that I checked into his whereabouts when Royce was murdered. George was off work that evening, so I wasn't able to conclusively confirm that he couldn't have done it. When I indirectly asked him where he had been when Royce was murdered, he said that he was home with his wife. I'm sure she would have confirmed his alibi. What wife wouldn't?"

"What did you think?" Clarissa asked.

Raymond glanced at the table next to his chair. "Would you be so kind as to pour me another cup of tea?"

"Of course."

He stayed silent while Clarissa poured them each more tea. He took a couple of sips before resuming. "I'm afraid that I always thought it was possible that George had killed Royce," he said softly. "They really didn't get along because they both wanted the same thing. I was much relieved when the police concentrated their investigation on the staff members Royce had fired. They never even questioned George or myself. Just as well—I wouldn't have lied for my son, and now I'd have something else to regret. Although I suppose none of it matters, now that George is dead."

Clarissa sat there for a long moment, uncertain whether she should say more.

Raymond studied her. "You're holding something back. Is there more that I should know?"

Despite her promise of confidentiality to Detective Baker, she felt that this was one of those times when it would be beneficial to share information in order to get information. She made her decision.

"David Ames didn't die of heart failure," she finally said. "He was murdered in the hospital, and I think he was killed because he'd been blackmailing the killer of Royce Llewellyn for the last fifty years."

Raymond sat for a moment, absorbing what he had been told, and then he smiled in relief. "So the killer couldn't have been my George. He's been dead for over twenty years."

"Some things are passed on in families," Clarissa said.

"Ah, you mean that Harry could have taken up his father's mantle in order to protect the reputation of the family?"

"Would he have come to you and told you what he was doing?" she asked.

Raymond shook his head. "He knows I don't fully approve of his values, and he knows that I would never condone blackmail under any circumstances. But why would Harry kill David Ames after paying blackmail for thirty years? Why not just wait for the man to die?"

"I believe Ames was going to pass along the information to someone else who would continue the blackmail," Clarissa said. "So the killer silenced him before that could happen."

"Who was Ames going to tell?"

"His old friend, Jack Spurlock."

Raymond frowned. "Didn't he recently die in an accident where he fell from a ladder?"

"It was no accident. The ladder was pushed."

The old man slumped back in his chair and closed his eyes. He looked every bit of his ninety-something years. "My grandson is many things: foolish, greedy, impulsive, and small-minded," he said. "But I can't imagine him being a multiple murderer."

"Maybe he isn't. It's only a hypothesis, and so far there's no hard evidence to back it up. I haven't presented my ideas to the police," Clarissa reassured him.

"Thank God for that. Would you leave the police out of it until you've talked with Harry?"

"I'm not sure he'll see me after this church land business," she said.

"He'll see you. I guarantee it. He expects to inherit a sizable estate after I go, and that gives me a great deal of influence over him," Raymond said drily. "Oh, yes, he'll talk to you. I'll have him give you a call to set up a meeting, but I won't tell him what it's about. You can approach it in your own way. All I ask is that you be fair and honest. Beyond that, let the chips fall where they may."

"Thank you. I greatly appreciate your help," Clarissa said.

Raymond gave her a thin smile. "This has certainly not been a typical pastoral visit."

"I'm sorry if I distressed you," she apologized.

"No, no. You've just reminded me of something important that I let slide in the past—ascertaining whether my son was guilty of murder. And that's made me very aware that I shouldn't make the same mistake in the present with my grandson."

Clarissa stood.

"Please forgive me if I don't stand," Raymond said. "I'm feeling rather tired right now."

She walked the few steps between the chairs and took his hand. "I look forward to seeing you again. Thank you for all your help," she said.

"No, no. Thank you, my dear. Thank *you*."

Chapter Twenty

As Clarissa looked out her window at the dawn on Monday morning, she saw that it was slightly overcast, and wondered if there was a possibility of rain in the afternoon. That would make it the kind of day at the beach that everyone on vacation dreaded.

She watched the sun appear as a fuzzy pink ball just above the horizon, and thought about yesterday's conversation with Raymond Blanchard. It certainly seemed as if his son, George, had a motive to kill Royce Llewellyn, since he had very much wanted to be in charge of running the hotel. However, it struck her as odd that he would happen to choose the day after David Ames was fired to commit the crime, unless he hoped the blame would fall on Ames. Of course, if Ames had nothing to do with the murder, there wouldn't necessarily be a connection between the two events. It could have been happenstance that the killer struck right after Ames was fired, and just luck that Ames went off to attack Llewellyn on the night that the killer decided to strike. Coincidences did happen, Clarissa reminded herself, but she couldn't rid herself of the suspicion that the two events were somehow connected.

Clarissa showered and dressed. She went down to the kitchen, where Mrs. Gunn was pouring herself a cup of coffee.

"I enjoyed your sermon yesterday on rebirth," Mrs. Gunn said, filling Clarissa's cup. "It's good to be reminded as we get older that things don't have to go on the way they are until the end."

"That's right. No matter what the past events in our lives, or how long one has been following a particular path in life, there is always the possibility of change if we remain open to it." Clarissa gave the woman a curious glance. "Were you thinking about this in a personal way? Are you contemplating a dramatic change in your life?"

Mrs. Gunn blushed and looked almost girlish. "Don't know how dramatic it is, but I did have a date yesterday afternoon. The first I've had since Mr. Gunn died ten years ago."

"How nice," Clarissa said, smiling. "Were you out with anyone I would know?"

Mrs. Gunn nodded. "Joe Morgan. He's a member of the church. I don't know if you remember him."

Clarissa nodded. She pictured a tall, gray-haired man with a kind face who had greeted her warmly each Sunday she had preached so far. "He seems like a nice man," she volunteered.

"He is. At least I think so. We haven't been seeing each other except at church up until now."

"Have you ever thought about remarrying?"

Mrs. Gunn paused. "For a long time I couldn't bear to think of the idea. Adjusting to living with another person just seemed more trouble than it was worth. Mr. Gunn and I got along pretty well, but the early years took some work, and I just didn't feel I could go through that all over again."

"But now you do?" Clarissa asked.

"Let's just say I'm willing to consider it," Mrs. Gunn replied. "Joe is a pretty accommodating sort, and I guess I've kind of gotten tired of living alone. A lot of women my age are determined that once is enough. A boyfriend is all right, but they don't want the responsibility of a husband. I know Joe would like for us to get married. But things like this seldom run in a straight line. It took me a couple of years before Mr. Gunn managed to convince me to marry him. Of course, I haven't as much time now to be making up my mind. But the security of having a husband sort of appeals to me."

"I can understand that."

"How are you and your young lawyer doing? Have you made things up?"

"We've taken the first step. We've agreed to go out again."

Mrs. Gunn nodded wisely. "At your age you need to be part of a couple. Just be real careful when you make your choice."

Clarissa didn't know how true that first part was, but smiled anyway. "I intend to be," she told the older woman.

After breakfast, Clarissa walked over to the office and checked the answering machine. There were a couple of notifications from family of members in the congregation who were in the hospital, so Clarissa put it in her schedule to visit them a bit later in the week.

A few minutes later, Ashley came into the office. "How did your visit with Raymond Blanchard go yesterday afternoon?" she asked as she settled in behind her desk.

"It was worthwhile. I think I've got another clue." Clarissa gave her a summary of their conversation.

"Do you think Raymond's son George could be the one who killed Royce Llewellyn?" Ashley asked.

"He had a motive and a rather weak alibi, so I suppose it's possible."

"But that would mean that Harry is the one who killed Ames and Jack Spurlock." Ashley looked dubious. "I can imagine Harry doing a lot of unsavory things. I can certainly imagine him paying blackmail to protect the family name, but killing two people seems like a stretch. He seems more sneaky than dangerous."

"I'm inclined to agree," Clarissa said, "but you can't be sure what someone will resort to when they're desperate. I guess the only way to find out is go and question him."

"Will he even see you?"

"I think so. His grandfather promised to put pressure on him. When I ask him to meet with me, I'll say that it's just part of my efforts to visit everyone in the congregation."

"But if he *is* a killer, do you think it's wise to go alone to accuse him of being one?"

"I don't think he'd hurt me if I made it clear that people knew I was meeting with him."

Ashley shook her head. "Harry is volatile. He acts before he thinks, so he might attack you in a fit of temper."

Clarissa paused. "You might be right, but I can't really bring along Detective Baker. Harry would be furious if he thought I'd gone to the police with my unsubstantiated suspicions. He'd get a lawyer, and we'd never find out anything."

"Why don't you take me along? I'm your silent partner in all this anyway," Ashley said with a smile.

"I don't know," Clarissa said doubtfully.

"You don't think the two of us could handle Harry? Even without pepper spray, we could have him on the ground crying 'uncle' in five seconds if he starting acting up."

"But would he talk in front of you?" Clarissa wondered. "He might talk to me after his grandfather gives him a call, but I'm not sure he'd be willing to say anything sensitive in front of you."

"Why not? We're both church employees, and this is sort of church business. I'm ready to go, unless you have a better idea."

In her black blouse, black pants, and ultra-black hair, Clarissa thought Ashley definitely looked ready to go if they were planning a ninja attack.

"Okay," she relented, "we'll give it a try."

"Great!" Ashley said. "What do we do next?"

"Raymond said that he would get Harry to call me, so all we can do now it wait."

"Okay. That's not something I'm good at, but I guess we have no choice. What would you like me to work on this morning?"

"How about you use the updated list of church members on the computer and set up a schedule of visits for me, figuring that I'll go out two afternoons a week and visit three families in an afternoon?" Clarissa replied.

Ashley gave her a dubious look. "I don't think you can do three in an afternoon. People who are home all day love to chat. Plus, you'll never get to see folks who work if you only go on weekday afternoons."

"Good point," Clarissa said. "Let's do one weekday afternoon and make the other one a Sunday afternoon. And I'll cut back to doing only two in an afternoon."

Ashley nodded. "And where do you want me to start?"

"Let's do it in alphabetical order. That way no one will be offended."

"I thought you were going to go by age since you began with Raymond Ballard."

"He was special. Plus, I don't think our records give ages."

"And if we did ask for ages, most of the female members wouldn't give an honest age anyway." Ashley winked.

Clarissa smiled. "No sense putting anyone on the spot."

"You do realize that visiting everyone is going to take a year?"

"Doesn't matter. When I get done, I'll probably start all over again from the beginning. It's a great way to stay in touch and hear about people's concerns and needs."

Ashley rolled her eyes. "Better you than me. I guess that's why they call you the pastor."

Clarissa smiled and went into her office. It was time to formulate some ideas for next Sunday's sermon.

She was so focused on her work that she didn't hear the phone in the outside office ring and know a call had come in until Ashley buzzed her and said Harry Blanchard was on the line.

"My grandfather said that you wanted to speak with me," Harry Blanchard said right away, skipping over "hello" and making it clear that only because his grandfather strongly suggested it was he willing to speak with her.

"Thanks for calling, Harry," Clarissa said graciously. "I'd like to meet with you for a few minutes, when you have time."

"This isn't to gloat about the Rogers' deal falling through, is it?" he said. "If so, I want you to know that I still think it would have been great for the church. I think those of you who were against it had your heads in the sand."

Clarissa sighed. "It has nothing to do with that. I'm visiting all the members of the church, and as someone who is very involved in church matters, I wanted you to be one of the first."

"It's hardly necessary for us to meet, is it? We already know each other, and you see me every month at board meetings," Harry retorted.

"But only to discuss business. I'd like to learn more about the backgrounds of the members, especially those who have been part of the church for a long time. I was hoping you could tell me something about your father."

"My father," he said, a sudden note of warmth in his voice. "He was a wonderful person. He made me the man I am today."

Clarissa thought—a shade unkindly—that not everyone would consider this great praise, but then chided herself for being so uncharitable.

"Why don't we meet at my office?" Harry said. "I'm right near the middle of the pedestrian mall at Blanchard Properties. I have some time at eleven o'clock."

"That sounds fine. And I'd like to bring along Ashley Williams, the church administrative assistant. She'll be taking notes, so we can incorporate what you tell us into a short history of the church that we're working on."

"That's the girl who always dresses in black like some kind of witch, isn't it?"

"She's my assistant," Clarissa said firmly.

"Well, if you feel she's absolutely necessary," Harry said, suggesting that he certainly didn't. "I'll see you right at eleven."

"I'll be there."

After hanging up, Clarissa went out to Ashley's desk, where she was working on a chart to schedule pastoral visits.

"We're all set to meet with Harry Blanchard at eleven," Clarissa informed her.

Ashley made a face. "Oh, joy. The perfect way to start a week."

"You can still beg off. I think I'm able to do this on my own."

"And what if you didn't come back, or end up buried in Harry's basement? I'd never forgive myself— because my aunt would never let me."

Clarissa grinned. "Nice to know you care. I'm sure everything will go fine, but you'd better bring a notebook. I told Harry that you'd be taking notes for a church history we're going to do."

"I hope that's something you made up just to get him to meet with us," said Ashley.

"Actually, I've been thinking that a church history might be a good idea," said Clarissa. "I was rooting around in the storeroom last week and came across a history done in the 1920s. I think it's time we came out with an updated one. An institution can often learn where it should go by seeing where it's been."

"That sounds like an advertising slogan to me," Ashley said.

Clarissa smiled. "I guess it does a bit, but I still think there's kernel of truth in it. Plus, it will help me get a better idea of what I have to deal with here."

"I'm more of a numbers person," Ashley warned.

"No problem. You can sift through the facts, and I'll put them in an acceptable literary form."

"Is it okay if I bring a small laptop to our meeting with Harry?" Ashley asked. "I'm not much for writing things down by hand."

"That sounds fine."

"Plus, it will give me something to hit him with in case he gets rowdy," Ashley said with a grin.

***

Clarissa and Ashley got to Blanchard's office right at the stroke of eleven. They'd walked the six blocks from the church, enjoying the exercise and the beautiful day.

Several tourists had cast curious glances at Ashley in her ninja garb; she wore a matching black backpack to hold her laptop. Clarissa thought, not for the first time, that one of the advantages in wearing only one color was the ease of accessorizing. Whenever she found herself wishing that her assistant were a bit more conventional in appearance, she reminded herself that Ashley came as a package. If you wanted her intelligence and good humor, you had to accept the eccentric getup.

"How do you want to play this, Boss?" Ashley asked, licking her lips a bit nervously.

"Like I told you, Harry thinks the only reason we're here is to work on a history of the church," Clarissa told her. "You're here to take notes. In order to write that history, we need to ask him about his father. I think it's a subject he enjoys talking about. We'll let him rattle on as long as he likes, then gently guide him to the time of Royce Llewellyn's murder."

"How are you going to gently ask him if he and his father are the victims of blackmail, and possibly multiple killers?" Ashley demanded.

Clarissa frowned. "I guess I'll play that part by ear."

Ashley shook her head as if that were no plan at all. "Well, don't worry. If he gets upset, I've got my pepper spray in an outside pocket."

"Let's hope it doesn't come to that."

"Yeah, that wouldn't make it much of a pastoral visit."

They opened the door to the office, which caused a bell to ring above the door. A well-dressed young woman sitting behind a desk in the center of the surprisingly spacious reception area looked up and smiled. "How may I help you?" she asked.

"I'm Clarissa Abbot and this is Ashley Williams," Clarissa said. "We have an appointment with Mr. Blanchard."

"I'll let him know you're here," the receptionist replied. She picked up the phone, pushed a button, and told whoever answered that the eleven o'clock was here. "He'll be with you in a moment, if you'd like to have a seat," she said.

Clarissa and Ashley settled into chairs off to the side of the reception area, where they sat and sat.

Ten minutes must have gone by when Ashley whispered, "Just like the little twit to make us wait. He's probably in there reading the sports pages."

"Patience," Clarissa advised with a smile. Ashley's response was a disdainful snort.

A few minutes later, during which time Ashley twitched and fussed constantly, Harry came out into the waiting room.

"Sorry to keep you waiting," he said. "I had a few urgent items of business I had to attend to."

Clarissa tried to avoid looking at Ashley, who must have been rolling her eyes. Harry shook hands with Clarissa, and reluctantly touched Ashley's offered hand with two fingers, as though afraid of being infected with eccentricity.

He led them through the double doors behind the receptionist's desk and down the hall to a large corner office. There were no windows on the side because his building was sandwiched between two others, but a large set of windows looked out on the pedestrian mall, and an even larger set above revealed a surprisingly unobstructed—if somewhat distant—view of the ocean.

Harry settled into the ergonomic office chair behind his desk and smiled reminiscently. "So you wanted to talk to me about my father."

Clarissa realized that this was the first time she had ever seen the man smile, his normal expression being that of a man with severe heartburn. It transformed him into a rather pleasant-looking individual.

Clarissa glanced at Ashley, who appeared stunned, as if a snake had suddenly grinned at her. She stared at Ashley until she got her attention, then nodded toward the laptop. Her assistant got the point. She whipped it open and booted it up.

Harry noticed none of this because he was staring at the ceiling, as if seeking divine inspiration. "My father was an innovator," he finally began. "He was the chairman of the planning board that came up with the idea of blocking off part of the downtown and creating a pedestrian mall."

"Really," Clarissa said, impressed and a little surprised that Raymond hadn't mentioned his son's significant contribution to Shore Side.

Harry nodded and went on for the next ten minutes about the various town projects that his father had been instrumental in developing.

"But his actual job was running The Harmony of the Sea Hotel, wasn't it?" Clarissa finally interrupted.

"Of course, he did run the hotel for much of his life," Harry granted with a casual wave of his hand, as though that hardly mattered compared to his father's community contributions. "But in the last ten years of his life, he devoted much of his time to founding this company."

"However, *you're* the one who had made it into the success that it is," Clarissa said.

Ashley glanced at her, as if not believing she was laying the flattery on so thick.

Harry's confused expression showed that he was uncertain whether to accept such praise or defer to his father. "I suppose that's true," he said with a modest smile, "but I was only building on the foundation that my father had already laid."

"I'm sure your father must have really enjoyed commercial real estate to have worked so hard to build up this enterprise. But he must have also gotten a great deal of satisfaction from running the hotel. I gathered from what your grandfather said that when your father was the assistant manager, he urged your grandfather to buy out Royce Llewellyn several times, but Llewellyn refused to sell. That must have been very frustrating for your father," Clarissa said in what she hoped was a sympathetic enough tone.

Harry eyed her suspiciously. "That's all ancient history. Grandfather bought out Llewellyn's share from his widow, and my father became the hotel's general manager, a job he held until my grandfather sold the hotel to a developer."

"And it was a job that he enjoyed?" Clarissa asked.

"Of course. My father was a natural leader. Running a hotel is very complicated. You have to manage a wide variety of moving parts and make sure that everything is functioning efficiently. You also have to provide inspiration for your employees, so each feels that his or her individual contributions are valued. It's an extremely demanding job that requires a certain type of personality."

"A kind of personality that Royce Llewellyn didn't possess?"

"He was too busy using his position to satisfy his . . . appetites." Harry spat out the last word with disgust.

"So his sudden death was very fortunate for everyone, including your father."

Harry popped forward in his chair. Out of the corner of her eye, Clarissa saw Ashley reaching into the pocket of her jacket, no doubt for the pepper spray.

"What are you implying?" Harry asked in an ice-cold voice.

"Nothing," Clarissa said, keeping her tone level and calm. "I was simply pointing out that Royce Llewellyn, in the normal scheme of things, could easily have lived for another twenty-five years and continued to manage the hotel. You seem to be suggesting that would have been very bad for the business."

"I suppose," Harry said, settling back slightly in the chair but still on alert. "Look, I don't really see how this line of inquiry is relevant to establishing my father's role in the community."

"Did you know David Ames?" Clarissa asked pointedly.

At first she thought Harry wasn't going to answer, but then he shook his head as though bemused by the line of questioning. "I saw him around town," he said. "He was an occasional member of the church, but I didn't know him well. We hardly traveled in the same circles."

Clarissa took a deep breath. "We believe that Ames knew who killed Royce Llewellyn and was blackmailing that person. Did you father know David Ames?"

The coin dropped and Harry shot to his feet, his face turning a livid red. "Are you suggesting that my father had something to do with the murder of Royce Llewellyn?" he demanded.

Out of the corner of her eye, Clarissa saw Ashley's hand move again toward the pocket with the pepper spray.

Clarissa kept her voice low. "Your grandfather didn't think the idea was so outrageous," she said.

It took a moment for the words to sink in; then confusion replaced anger on Harry's face, and he sank back into his chair.

"Your grandfather felt that your father was desperate to take over management of the hotel and would stop at virtually nothing to achieve it," Clarissa continued.

Harry rubbed a hand over his face and stared across the room. Suddenly he seemed subdued, as if all the fight had gone out of him.

"My father lived for that job," he finally said in a faraway voice. "He never forgave my grandfather for selling the hotel. Setting up this real estate company was never an adequate substitute for him. He also had nothing but contempt for Royce—but I can't believe he murdered him. My father was an ambitious man, but not a violent one."

"We think David Ames was blackmailing whoever killed Llewellyn. Did you father ever give any indication that he had business dealings with Ames?" Clarissa asked.

"I can't remember him ever mentioning Ames to me." Harry gave a wan smile. "But he probably wouldn't have if the man was blackmailing him, would he?"

"So no one ever approached you after your father's death and demanded that you give him money or there would be a scandal involving your father?"

"No, of course not. This is the first time I've heard anything about my father being involved in such a thing, and I still don't believe it."

Clarissa could tell that Harry was starting to get heated again, so it was time to end the conversation. She glanced over at Ashley who was assiduously taking notes on her laptop.

But Clarissa still wanted to push her point a bit more. "We believe the killer of Royce Llewellyn murdered David Ames *because* Ames had been blackmailing him, and he intended to pass his secret along to a new blackmailer," she told Harry.

"Ames was murdered? I never heard that," he replied.

"The police think so." Detective Baker wouldn't be happy at her letting the cat out of the bag, again, but she thought it was high time. "Are you certain that your father had no contact with him?" she asked.

"None that I know of, and if my father was being blackmailed, it would have been all over ten years ago when he died."

"Unless Ames began to blackmail you."

"Are you implying that *I* killed him?" Harry jumped to his feet again. "I think it's time both of you left."

"If Ames had approached you with evidence that your father had killed Llewellyn, would you have paid to preserve you family's good name?" Clarissa demanded.

Harry looked thoughtful for a moment, and Clarissa thought he might answer. But then he simply pointed to the door.

Ashley slowly packed up her laptop, probably trying to show she wasn't intimidated, and they both left.

"What do you think?" Clarissa asked Ashley once they were both out on the street heading back toward the church.

"I hate to say it, but I believed him," Ashley said. "I think he would have paid blackmail if Ames had approached him, but I don't think he did. He seemed genuinely surprised at the very idea that his father had killed Llewellyn."

Clarissa nodded her agreement. "I don't think Harry's father killed Llewellyn, although the man's death definitely helped him by allowing his grandfather to buy the hotel and put him in charge."

"So who remains on our suspect list?" Ashley asked.

Clarissa shrugged. "I'm pretty much out of names. There's still the widow, Doris; I suppose she could have killed her husband because of his cheating. But she's close to her nineties now and rather frail, so she couldn't have killed Ames and Spurlock."

"What about Maggie Preston? She could have murdered Llewellyn if she thought he was going to dump her. She could have been the one paying blackmail to Ames all these years. She's up in her seventies, I guess, but you said she was still active. Maybe she killed Ames and Spurlock to end the blackmail," Ashley suggested.

Clarissa frowned. "I suppose she's physically capable of killing the two men. I guess I could go talk to her again—if she's willing to see me."

"Might be worth a shot," Ashley said. "Even if she isn't the killer, she was on the scene when the original murder took place. Maybe she could suggest another suspect."

"Last time I talked to her, she seemed to be certain that Doris Llewellyn had killed her husband because he was going to leave her for Maggie. And we already know that Doris didn't kill Ames and Spurlock."

"Press her harder. She might know more than she realizes."

Clarissa checked her watch. "Maybe I'll go by her place for lunch. She's sure to be there, and if she doesn't throw me out again, she might tell me something worthwhile."

"Want me to join you?" Ashley offered.

Clarissa thought for a moment. "I'd better go alone. She won't be happy to see me in any case, so she certainly won't be thrilled to see that I've brought a friend."

"Good luck, and be careful," Ashley said.

Clarissa nodded headed in the direction of the beach. Who knew this sleepy little coastal town could hold so many secrets?

Chapter Twenty-One

Clarissa walked along the boardwalk, wondering how she was going to get Maggie to speak with her. She found herself envying the people who walked past, obviously intent on enjoying the beautiful day at the beach with nothing more pressing on their minds.

When this is all over, Clarissa thought, *I can go back to being just a pastor.*

Oddly, along with a sense of relief, there was also a feeling of disappointment. She had to admit to herself that, although it had provoked some anxiety, she also enjoyed solving a mystery. Just as she had gotten pleasure from the challenge of writing a good research paper in seminary, she was getting satisfaction from delving deeper and deeper into the death of David Ames. It was probably because both activities were focused on finding the truth.

She entered Maggie's Luncheonette just as the lunchtime rush was coming to an end. The waitresses were busy clearing the tables, although there were still a few people eating.

"What can I get you, honey?" a middle-aged waitress asked her.

"I'll have a ham and cheese on rye and a cup of coffee."

"You've got it."

"Would Maggie be around?" Clarissa asked as the woman turned to go.

"She's working in the back."

"I'd like to see her, if she isn't too busy."

"We're not hiring right now, if that's what you want to see her about," the waitress said, pushing her hair into place. "Not that we couldn't use another girl."

Clarissa smiled. "I'm sure you could. But what I want to see her about is something personal."

The woman gave her a long look, as if trying to decide whether she was trouble. "Okay, honey, I'll see if she's available."

A couple of minutes later, Maggie came out of the kitchen and walked into the dining room. When she saw Clarissa, she stopped in her tracks. For a moment, Clarissa thought she was going to turn around and head back into the kitchen. But after clearly debating with herself, Maggie advanced toward the table.

"What do you want this time?" she asked.

Clarissa was still uncertain about the best approach to get Maggie to talk to her. Finally, she decided on directness. "There's a killer in Shore Side," she said, "and I want you to help me catch him."

Maggie paused, then sat down in the chair across from her. "I already told you, Doris killed her husband," she said. "Any more recent murders, I've got no idea about."

"I think whoever killed Royce has killed two other people in the last week, and I don't think that person is Doris," Clarissa told her. "A man like Royce, who liked to be in charge of things, must have had some enemies. Wasn't there anyone else with whom he came into conflict?"

Maggie stared across the room, and Clarissa could almost see her mind traveling back across the years.

"Morris Hazelton, who owned the Orion Hotel just down the beach from us—he wasn't a big fan of Royce's," she said. "He came by one time and point-blank accused Royce of trying to put him out of business."

"Was that true?" Clarissa asked.

Maggie smiled gently. "It probably was. The Orion was our nearest rival, and Royce could be a pretty tough competitor."

"What did he do?"

"Oh, he ran ads saying that our hotel was the best on that stretch of the beach. He'd lower our prices to undercut the Orion at the height of the season, and send out flyers to lists of former Orion guests letting them know we were cheaper."

"How did he get a list like that?"

"I don't know for sure, but there was lots of talk that he would bribe Orion employees to get him the information," Maggie said. "There were even some who claimed that he bribed Morris' people to make mistakes, so the Orion would get a bad name. In fact, David Ames worked at the Orion before he came over to us, and some said he was actually working for Royce the whole time to sabotage the Orion."

"Sounds like a pretty hardball approach for a hotel in a small beach community," Clarissa said.

Maggie smiled and Clarissa thought there was more than a hint of admiration in her eyes. "Royce never did anything halfway."

"If Royce and Ames were so close, why did Royce fire him right before the murder?" Clarissa asked.

"Royce's daughter, Elise, started hanging around the hotel when she wasn't in school. She was only fifteen and couldn't officially work, but Royce would give her little jobs to do to make her feel important," Maggie explained. "From what I saw, she spent most of her time flirting with the busboys and lording it over people that she was the boss's daughter. To be fair, she seemed pretty attached to her father. I think she hung around the hotel because it was better than being at home with her mother."

"Were David Ames and Elise starting to get involved?" Clarissa asked. "Did her father feel he had to break them up?"

"Not exactly. David Ames was a good-looking guy when he was young, and I think Elise was kind of attracted to him. But what got Royce so angry at Ames is that he told Elise about us."

"About you and her father?"

Maggie nodded. "That was right after Royce had set me up in my own place. The last thing Royce had wanted was for Elise to find out that he was cheating on her mother. Family was important to him, in a funny sort of way. We were always careful not to show how we felt about each other in front of the girl."

"But, if you'll excuse me for saying so, he'd had other girlfriends. Didn't his daughter already realize her father cheated?" Clarissa asked.

Maggie shook her head. "Royce was always pretty careful, and Elise only started coming to the hotel in the month or so before the murder."

"And David told her about the two of you. Why would he do that?"

"From what I heard, Dave was making a play for her, and she said something about how he wasn't the man her father was. Dave always had a hot temper, and I guess he couldn't resist disillusioning her. I don't know exactly what he said to her, but it was enough that she confronted Royce right on the spot in the center of the lobby. They had quite a public argument, and when she was angry, Elise had a voice that would shatter glass. Everyone on the staff knew about it. Back then, this was a smaller town with a tight grapevine. The whole story had traveled up and down the beach by the next day. Morris Hazelton even stopped in the next morning for breakfast in the dining room just to gloat."

"And the next night Royce was killed."

Maggie nodded. "And my life changed forever."

***

By the time Clarissa returned to the church, both Mrs. Gunn and Ashley had left for the day. She sat in her office, wondering what to do next.

Finally, she took out a phone book and looked up the name Hazelton. There was only one listing in Shore Side, and she called the number.

"Hello, I'm Clarissa Abbot, pastor of the Shore Side Community Church," she said to the man who answered. "I was wondering if you were related to the Morris Hazelton who used to run the Orion Hotel. I'm trying to get in touch with him."

The man chuckled. "I'm afraid you're going to have to rely on the power of prayer. Morris was my grandfather, and he passed away over fifteen years ago. I'm Ronald Hazelton."

"I'm very sorry to hear that," Clarissa said. "I'm doing some research on the town of Shore Side as part of my history of our church. Would you know anything about the period of time when your grandfather owned the Orion?"

"I was only a boy when he sold the hotel, but my grandfather certainly talked to me a lot about it in his later years," Ronald replied. "I might be able to help you." He told her his address and they agreed to meet in about an hour.

Clarissa went back to working on her sermon. She wanted to get a head start because tomorrow morning would be devoted to hospital visits, and the afternoon to going to the homes of congregation members. She started working on her topic, which was how your faith could help with making good decisions. She became so engrossed in the subject that forty-five minutes had gone by before she glanced at the clock, and she had to immediately set off to see Ronald Hazelton.

He lived in a condominium that overlooked the small harbor in the northern part of Shore Side. As she rang the bell and took in the view from his front door, she could see the fishing boats coming in from a day at sea and could clearly see the yacht basin. Clarissa was willing to bet that one of the slips down there belonged to Hazelton. Apparently, he had done very well for himself—or else his grandfather had left him well-off.

The man who opened the door was a plump, jovial fellow in his mid-thirties who invited her into the living room, where he offered her tea and cookies that he said he had made himself.

"This is a wonderful cookie," Clarissa said after taking a bite. "I'm impressed that you made them yourself."

Ronald smiled. "Well, there is no Mrs. Hazelton, so I've had to learn to take care of myself. Plus I enjoy puttering around in the kitchen." He paused and took a sip of tea. "You wanted to talk to me about Grandpa Morris?"

"That's right, particularly about the time when he owned the Hotel Orion," Clarissa replied. "I'm quite interested in his relationship with Royce Llewellyn."

Ronald laughed. "I'm not sure there *was* a relationship, unless you consider hatred to be one. Grandpa was convinced that Llewellyn was determined to put the Orion out of business, by fair means or foul."

"Did he ever tell you why?"

"The hotels were on the same block of beach, so they were direct competitors. But I'm not certain that was all of it," he said. "I think what it came down to is that they just didn't like one another. They were probably just too much alike: domineering, competitive, and aggressive. I only really knew Grandpa in his later years, after he'd begun to mellow, but even then, you didn't want to get on the wrong side of him."

"So he probably wasn't very upset when Royce Llewellyn got murdered?"

"Of course, I don't know what he actually felt because it was before my time," Ronald said, "but he told me later that he wasn't surprised that things turned out that way. He said that Royce wasn't above dealing with some pretty unsavory characters, so it was no surprise that all his double-dealing finally caught up with him."

"Did your grandfather ever mention David Ames?" Clarissa asked.

"Did he!" Ronald exclaimed. "He still talked about him with disgust thirty years after the event. He was always telling me how Ames worked in the Orion for six months, and during that time he had rats in the kitchen, bugs in the beds, and a huge uptick in the number of clogged toilets. Granddad had a private investigator work undercover to find out what was going on, and he determined that Ames was sabotaging the hotel. My grandfather fired him. He probably would have had him arrested if there had been more proof. A week after he was fired, Royce Llewellyn hired him. Granddad was always convinced that he had been in Llewellyn's employ all along."

"Your grandfather must have been furious." Clarissa paused, unable to think of a tactful way to put the next question. "Would he have been angry enough to kill Royce Llewellyn?"

Clarissa had been half expecting Ronald to be offended, and she was relieved when he laughed. "You never knew my granddad or you wouldn't ask that," he chuckled. "Like I said, he could be tough and competitive, but his anger always burned out quickly. In many ways, he was the gentlest, wisest man I ever knew. He was always able to put things in perspective. Actually, I think he felt sorry for Llewellyn because the man was never satisfied with what he had. He always wanted more and couldn't be content. Granddad was happy just to have the Orion doing well. It was his baby."

"Did your grandfather have any contact with David Ames after he fired him?" asked Clarissa.

"I suppose he saw him around town. We all did at one time or another. One thing about living in Shore Side, you're bound to see both your friends and enemies on a regular basis," said Ronald. "But as far as I know, he never had any further contact with him. I think he always figured that it was at least half-possible that Ames killed Llewellyn after getting fired."

"What happened to the Orion? It's doesn't exist any more, does it?"

Ronald looked sad. "My grandfather continued running it until he was in his late seventies and it became too much for him. Neither my father nor I wanted to go into the business—my dad's an accountant and I'm a high school history teacher. So Granddad sold the hotel. It was renovated and renamed the Claremont. My dad gave me some of the money he inherited from the sale to buy this place." He gestured around him.

"I've heard of the Claremont," Clarissa said. "Folks say it's a good hotel."

"It probably is, but my grandfather always thought it went downhill after he left the business. I suppose it's only natural to feel that way."

Clarissa stood up and thanked Ronald for his hospitality and help.

"Don't mention it," he said. "I *am* a historian, after all. I like talking about the past." He gave Clarissa a shrewd glance. "I hope you find out what you want to know. But lots of people have been curious about the

Llewellyn murder over the years, and it's never been solved."

"Maybe I'll have better luck," Clarissa said.

He reached out and shook her hand. "I hope you do, Pastor."

She hoped so, too.

Chapter Twenty-Two

The next morning, Clarissa sat in the outer office facing Ashley, who was seated in front of her computer as usual. Clarissa had just told her about her conversations with both Maggie Preston and Ronald Hazelton.

"So Maggie said that Ames told Elise Llewellyn about her father's affair, and *that's* why Royce fired him?" Ashley said, looking somewhat puzzled. Clarissa understood; it was a lot of names to keep track of.

"I guess Royce took his family life seriously, even if he wasn't faithful, and he wanted to protect his daughter from his infidelities," she said.

"That certainly gave Ames a motive for murder—especially since he was apparently kind of a hothead to begin with," Ashley mused. "Is there any way that Ames *is* the murderer and someone killed him in revenge? Maybe Maggie Preston? She still seems to be carrying a torch for Llewellyn."

"But over forty years is a long time to wait for revenge."

"Don't they said it's best served cold?" said Ashley.

"After all that time, it would be frozen. Plus, we already know that David Ames was blackmailing the killer, so he couldn't have been the one who murdered Royce Llewellyn," Clarissa said.

Ashley toyed with a paper clip for a few moments, and then her eyes lit up. "Do we really know that Ames was blackmailing anyone?" she said. "All we have to support that is Owen Chandler's speculation that Ames was getting extra money that way. The only confessed blackmailer we have is Chandler himself, who was blackmailing Ames by threatening to expose the fact that Ames wasn't in the bar at the time Llewellyn was killed like he'd claimed."

"But Ames was clearly getting extra money from somewhere; both Chandler and Ames's last girlfriend, Sharon Meissner, were pretty sure of that," Clarissa pointed out.

"Sure, Ames was a crooked guy, there's no doubt about that. But who knows what he was involved in to make extra cash? It didn't have to be blackmail."

Clarissa paused. "Okay, let's say that you're right. But if Ames wasn't blackmailing the killer, why was he murdered? If we take both revenge and blackmail off the table, there's no reason left for anyone to kill him. But someone obviously did."

Ashley gave a weak smile. "Yeah, I guess I've talked myself into a corner here."

"The problem is that we have no idea who Ames was blackmailing," Clarissa said.

"Well, we do have a few candidates," Ashley replied. "Ames could have seen George Blanchard kill Llewellyn and have been blackmailing him for years. Harry might have taken over the job after his father died."

"But Harry seemed pretty surprised at the notion that his father was a killer."

"Mostly he seemed angry. There's a difference," Ashley said.

"Fair enough. I guess Harry has to stay on our list, even if he seems to act innocent." Clarissa paused. "And I suppose our other prime suspect would be Morris Hazelton. He might have killed Llewellyn because he was using underhanded methods to destroy Hazelton's hotel."

"Right. His grandson Ronald might have been continuing to pay the blackmail, and finally got fed up when Ames decided to pass on the information to Jack Spurlock."

"But Ronald Hazelton is a high school teacher."

Ashley smirked. "I've known some pretty desperate high school teachers in my time."

"Okay," Clarissa said with a smile. "He stays on the list. And there's always Maggie Preston. What if right after he had that big blowout with his daughter, Royce went to her and said that it was all over—he was going to choose his wife and daughter over her? Wouldn't that be enough motive for murder?"

"The woman scorned angle is always a good one. But could Maggie really have afforded to pay blackmail forty years ago?" Ashley asked. "Now she has a thriving business, but I'll bet that in the early years, she didn't have much."

Clarissa stared across the room. "You're right about that, but you know, one of the odd things about Ames as a blackmailer is that he must not have been asking for much. He wasn't living an extravagant lifestyle. It was more like he used the blackmail money to supplement his income, just so he could have a few extras. And, of course, some of it had to go to Owen."

"So you're saying that whoever he was blackmailing didn't find it hard to meet his demands. So what changed to make this person decide to kill him?"

"Ames' decision to pass along his information on his deathbed to a new blackmailer."

"Jack Spurlock," Ashley finished.

Clarissa nodded. "I personally doubt that Jack would have continued the blackmail. His wife had pretty much reformed him, but the killer must have been worried that he would."

"So by passing along the one thing of value he had to an old friend, Ames signed his death warrant."

Clarissa nodded again.

"But how did the killer find out that Ames was going to pass his information on to Jack?" Ashley asked.

"Well, David's nurse told me that he asked for his cell phone right after I was there. She plugged it into the charger for him." Clarissa paused. "I guess I assumed that he contacted the person he was blackmailing to let them know that he was passing on the information to someone new."

Ashley looked doubtful. "Do you really think he'd do that? Wouldn't he be putting himself in danger? And if he told this person that he was handing on the information to Jack, he'd also be putting Spurlock's life at risk."

"And that's exactly what happened," Clarissa said.

"Yeah, but would Ames really be stupid enough to have volunteered that information? Did anyone actually *see* him make the call?"

"I'm not sure," Clarissa admitted. "I think Wanda Bascomb said she didn't, and I doubt that anyone else would have been around to know. The guy sharing his room seemed pretty out of it."

"So we don't actually know that he called anyone?"

"Correct."

"Who has the phone now?" asked Ashley.

"I imagine it's in the hands of the police."

"Maybe you should contact Detective Baker to find out if they checked the call history to see who Ames spoke to last."

"I can't believe they wouldn't have done that," Clarissa said doubtfully.

"They probably did, but they might not be approaching things the way we are, so it might not mean as much to them," Ashley said.

Clarissa nodded. "That's a good idea. I can't believe I didn't think of that."

"That's what partners are for. They remind us of things we already knew." The younger woman looked satisfied with herself.

"I think I'll give Detective Baker a call right now and see what they found on the phone," Clarissa said.

Ashley gave her a thumbs-up, so she headed into her office and closed the door.

"What can I do for you today, Pastor?" Baker asked when the call was put through. "Let me take a guess. It has something to do with the David Ames case."

"You're right," Clarissa admitted, feeling a bit sheepish. She thought she heard a deep sigh come from the other end of the phone.

"Fire away, then. I'll answer it if I can," Baker said.

"I was wondering about David's cell phone. You did find one, right?" she asked.

"Sure. It was packed up with his things. The staff had cleared away his stuff when he died, but we took the bag with everything he had there. The phone was inside."

"And I'm sure you checked his call history."

"Of course."

"Whom did he call last when he was in the hospital?"

"No one."

"You mean his call history was erased?" Clarissa asked in surprise.

"No," Baker replied. "There were several calls from before he went into the hospital. There was one call to his girlfriend right before he went into the hospital, and apparently he called out for pizza rather frequently. He also received a couple of robocalls, but apparently he didn't make or receive any calls while in the hospital."

"But the nurse said that he asked her to plug his phone into the charger shortly before he died."

"Well, apparently he never used it."

"Because he was murdered before he got a chance to."

"That's very possible," the detective admitted.

Clarissa sat there in silence for a moment, thinking. "Did he have any visitors?" she asked.

"We talked to all the nurses who worked on his floor. They don't keep a record of visitors, and no one was sure whether anyone came to see him. The other man in the room had some folks come to see him."

"The man who seemed comatose?"

"That's right. Apparently he has a very dedicated family. Ames had no family to speak of, at least in the area, and apparently very few friends."

"I don't think he wanted to be seen when he was that sick. He even warned his girlfriend to stay away," Clarissa said.

"The only possible visitor is that guy in the hoodie that the nurse thinks she may have seen enter his room shortly before his death. But we've had no luck confirming that." Detective Baker cleared his throat. "Do *you* have any information, Pastor, that might be helpful to our investigation? If so, I'd like to hear about it."

Clarissa told him about her visit to Maggie Preston and Ronald Hazelton.

"I'll have a conversation with each of them and see if I can find out more," Baker said. "That might be helpful, although I have my doubts about Ron Hazelton being a murderer. He's quite a pillar of the educational community."

Clarissa almost said something about even pillars having feet of clay, but decided it was a mixed metaphor.

"You haven't received any more threats, have you?" the detective asked.

"No," she said. "I think the killer has probably decided that I'm never going to solve this thing, and he may be right. I'm certainly close to a dead end right now."

"Maybe it would be best to leave it at that," Baker suggested. "Our investigation is still ongoing, and eventually we'll identify the killer."

"I hope you're right."

"And there's no sense in putting yourself at risk."

Clarissa agreed with him and ended the call. Then she sat and stared at the mahogany walls; she'd found herself doing a lot of that lately.

She wondered whether it was worthwhile during her visit to the hospital today to seek out Wanda Bascom, the nurse who had been in charge of caring for David Ames. The same one who claimed to have seen the mysterious visitor and had plugged his phone into the charger. Clarissa decided that such an interview would be worthwhile. After all, people sometimes remembered new things after an event and didn't bother notifying the police.

The fact that David had apparently not made a phone call to the person he was blackmailing left open the question as to how the killer had known Ames was going to share his secret with Jack Spurlock. Perhaps the murderer had visited David at some point before returning to kill him. Yes, Clarissa decided with a firm nod of her head, she would definitely go to see that nurse today.

Her office door opened, and Ashley stepped into the room before carefully closing the door behind her. "There's someone here to see you," she said.

"Who is it?" Clarissa asked. "I don't think I had any appointments this morning. Is it a member of the congregation?"

Ashley shook her head. "He says that he's got something personal to discuss with you." She gave a wicked grin. "He's dreamy. Shall I show him in?"

Clarissa stood. "No, I'll go out and deal with this," she said. "It could be one of Kenneth Rogers' flunkies up to something. He seems like the type of man who never gives up."

Putting on a stern face, Clarissa strode into the outer office. When she saw the man standing there, though, she came to a sudden stop, causing Ashley to bump into her.

"Hello, Clarissa," the man said softly. He came toward her and gave Clarissa an awkward hug.

She didn't respond and quickly stepped back from him.

She turned to Ashley. "Ashley, I'd like you to meet Tyler Hamilton, my former fiancé," she said, hoping her voice wasn't wavering.

Ashley put out her hand, her eyes going wide. "Nice to meet you," she mumbled.

"Likewise," Tyler said, giving her a pleasant smile while quickly glancing over her black dress. He hesitantly shook her hand.

"Tyler is also a minister," Clarissa said to Ashley.

"But I'm not currently working as one," he said.

"Oh, really?" Clarissa gave him a surprised look.

Tyler glanced meaningfully toward her office door. "Perhaps you can give me a few moments to explain?"

Clarissa considered the request for a moment and then nodded. She directed him into her office and motioned for him to take the chair in front of her desk. She sat behind her desk, hoping that physical distance would give her emotional distance.

She took a long look at him as he settled into the chair, noticing (almost against her will) that his skin had begun to tan to a golden glow, as it always did in the summer. She'd often referred to him as her "beach boy."

"Why are you here, Tyler?" she asked, not seeing any point in beating around the bush. She was concerned that the longer she talked to him, the less rational any decision she made would be.

He frowned, as if not sure how to express himself. "I've come to win you back," he finally said in a firm voice.

Clarissa shook her head. "Maybe you don't realize how deeply you hurt me, but one quick visit isn't going to sort it out."

"I understand," he said. "That's why I've given up my job as assistant minister up North and taken a job down here. I thought it would give us a chance to start over again."

Clarissa felt breathless for a moment. She wasn't sure whether this news was appealing, disturbing, or some combination of the two.

"What kind of work are you doing?" she asked, partly out of genuine interest and partly to buy some time to recover from the shock of his audacious plan.

"I'm currently working for a private youth services organization," he said. "We provide places for at-risk young people to go after school for recreation, help with their homework, counseling—pretty much whatever they need. In some ways, it's not a lot different from what I was doing in the church, just for a different population."

"How long have you had the job?" Clarissa asked.

"Two weeks."

"So you didn't stay in your ministerial assignment very long?"

Tyler gave a short laugh. "I stayed for two of the longest months of my life," he said. "I realized right after I took the job what a fool I had been for letting work get in the way of our relationship. I knew that I couldn't just call you and ask you to take me back. I had to do something to prove to you how committed I was to us."

"So you've moved down here to show me how much you've missed me," she said in a cool tone.

He blushed. "That was the idea."

Clarissa smiled slightly. "Well, I appreciate how hard that must have been—really, I do. But maybe you should have phoned first, so we could have talked it over before you made such a drastic move. Because moving down here really doesn't solve our problem," she said. "We both want to be ministers, and it is extremely unlikely that we'll get churches close to each other. So if we're going to be together, someone has to give up his or her dream. We had an agreement that, when the time came, the person with the lesser job would give up their position, but when that time came, you refused. Do you think it would be any different in the future?"

Tyler held up a hand. "I know that backing out of our agreement was wrong, and I apologize."

"Maybe it was wrong, but it was also completely understandable. We were being hopelessly unrealistic in expecting one of us to give up what he had hoped and dreamed about in order for us to be together."

"But I *have* given up everything by coming here," Tyler insisted.

"Do you see yourself working in youth services for the rest of your life and not in the ministry?" Clarissa asked.

"I don't know. They're not the same." He paused for a moment and looked down. When he glanced up again, he was obviously in pain. "Okay, I'll admit it. I still want to be a minister."

"So there we are," Clarissa said glumly. "We still have the same intractable problem."

"But look, can't we just see how it goes for a while?" Tyler pleaded. "I'll keep doing what I'm doing, and you keep being a minister. We continue to see each other and find out what happens."

"Won't we just be torturing ourselves? This problem isn't going to just disappear over time," she said.

"Please, Clarissa, let's give it a try. You never know what options the future might bring."

Clarissa stared at the top of her desk. She had to admit, sometimes the future *did* bring new and unimagined options. But she still felt that by giving in to her emotions, she was making a mistake. "Okay, we give your way a chance," she relented with a sigh. "But only on one condition."

"Name it," Tyler said with a relieved smile.

"We continue to see each other, but we remain free to date other people."

"Is there someone else?" he asked with a quick frown.

"No one serious, but I don't want to miss out on any of those 'future options' while waiting to find out what happens with us," Clarissa said carefully.

After a moment's hesitation, Tyler thrust his hand across the desk. "I'll admit that I'm not happy with your condition, but if that's the way it has to be, it's a deal," he said.

Clarissa shook his hand, wondering once again if she had just made a big mistake.

***

"Wow, now you've got two hunks on the line," Ashley said once the door had closed behind Tyler. "Some girls have all the luck."

"I'm not so sure that I'm all that lucky," Clarissa replied with a frown.

"Well, if you'd like to pass one of them along to me, feel free. I'll take either, I'm not fussy." Clarissa had to smile at the exaggerated eagerness on Ashley's face. "But seriously," she continued, "how is this a bad thing?"

"They're bound to find out about each other eventually, and then there will be some kind of macho contest to see which one I'll pick," Clarissa said with a roll of her eyes.

"Just like in the wild, with rams butting heads," Ashley said, bumping her fists together.

"Hopefully nothing quite that violent. Of course, it could happen that each will decide I'm not worth the effort, and I'll end up with nobody."

"If that should happen, I'm sure a replacement will come along soon enough. Men are attracted to women in authority."

Clarissa gave her a curious look. "That hasn't been my experience."

"Boys aren't, but real men are," Ashley said with confidence.

"The other problem is that I'm not sure whether either one of them is a good long-term prospect," Clarissa said. "Andrew sort of messed up on our last date, and Tyler didn't do too well when push came to shove."

"What do you mean?" Ashley asked.

Clarissa explained about Tyler refusing to give up his church position to be with her.

"I can see where that would have been a hard decision for him," Ashley said.

"I would have done it if our positions were reversed," Clarissa pointed out.

"Probably so, but you know how men are; their jobs are everything to them. And if you *had* given up the ministry to be with him, don't you think you would have eventually come to resent him? You would have spent every day watching him do the job that you wanted to have."

"I never really thought about that," Clarissa said after a moment. "You might be right. But that just goes to show that we shouldn't be together because one of us will end up resenting the other, whichever way it works out."

"Maybe, but I think you're right to give it some time," said Ashley. "Things usually have a way of working themselves out. Both of these guys are attractive and educated, and you've found things to like about both of them. And you've already decided to give both of them a second chance, so why don't you just go with the flow and see what happens?"

"I guess that's what I'll try to do." Clarissa looked at the clock. "It's time for me to head to the hospital. I want to visit with Vera Sanford." She was one of the more elderly members of the congregation.

"What's she in the hospital for?" Ashley asked.

"A hip replacement."

She scrunched up her face. "Sounds painful."

"I suppose it is, but from what I've heard from Mrs. Gunn, Vera has had pain from her bad hip for many years," said Clarissa. "I'm sure she'll be better off now that it's replaced."

"Well, say 'hello' for me. Vera is a friend of my aunt's."

"Will do," Clarissa promised. "While I'm there, I'm going to see if I can have another chat with that nurse, Wanda Bascomb."

"Is she the one who saw the mysterious hooded figure coming out of Ames' room right before he died?" Ashley asked.

Clarissa nodded. "I'm hoping she can give me some idea of who his previous visitors might have been."

"I thought you already asked her about that."

"I did, right after David was killed, but she might have remembered something new by now."

"Good luck," Ashley said. "Is there anything I can do to help? All I've got on the agenda for today is to type up the minutes of the last board meeting."

Clarissa stood for a minute, lost in thought. "You know," she said, "ever since I spoke with Maggie Preston yesterday, I've been thinking about Elise Llewellyn, Royce's daughter. It must have been very traumatic for her to find out that her father was unfaithful to her mother."

"You said that she got in a public shouting match with him at the hotel. That's a pretty good sign that she was upset about his relationship with Maggie," said Ashley. "Are you suggesting that she was upset enough to kill her own father? That's pretty extreme."

Clarissa nodded. "I realize that, and I'm not jumping to any conclusions. But I was wondering if you could sort of poke around—maybe ask your aunt—and see what you can find out about Elise. The one time I met her, she seemed rather withdrawn," Clarissa recalled, thinking back to her visit at Doris' house. "Elise's mother told me that she'd sent her away after the murder because of all the publicity. I'm sure some of the kids in school here were rather cruel to her. I'd just like to know what happened to her after that."

"What my aunt doesn't know, she'll have a way of finding out. She's got more contacts than the CIA," Ashley said.

"Great. Well, I'm off to the hospital, then. I shouldn't be very long."

"Okay, Boss. Don't worry, I'll hold down the fort."

Clarissa smiled. "I'm counting on it."

As she left for the hospital, she realized how much better she felt about her position in the church and the community now that she had a partner in crime.

Chapter Twenty-Three

Because of Tyler's unexpected visit, Clarissa found herself running a little late for her visit to the hospital, so she decided to take her car rather than walk, even though it was a beautiful day. After traveling the half-mile to the hospital and parking in the lot, she hurried inside and asked at the desk for the number of Vera Sanford's room. She was directed to the third floor. When the elevator doors opened, she followed the numbers to the room she was seeking.

Walking into the room, the first person she saw was a plump woman in her late sixties, with rosy cheeks and glasses perched upon her nose. She was reading a paperback book. Although she couldn't quite remember what Vera looked like, Clarissa gave her a tentative smile, hoping she had the right person.

"Hi, Reverend Abbot, nice of you to come to see me," the woman quickly responded.

"Call me Clarissa, and it's my pleasure. How are you doing?" she asked.

Vera gave a faint smile. "Better now. The first couple of days after the surgery, I had a lot of pain, and the medicine they gave me upset my stomach. But things got a lot better starting yesterday. They even had me up and walking down the hall this morning." She grinned. "They probably can't wait to get me on my feet so they can get me out of here."

"Well, that does sound like progress," said Clarissa. "Do you think you will be going home soon?"

"There's a bit of a problem there. My apartment is on the second floor, and the doctor doesn't want me going up and down the stairs a couple of times a day."

"Do you have anyone who can bring you what you need?" Clarissa asked.

"My daughter lives in Pennsylvania. She can come over to see me on the weekend, but more often than that would be difficult for her. She works and has a family," Vera said.

"So what's the doctor's plan?"

"He thinks I should go into a nursing home for a month of rehabilitation. They would make me do the exercises and take care of me until I'm fit enough to go home. I guess my insurance would pay for it, but I hate the idea of going into a nursing home," Vera said with a scowl. "My mother was in one shortly before she died, and I just don't like the idea of being in one."

"Going into a nursing home for rehab is probably a good idea since you live alone, but I bet our church women's group could organize something so people could bring you food and visit with you after you're out. Maybe that way you'd be able to get home sooner," Clarissa suggested.

"That would be swell!" Vera gave her a bright smile.

"I'll get in touch with Mary Parks, the chair of the women's group, and have her give you a call," Clarissa promised. "Do you have a cell phone number?"

Once Clarissa had Vera's number, she settled back in her chair.

"So, have you lived in Shore Side a long time, Vera?" she asked.

The woman nodded. "My whole life. I met my husband right after I graduated from high school. We worked in town, bought a house here, and raised our family. He passed away five years ago. He had a bad heart."

"I'm sorry."

"So am I. I still miss him every day."

"But it is nice to put down roots somewhere. It gives you a sense of belonging," Clarissa said. Then a thought occurred to her, and she asked, "Did you by any chance know Elise Llewellyn when you were in school?"

Vera's face clouded. "I was a year ahead of her," she said. "That's such a sad story. You know about her father being murdered, and then all that scandal coming out about his having so many girlfriends."

"It must have been terrible for Elise."

"She was devastated," said Vera. "And it was different then. People were a lot less tolerant about anything improper. And kids can be so cruel. There were some who teased her about her father's cheating, and even questioned whether she was legitimate. She left school a week or so after his death when her mother sent her to a private school out in Pennsylvania."

"Moving to a new environment must have been difficult for her as well," Clarissa mused.

Vera nodded. "Someone in our school had a cousin who went to the school Elise was sent to. She said that before Elise was there a month, she went wild— running around with boys, drinking alcohol, using drugs. I heard that she had a complete mental breakdown at the end of her sophomore year and never returned to school."

"But she did return to Shore Side."

"Yes, but that was a long time later, at least a year," she said. "The rumor was that she was institutionalized for a while. When Elise did come back to town, she never returned to school. Her mother got her tutors, and I guess eventually she earned an equivalency degree. But she spent all that time living in that big house with her mother."

"That sounds like a very lonely life," Clarissa said. "But she must have started going out on her own at some point, because when I met her last week she was coming back from shopping."

"Eventually she started going out, but I hear that was only after years of therapy," Vera replied. "I'm afraid she's still rather odd. She refuses to recognize anyone she knew at school, even people who were always nice to her, like myself. She's sort of like a zombie, walking around town in a world of her own. She really can't cope for herself. I don't know what's going to happen to her when her mother passes away. They'll have to appoint someone to take care of her."

"Does she have any relatives other than her mother?"

Vera paused. "You know, it seems to me that she had an uncle on her father's side, but he didn't live around here."

Clarissa decided that was enough on the matter for now, and talked with Vera for another ten minutes or so about how she was doing, her family, and whatever seemed to interest the older woman. Vera clearly enjoyed herself, and Clarissa enjoyed learning about her life and the history of Shore Side.

After finishing the conversation, Clarissa stood up. "It's been great talking with you, Vera," she said. "I'll be sure to visit you in the nursing home, so give me a call when you get settled, and I'll make a point of having the women's group help you out. You won't be forgotten."

Vera reached out and took Clarissa's hand, her eyes filling with tears. "Thank you. It means a lot to hear that." She tapped her thigh. "Talking about poor Elise has made me realize that even though I have this problem, there are others whose problems are a lot more serious. It really puts things in perspective."

"I suppose it does," Clarissa said, patting her hand. "I suppose it does."

Leaving Vera's room, Clarissa went up one floor to where David Ames' room had been. She walked past the door to his former room and up to the nurses' station.

She was pleased to see that Wanda Bascomb was there, sitting at the computer. She glanced up as Clarissa approached, and smiled in recognition.

"What brings you here today, Reverend?" she asked.

"Hi, Wanda. Please call me Clarissa."

The nurse nodded and continued to look at her with curiosity. "Are you here to visit another patient?" she asked.

"Actually, I already have, but I thought I'd stop by to talk to you again about David Ames," Clarissa said.

"I'm afraid that I've already told both you and the police everything I know," said Wanda.

"You did say that you might have seen someone wearing a hoodie coming out of his room shortly before his body was discovered."

Wanda nodded, and then leaned forward to speak in a hushed voice. "Apparently, the police found out that Dave was murdered, so everybody has been questioning me about what I saw. The hospital administration is really upset, and they're making plans to ramp up security. They keep trying to make it sound like it was my fault that I didn't keep a better eye on his room, but I can't sit here all day staring at one door."

"So you have no idea who it was that you saw?" Clarissa asked.

"Not a clue. I'm not even sure whether it was a man or a woman."

"No one else saw anything?"

"Nope. My station is the only one that directly faces toward Dave's room."

Clarissa paused. "What about other visitors during his time here? Did David have any?"

"Only one," said Wanda. "A woman came to see him shortly after he entered the hospital. Her name was Sharon. That's all I know. And I only happen to know that because the two of them got into an argument, and I heard Dave shout her name."

"What were they arguing about?"

The nurse shrugged. "All I know is that Dave said he'd told her not to come to see him, and couldn't she at least respect his last wishes."

Clarissa thought the visitor had to be David's girlfriend. Sharon had said that David broke it off with her before going into the hospital—but she hadn't mentioned going to see him. Clarissa decided that it was time to pay her another visit.

"You didn't see David make any phone calls?" she asked Wanda.

"Like I said, he asked me to plug in his phone. I did that, but I never actually saw him use it."

"He didn't mention needing to contact anyone?"

"Not to me. To be honest, I didn't think he had anyone close to him in his life. It was really sort of sad. But there are lots of older people like that who end up in the hospital without family close by and no real friends to visit. I guess that's why you come to see them," Wanda said with a smile.

Clarissa nodded and returned the smile. "Yes, that's why it's an important part of what I do."

"Do you think the police will ever find out who murdered Dave?" Wanda asked.

"I'm sure they're doing their best."

"Well, I hope they catch him. You know, it's terrible to say, but it's lucky for me that Dave turned out to be murdered."

"Why's that?"

"The administration was getting ready to come down hard on me because his monitor was unplugged," Wanda said. "I told them about Dave getting out of bed on his own to use the bathroom and unplugging himself, but they didn't want to hear it. They said it was my responsibility to see that he was plugged into the monitor at all times. You'd think I had only one patient to look after. We're so understaffed, it's almost impossible to keep up as it is."

"But since the killer must have unplugged it, you're off the hook."

"Like I said, it's a terrible thing, but it probably saved my job," the nurse admitted.

"Well, I'd better let you get back to it," Clarissa said. "Thanks for all your help."

Wanda nodded, but her eyes had already returned to the computer screen.

***

Clarissa decided that her next stop would be at Ocean Breeze Realty to have another chat with Sharon Meissner to find out why she had failed to mention her visit to the hospital. Clarissa called from her car to make sure that the woman was available. Although somewhat reluctant, Sharon agreed to meet with her if she could make it within the next half-hour.

When Clarissa arrived, Sharon greeted her coolly and directed her toward the back office. Clarissa wondered what the problem was, and didn't have long to find out. When they were settled in the office, the realtor spoke first.

"The police have been here to see me. Apparently, they are treating David's death as a murder. You didn't tell me that the last time we spoke. In fact, you led me to believe that you were simply looking to gather information for his eulogy." Sharon paused and gave Clarissa a long accusatory look.

"Actually, I *was* trying to get information for his eulogy, but I'm also trying to help the police discover who killed David," Clarissa responded. "Detective Baker made me promise not to tell anyone that David's death wasn't due to natural causes."

Sharon's eyes stayed hard. "Well, it was still deceptive."

"I'm sorry about that, but it was not as deceptive as your telling me that you hadn't seen David after he went into the hospital," Clarissa retorted.

"I didn't."

"Don't bother to lie. A nurse saw you there and heard David say your name. Did you fail to mention that to the police when they came to interview you?" Clarissa demanded. "Because if you did, you're guilty of lying to the police, and that could get you in a lot of trouble."

Sharon's stone-faced expression collapsed. "I didn't mean to lie," she said, her lower lip trembling. "I just didn't want to tell anyone that I'd been to see David because he'd virtually thrown me out of the room. I was just too embarrassed to admit it."

"Why did he throw you out?" Clarissa asked.

Sharon shrugged. "I'm not sure. He didn't actually tell me. All he said is that he had something going on that involved his past life from before he knew me, and he didn't want me getting involved."

"He wasn't any more specific than that?"

"No. I kind of assumed that it had something to do with a previous girlfriend. I was jealous and got angry with him." Her eyes filled with tears. "The poor guy was dying, and I accused him of cheating on me. How stupid is that? Now that I know he was murdered, I think he was just trying to protect me."

"You're probably right," Clarissa said gently. "David must have really cared for you."

She nodded. "I know that now, especially after I heard from the lawyer."

"What lawyer?"

"David's. He's a guy from out of town. His name is Kevin Harding. David had him listed as the person the hospital should notify if anything happened to him. When Harding heard that David had died, he contacted me. Apparently, I'm David's sole heir."

"Did you tell the police about this?"

"I didn't know about it when they spoke with me," Sharon said. "After I found out, I was afraid to tell them because I thought it would make me look guilty. After all, I was the only one who had something to gain from David's death."

"If you don't mind my asking, did you inherit a lot?" asked Clarissa.

"Fifty thousand dollars." She smiled crookedly at the surprised expression on Clarissa's face. "I know, who would ever have thought that David had that much? He lived in a cheap rented room like he had next to nothing."

"He must have been squirreling money away for some time," Clarissa mused.

"But where did he get it from in the first place?" asked Sharon.

"If we knew that, we might know who murdered him."

The realtor's eyes went wide. "You think he got it by doing something illegal?"

"It's possible."

"Well, I shouldn't take it then. I don't want someone's ill-gotten gains," Sharon said. "What if he stole it from some drug cartel, and they came after me to get it back?"

Clarissa suppressed a smile. "Let's not jump to conclusions," she said gently. "Let's see how this whole thing works out first."

"But what am I going to do?" Sharon asked forlornly.

"You have to go to the police and tell them just what you've told me," Clarissa told her. "Ask to see Detective Baker. He's in charge of the case."

"I'll do that right away," Sharon promised.

Clarissa stood up and gave her a comforting smile. "Try not to worry too much; I don't think things are as bad as they might appear. You never saw David again after that day in the hospital, did you?"

"Oh, no."

"Then I'm pretty sure the police will just take a statement and not make any more of it." Clarissa wasn't absolutely sure about that, but she saw no point in needlessly worrying the woman.

Sharon also stood and took Clarissa's right hand in both of hers. "Thanks for your advice," she said. "I did a stupid thing, but I've been really confused about all of this."

Clarissa nodded. "That makes two of us."

***

As Clarissa drove back to the church office, she mulled over the fact that David had left all his money to Sharon. He'd apparently cared about only two people in the world: Jack Spurlock, whom he was going to have take over his blackmail scheme, and Sharon Meissner, who would receive what he had already managed to extort.

She could understand Sharon's reluctance to accept money gotten illegally. Clarissa didn't have enough knowledge of the law to know whether Sharon could legally keep the money, but if she did, Clarissa would advise her to give it to charity.

When she arrived at the office, it was well after one o'clock. She was surprised to find that Ashley was still there.

"I thought you'd be gone by now," she remarked.

"Don't worry, I'm keeping track of my hours, and Mrs. Gunn is keeping track of you," Ashley said. "She was over here at noon, all in a tizzy because you hadn't shown up for lunch. I told her you were doing hospital visits and probably got tied up in some emergency."

"I should have called her to let her know I wouldn't be back for lunch," Clarissa groaned.

"Did you get some good information from the nurse?" Ashley asked.

"Let me take it in order. Vera Sanford went to high school with Elise Llewellyn, so she was able to fill me in about that time in her life." Clarissa went on to tell Ashley about Elise going away to a private school and having a nervous breakdown.

Ashley looked disappointed. "Darn, I got the same information from my aunt, and I wanted to surprise you," she said. "But you're right—according to some people my aunt knows, Elise hasn't been right in the head ever since the death of her father."

Clarissa paused and looked thoughtful. "You know, I've been wondering if the problem started earlier than that."

"What do you mean?"

"What if hearing about her father's cheating from David Ames tripped something in her, and she went over the edge?"

"You mean over the edge as in shooting her father?" Ashley asked in surprise.

"They were very close," Clarissa said. "Maybe she shot her father on the doorstep that night, and that's the real reason why she's never recovered."

Ashley nodded. "I suppose kids kill their parents every day in the world, and I imagine that Royce Llewellyn was a difficult guy to have as a father. So do you think Ames was lurking outside the house, maybe getting ready to attack Llewellyn himself, and he saw her do it?"

"That's what I figure."

"And he's been blackmailing Elise ever since."

Clarissa frowned. "Her mother probably controls the family money. I doubt that Elise has anything more than a small allowance, given her condition. I think Doris Llewellyn is the one who conducted business with David Ames for the last forty-five years."

"But she couldn't have killed him," Ashley protested. "Even in his weakened condition, we know she couldn't have suffocated him or rushed out of the hospital afterwards. Could Elise have done it?"

"She looked like a strong woman and seems healthy enough."

Ashley frowned. "But you said Vera told you that she's like a zombie. Now, I know zombies supposedly kill people, but they aren't exactly subtle about it. They don't sneak into hospital rooms and suffocate folks. They sort of stomp down the hall and take a bite out of you."

Clarissa smiled at Ashley's vivid description. "Maybe Vera was exaggerating a bit. It would help if we knew where Elise was at the time David was murdered."

"Maybe I can help you with that," Ashley said. "My aunt told me that neither Elise nor her mother drives. Agnes Coleman, a friend of my aunt's, takes them wherever they have to go. Let me get my aunt to check with her to find out if she was driving them anywhere on the day Ames was killed. If Elise was somewhere else, then we'll have to come up with a new suspect.

So, what did you find out from the nurse? Wanda, was it?"

"She still can't tell us any more about the person who slipped out of David's room around the time he died," Clarissa said. "But she did tell me that David's girlfriend was there to see him a couple of days before, and they had an argument." Clarissa filled Ashley in on her conversation with Sharon. She also explained about David's wish that Sharon stay away from the hospital, and about the terms of his will.

"So Sharon stands to inherit a cool fifty thousand," Ashley said with an eyebrow raised. "Some people have all the luck. All my relatives ever leave me are knickknacks. Maybe the money motivated her to come back a few days later and speed Dave on his way."

"But she didn't know about the terms of the will until after David's death."

"According to her. We don't know if she's telling the truth."

Clarissa nodded. "I believed her, but the police might suspect her of lying just as you do. She certainly had motive, and there's no reason she couldn't have come in that night wearing a hoodie and done the job. But there's something about that hypothesis that bothers me."

"What?"

"It strikes me as a tremendous coincidence that she would kill David hours before he was going to reveal his blackmail scheme to Jack Spurlock," said Clarissa. "I think the blackmail and the murder have to be connected."

"And that would seem to leave Sharon in the clear and direct suspicion back on Elise Llewellyn and her mom," Ashley said.

"Right. I hope for Sharon's sake that Detective Baker sees it the same way."

Ashley frowned. "And we'd better hope that Elise Llewellyn was free to go into the hospital that afternoon and murder David Ames. Otherwise we're out of suspects."

"Maybe, but maybe not," Clarissa said. "When you talk to your aunt, maybe you can have her ask around to find out if Royce Llewellyn had any family other than his wife and daughter. Vera believed Royce had a brother."

"You think there might be other family members involved. Clever," Ashley said with a grin.

"That's why I'm the boss," Clarissa replied with a wink.

Chapter Twenty-Four

After Ashley had left for the day, Clarissa went back to the parsonage and ate the chicken salad sandwich that Mrs. Gunn had left for her. While eating, she reviewed in her mind how the investigation had progressed so far.

Clarissa started out with the idea that the Llewellyns had been David Ames' blackmail victims, and as such, they had a strong motive to see that David did not pass on his information to Jack Spurlock. She could also imagine that, after killing David, they might have wondered if Jack already knew more than they thought, so to protect themselves, they staged his accident. So far, Clarissa thought, that seemed plausible. The problem with the theory was that Doris Llewellyn wasn't fit enough to murder the two men, and her daughter, according to all reports, was not in any mental shape to do so.

Clarissa sat at the table, slowly chewing her sandwich and wondering if she could have gotten off on the completely wrong track. Could the killer be Maggie Preston, Harry Blanchard, or Ron Hazelton? Maggie might have shot Royce Llewellyn herself if he dropped her after his daughter found out about their relationship. David Ames could have seen her do it, and been blackmailing her ever since. Although Blanchard and Hazelton were too young to have killed Royce Llewellyn, their grandfathers were of the right age and had motive, so the grandsons could have been the victims of Ames' blackmail and decided to finally put a stop to it. But how would any of the three have known that David Ames planned to pass along his information?

And, for that matter, how did the Llewellyns know? Unless David had managed to make a last-minute phone call to threaten one of them, it seemed impossible that anyone would have known that it was essential to silence him before he met with Jack Spurlock.

Exhausted after half an hour of going over and over the evidence in her mind without coming up with any new insights, Clarissa decided to return to her office and work on her sermon. At least there, she had a pretty good idea of how it was going to end.

An hour later, she had a completed outline of her sermon, with all the Biblical citations checked. She was about to start putting it in a more polished form when the phone rang.

"Hi, this is Tyler," an exuberant voice said when she answered. "Are you having a good day?"

"Pretty good, Tyler," she replied, trying to sound cautiously friendly. "How about yourself?"

"Very good. Look, I know it's kind of late notice, but would you like to go out to dinner on Wednesday night? I remember how you don't like to go out on Saturday nights because of preaching the next day, so I thought Wednesday would be a good alternative."

Clarissa didn't have to consult her calendar to know that she was going out to dinner with Andrew that day. This attempt to date two guys was already getting awkward.

"Thank you for remembering that I don't usually go out on Saturday nights," she said. "That's very considerate. Unfortunately, I have another commitment this Wednesday."

"Church business?"

It would have been so easy to grunt an ambiguous affirmative, but she wasn't going to lie. "No, actually I have a dinner date."

"I see," Tyler said, his voice suddenly frosty. "So I guess you *did* have a good reason for keeping our relationship non-committed."

"I did warn you," she said in a studiously calm voice.

"That you did. Well, I'll give you a call towards the end of the week, if that's okay. Maybe you can fit me into your social calendar for next week."

Clarissa suppressed a sigh at his hurt tone. "That will be fine," she said. "I'll look forward to it."

Hanging up the phone, she stared at the mahogany walls of the study. She'd actually grown to find them rather soothing over the last few weeks, and soothing was exactly what she needed at the moment.

Tyler had suddenly and without warning launched himself back into her world, and now expected everything to be as it had been before. But Clarissa was starting to realize that in the three months they'd been apart, she'd moved on. That it had happened so quickly seemed to indicate that their relationship hadn't been all that solid even before their disagreement over careers. Looking back, she could easily recall a significant number of times when Tyler had expected her to be the one to compromise on matters both small and large, and she could remember very few times that he had been willing to make a sacrifice, except occasionally over what to order at a Chinese restaurant.

Yes, she warned herself, she might have to give some serious thought as to whether attempting to get back together, even in a tentative way, was really a good idea. There was no point—in fact, it was cruel— to encourage Tyler in his dream if it wasn't one that she could realistically see herself sharing.

The phone rang again. For a moment, Clarissa considered letting the answering machine pick up in case it was Tyler again, either apologizing or attempting to guilt-trip her again. Deciding that she wasn't going to be a captive in her own office, she answered.

"Hi, Pastor, it's Josh Baker here," came the reply.

"How are you, detective?" she asked, breathing a sigh of relief that this wasn't going to be a painfully personal conversation.

"Oh, you know, fighting the good fight," he said good-naturedly. "I just wanted to thank you for urging Sharon Meissner to come in to see us. It's helpful to know that Ames had a pile of money stashed away. That makes it more likely he was involved in a blackmail scheme, like you suspected."

"Glad it helped. Is Sharon going to be charged with anything?"

"Probably not, unless we find a lot more evidence incriminating her. She should have told us about going to see Ames in the hospital, but I guess that was innocent enough," Baker said. "I can understand that she cared for him and didn't want to desert him in his time of need. Of course, the inheritance gives her a motive for wanting him dead, but I spoke to the lawyer who wrote the will, and apparently Ames made it clear that he had every intention of keeping it a secret from her. He didn't want her to know about it until after his death. I guess he thought about it as a pleasant surprise from beyond the grave."

"So she didn't know she was going to inherit, and would have had no motive to murder him."

"Exactly."

"Well, I've been following up on the blackmail angle," Clarissa said, and proceeded to summarize her conversations with Maggie Preston, Harry Blanchard, and Ron Hazelton.

"That's interesting," Detective Baker said slowly, "but I wish you would have included me in your investigation. Or at least you could have informed me right after they took place."

"Sorry," Clarissa apologized. "I would have, but they didn't really seem to lead anywhere. I think Maggie genuinely loved Royce Llewellyn, and still does, in fact. I don't think she killed Royce, so she wasn't being blackmailed. And I have doubts about Harry Blanchard or Ron Hazelton murdering two people just to hide a family secret."

"No one likes it to be known that they had a murderer in the family," Baker pointed out.

"Still, that seems extreme. It's not like Harry or Ron personally killed Llewellyn. At worst, it would be a long-dead father or grandfather who committed the crime. Maybe you wouldn't want the gossip spread around town, but it would essentially be ancient history. There'd be no trial to give it publicity."

"Yeah, it would be a much bigger deal if the killer were still alive."

There was a long silence on the phone.

"You still there, Pastor?" Baker asked.

"Yes, sorry, Josh," Clarissa replied. "I'm thinking about what you just said. That definitely leads me to my other two suspects."

"Who are they?"

"Royce's wife and daughter. If one of them killed Royce, she'd definitely go to jail. So they have something important to hide."

"Okay, but I assume we agree that Doris is too old to have killed Ames and Spurlock. That leaves Elise," Baker said doubtfully.

"I know she has mental problems, but disturbed people sometimes kill," Clarissa pointed out.

"Usually in an outburst, not after careful plotting. Plus, I've met her a few times, and she seems awfully fragile."

"I'm not going to write her off as a suspect until I find out that she couldn't possibly have done it. Ashley's aunt knows Agnes Coleman, the woman who drives the Llewellyns everywhere. Ashley's going to find out if Elise was out of town at the time Ames was killed. If she wasn't, I think you should question her," Clarissa said.

"I'd like a bit more evidence implicating her in the crime, beyond mere supposition, before I drag a mentally ill woman down to the station for questioning—especially a mentally ill woman whose mother still has considerable influence in the community."

"Couldn't you take Elise's fingerprints and check them against those you found in David's hospital room?" Clarissa asked.

"I could. But forcing Elise to be fingerprinted would also rattle her mother's cage," Baker explained. "Let me start by showing her picture around the hospital to see if anyone recognizes her. If anyone thinks they saw her there the night of Ames' death, I'll bring her in. Rudinski doesn't have much to do this afternoon; I'll send him right over to the hospital."

"Sounds great," Clarissa said, feeling encouraged. "Maybe you can help me with something else related to the case."

"What is it?"

"When the Llewellyn murder took place, were there any other family members in the area other than Royce's wife and daughter?" Clarissa asked. "It's a long shot, but I was just wondering if someone else in the family might have harbored ill will toward Royce. He doesn't seem to have been an easy guy to get along with."

"Let me check. I've got the file here somewhere."

Clarissa heard some shuffling around, and after a few moments, Baker came back on the line.

"Let me see," he said. "It looks like his only other relative was a younger brother living in Philadelphia. One of the investigators interviewed him when he came to Shore Side for the funeral. Apparently, he hadn't kept in close touch with Royce and had no idea who would want to murder him. That looks like a dead end to me."

"What about Doris Llewellyn's side of the family?"

"Nobody at all there."

Clarissa sighed. "Well, thanks anyway, and let me know what Officer Rudinski finds at the hospital. That may be our last chance of solving this thing."

"I'll call you first thing in the morning," Baker promised her.

Clarissa thanked him and hung up. Then she sat and wondered what the odds were that Elise would have attacked David while not wearing gloves. Anyone who watched television—heck, anyone who didn't live in a cave—knew about fingerprints and would be careful not to leave any. And as far as anyone spotting Elise slipping into the hospital wearing a hoodie went, well, that seemed like a pretty slim chance, too.

Deciding that she was only depressing herself, Clarissa returned to her sermon and, after a few minutes, was lost in the subject. Two hours later, she decided that it was in an acceptable form. She'd practice delivering it later in the week, but she was pretty sure that it would flow just fine.

Before leaving the office, she glanced at the list of two people she was scheduled to visit tomorrow afternoon. She hoped that her visits would be a pleasant distraction from this dead-end investigation.

Clarissa returned to the parsonage. After having a small portion of the gigantic casserole Mrs. Gunn had left for her, she spent an extended time in meditation and prayer, hoping to bring clarity to her mind and serenity to her soul before turning in for the night.

Chapter Twenty-Five

The first thing Clarissa noticed the next morning as she entered the kitchen was a loaf of just the kind of dark rye that she liked most sitting in the middle of the table.

"Good morning," Mrs. Gunn said. Seeing Clarissa staring at the bread, she smiled. "He said you would be impressed."

"Who did?" Clarissa asked.

"The young man who brought it to the door a few minutes ago," Mrs. Gunn answered. "He said his name was Tyler and that you were old friends. He also said that the bread was a peace offering because you'd had some kind of disagreement."

Clarissa struggled to keep her expression bland, although inside she was seething. Here was Tyler intruding into her life again, this time by coming right to the parsonage and telling Mrs. Gunn personal things.

"He seems like a nice boy," Mrs. Gunn said cautiously.

"He has his moments."

Mrs. Gunn gave her a quizzical look that Clarissa didn't respond to. Finally, realizing that the story would eventually come out and Mrs. Gunn would be hurt if she were the last to know, Clarissa decided to say something.

"We used to be engaged, but it didn't work out," she said flatly.

"Oh, I see. Well, that must have been very upsetting for both of you," Mrs. Gunn commented.

"It was, but I've moved on. Tyler apparently hasn't," Clarissa said. "He left his church job in northern New Jersey to move down here so he could be closer to me. I know it sounds very romantic, but . . ."

"You wish he would move on the same way you have."

Clarissa shrugged. She took two pieces of bread from the loaf and popped them in the toaster on the counter.

"In my experience, people very seldom agree on when a relationship started or when it should end. Often one person wants to cut the tie, while the other wants to have it remain in place," Mrs. Gunn said.

Clarissa leaned against the counter. "I'm not certain what I want. We had something wonderful once, but I'm not sure it can be brought back to life. I certainly don't like being pressured to move things along faster than I'm comfortable doing."

"Yes, the young man did have a kind of desperate optimism about him."

"I think he's convinced himself that, with a little effort, things are magically going to go back to the way they were." Clarissa shook her head. "That's not going to happen. If we even should get together again, it will have to be different than it was before."

"He is not going to be happy to hear that you're going out with that lawyer fellow," Mrs. Gunn observed.

"He already isn't. I warned him that I wasn't going to be exclusively seeing him, and he agreed. But when I told him I had a date, he got pretty huffy," Clarissa complained. "That's why he brought the loaf of bread—to make up. Why did he agree to my terms in the first place, if he was just going to get bent out of shape by my dating other people?"

Mrs. Gunn laughed. "He probably would have agreed to cut off a finger to keep going out with you. But that doesn't mean he would have done it when the time came. Men always want to sound reasonable, but when push comes to shove, they're more emotional than we are. It's got something to do with hormones."

Clarissa grinned and began buttering her toast.

"Would you like an egg to go with that?" Mrs. Gunn asked.

"No, thanks. I think this will be enough this morning."

Mrs. Gunn frowned, but said nothing.

The Ames investigation pressed on Clarissa's mind. "Do you happen to know if there were any other members of the Llewellyn family living in town back when Royce was murdered?" she asked.

Mrs. Gunn stared across the kitchen. "I don't remember hearing about any. Elise was the only Llewellyn in the school at the time as far as I know. Why do you ask?"

Clarissa didn't want to tell Mrs. Gunn about the extent of her involvement in the murder investigation, so she said, "I just heard about how badly off Elise is mentally, and I was wondering if there were any other family members to give Doris support."

"Poor Elise is a sad case. She's never been completely right since she came back to town. But I never heard about her having any other family." Mrs. Gunn poured herself a cup of coffee. "But—wait a minute, someone did tell me that the new owners of the Italian restaurant on the west side of town are named Llewellyn. I remember wondering if they were somehow related. It's not that common a name."

"What's the name of the restaurant?"

"The Florentina. It's on Sitwell, just inside the town line."

"That's quite interesting," Clarissa said. She was definitely going to visit the restaurant this afternoon.

"So, you have a date with Andrew the lawyer tomorrow evening," Mrs. Gunn said, turning the conversation back to Clarissa's love life. "Are you going to tell him about your ex-fiancé being back in town?"

Clarissa thought about it. "I guess it would only be fair to tell him. Since Tyler knows about him, I guess he should know about Tyler. Today that's what they call transparency."

"Sounds like a situation that could lead to a confrontation."

"That's what Ashley thought. She figured it would be like two rams butting heads."

A sly look came into Mrs. Gunn's eyes. "I don't think we've ever had two men fighting over who's going to date the pastor."

"How about two older women fighting over the handsome Reverend Hollingsworth?" Clarissa asked with a grin.

"Ah, now that's a different matter," Mrs. Gunn said. "I'll have to tell you about that some time."

After finishing breakfast, Clarissa went over to her office. She read through her sermon again in the cold light of morning to see whether it was actually as good as it had seemed the day before. Aware that sometimes what she considered to be her more brilliant sermons fell flat, while her less skillfully crafted ones were a big hit, she tried not to get too enthused over her work until it had actually been presented.

She heard the outer door open, and went into the outer office just as Ashley entered. She was wearing a black blouse and black jeans with black running shoes. Clarissa hoped Ashley didn't go walking like that at night; an inattentive driver could easily hit her crossing the street—if the police didn't pick her up first.

This morning, though, her expression was as dark as her clothes.

"What's wrong?" Clarissa asked. "Did your aunt make you eat bacon and eggs for breakfast?"

Her attempt at humor fell on deaf ears; Ashley didn't crack a smile. "I'm afraid our investigation has hit a major dead end."

"How's that?"

"My aunt got in touch with Agnes Coleman last night, and she checked her calendar of driving assignments for last month," Ashley said. "Apparently she's a stickler for keeping records; it's her only way of being certain she gets paid. And on the afternoon that David Ames was murdered, Agnes took Elise and her mother to Philadelphia for Elise's monthly visit with her psychiatrist. They left town at two o'clock and didn't get back until after eight. There was an accident on the road on the way back, and they got delayed. Do you know when someone last saw Ames alive?"

"Let me call Detective Baker," Clarissa said. "He's checking up on something else for me anyway."

Clarissa called the police station and quickly got through to the detective.

"I was going to call you in about ten minutes," he said on the other end of the line. "I didn't know what time you started work."

"Before you tell me about Officer Rudinski's search, could you tell me when David Ames was last seen alive?" Clarissa asked.

"Let me check; it's in the file."

While Clarissa waited, Ashley whispered, "Any time after two o'clock is going to be too late."

Detective Baker was back. "Nurse Bascomb checked on David at three-thirty," he said, "and he was doing okay. When she came in at four-thirty with his supper, he was gone."

Clarissa sighed. "Well, we can write off Elise and Doris Llewellyn as the killers, then, because according to Agnes Coleman, their driver, they were on their way to Philadelphia at the time of his death."

"Okay. I'll go talk to Agnes just to make sure that there isn't any mistake. And I'm afraid the news on this end isn't any better," Baker said. "Rudinski showed Elise's picture around the lobby of the hospital, on the floor Ames was on, and on both the floors above and below. He checked with the staff and any patients who were in that area of the hospital at the time of the killing. No one remembered seeing her. The hospital has a surveillance camera in the lobby and one in the back parking lot, so Rudinski went through the tapes for the day of the murder, starting at two o'clock and going all the way to five. There was no sign of Elise. Now, the cameras aren't complete in their coverage, but it does suggest along with everything else that she wasn't there."

"You're right. It does sound pretty conclusive. Unfortunately, it leaves us without any suspects," Clarissa sighed. "Thank Officer Rudinski for me. It sounds like he went above and beyond the call to do a thorough job."

"Yeah, he's got the kind of persistence needed to be a detective. Of course, in this case he knew it was something *you* were interested in, so he went all out. I think you've got a fan there."

Clarissa suppressed another sigh. All she needed was a third guy interested in her.

"Oh, by the way," she said. "Mrs. Gunn mentioned that someone named Llewellyn just opened up an Italian restaurant in town."

Ashley waved her hand to catch Clarissa's attention and whispered, "My aunt says he's the grandson of Royce Llewellyn's brother."

Clarissa passed the news along to Detective Baker. "I thought I'd stop in there today to see if he knew anything," she told him.

"All right," Baker said doubtfully, "but be careful. Don't make any accusations. Just find out if he's had any contact with the rest of his family. If he has, I'll take it from there. In fact, why don't you take Ashley along with you? She looks fierce enough to put the fear of God into any felon."

"Okay, I'll do that," Clarissa said, barely keeping a straight face.

After she hung up, Clarissa told Ashley what the detective had said, leaving out the part about her threatening appearance.

"Sounds good," Ashley said enthusiastically. "Let me call the restaurant and see if they're open for lunch. If they are, we might be able to talk to the owner then."

"If not, we'll make an appointment," Clarissa said. "I'm going to go into my office and sketch out a few questions I want to ask the two families I'm visiting this afternoon. I'll show them to you after I'm done to make sure they'll give us the kind of information we need to do the church history."

Ashley nodded, already punching numbers on the phone.

For the next hour, Clarissa tried to clarify in her mind exactly what she wanted the church history to be. Rather than a dry recital of statistics and official events, she thought it would be more valuable to have church members recount events from the past that stood out in their own minds, preferably events that were in some way relevant to the church. But she didn't want only good memories—conflicts, disagreements, and arguments were just as meaningful a part of the church's life.

The phone rang. When she picked it up, Ashley said, "Andrew Corrigan is on the line for you." Clarissa thought she detected a note of humor in Ashley's voice.

Ashley put him through and Clarissa greeted him: "Hi, Andrew, how are you?"

"Fine," he replied. "I just called to tell you how much I'm looking forward to our going out to dinner tomorrow night."

"So am I. You didn't think you had to call to remind me, did you?"

"No, of course not." Andrew chuckled. "Well, maybe I wanted to check that you really had forgiven me for that last fiasco, and weren't already regretting having agreed to go out with me again."

"Not at all. I'm a great believer in new beginnings." Saying those words reminded her of what she had said to Mrs. Gunn about being fair to Andrew by telling him about Tyler. "I'm glad you called, because I wanted to let you know that my former fiancé has moved to the area."

"I didn't know you'd had a fiancé," Andrew said, startled.

"Well, we didn't exactly have an opportunity to talk much about our pasts last time." Although to be honest with herself, Clarissa wasn't completely sure she would have told him about Tyler on a first date anyway.

"Is he definitely a *former* fiancé?"

"Oh, yes. But he still wants us to see each other."

"So he hasn't given up?"

Clarissa frowned. That was a blunt—but accurate—way to put it. "I guess you could say that."

"He isn't going to shoot me in a jealous rage, is he?" Andrew said.

"He's a minister."

"That doesn't answer the question."

"No, he's not a violent person, so you don't have to worry."

"That's fine, then. Let the best man win."

"Yes, I suppose so," Clarissa said, not sure she liked being depicted as a prize at a sporting event. "I'll see you Wednesday evening."

"Looking forward to it, and now I'll definitely be bringing my 'A' game," he said.

Clarissa hung up, wondering whether there was ever a time when men stopped being boys.

Ashley opened the door. "I got in touch with someone at the Florentina. They serve lunch and open at eleven-thirty. The owner, Noah Llewellyn, will be there, and is looking forward to seeing us."

"What reason did you give him for our visit?" Clarissa asked.

Ashley's eyes got a bit shifty. "I may have mentioned that the women's group is looking for a place to have their luncheon meeting next month."

"Is that true?"

"Well, they've been going to the same place for years, and my aunt mentioned that there's a significant faction that would like to have the meetings move around so they get to sample a variety of restaurants. Since she's in charge of organizing the luncheons, I could have significant input in the decision."

"So it's sort of true."

"If you come at it the right way."

Clarissa glanced at the clock on the wall. "We have an hour before we have to leave to see Llewellyn. Let me go over my visitation questions and talk a little about my concept of this history."

"Are you *sure* you want to do this history thing?"

The pastor gave her a level stare.

"Okay, Boss," Ashley replied, putting her hands up. "I give up."

Clarissa chuckled; she wasn't sure if Ashley *ever* gave up.

Chapter Twenty-Six

The Florentina looked like it was made out of plastic stucco. The outside was garishly shaped and decorated to resemble an Italianate palace. Clarissa had been to Italy on a tour with her parents back when she was in high school, and this looked like something you'd see along the Grand Canal in Venice—if you didn't look very hard.

"It's a bit tacky," Ashley said, "but you can't go just by that. Maybe the food is good."

They walked through the front double doors and into a large bar area. The carpeting underfoot was thick enough to slow them down, and overhead, the chandeliers were large enough to feel oppressive.

A young man working behind the bar spotted them. "Unless you're here for a drink, you took a wrong turn. The restaurant is to the left as you come in the door," he informed them.

"We have an appointment with Noah Llewellyn," Clarissa said in a crisp voice.

"I'll get him for you."

The bartender returned a couple of minutes later with a tall, thin man in his early thirties.

"I'm Noah Llewellyn," he said to Clarissa. "Are you Reverend Abbot?"

She nodded. "Clarissa will be fine."

The man smiled and took a longer look at Ashley.

"I'm Ashley Reynolds. The office manager," she said.

Llewellyn nodded and gave a slight smile, as if bemused by the incongruous couple. "Your message said that you're looking for a venue for a luncheon that the church's women's club is holding," he said.

"That's right," Clarissa said.

"How many would be attending?" he asked.

Not sure of the answer, Clarissa glanced over at Ashley.

"Twenty-five to thirty," Ashley said quickly.

"We have a private room that will hold that many," Llewellyn said. "If you'll come with me, I'll show it to you."

He turned and quickly led them through the bar, around a corner, and across the back of the dining room. Although she didn't have much time to look around, Clarissa had a sense of a certain uniformity of excess. Their motto in decorating seemed to be if a little is good, more is better.

Finally, Llewellyn stopped before a heavy door and shoved it open to reveal a spacious room with a dining table down the center that looked like it could easily hold forty people.

"This should be just fine," Clarissa said. She looked at Ashley for confirmation; she nodded.

"Here's a menu to take with you," Llewellyn offered. "I know how these things work. There's probably a committee that makes the decision, and they might like to see what we have to offer. We have all the usual Italian red sauce dishes, but for those who want something different, we have several northern Italian items and a few southern German selections."

"Thank you very much. We'll let you know soon." Clarissa glanced at Ashley.

"Within a week," her assistant added.

"I'd appreciate knowing sooner rather than later," Llewellyn said. "This room does tend to get booked in advance."

"Don't worry," Clarissa said. "We'll get right on it. By the way, I came into contact through the church with a couple of people in town who have the same last name as you: Doris and Elise Llewellyn. Are they related?"

The man's lips thinned into a straight line. "Distant relatives. My grandfather's older brother lived here years ago. Doris and Elise are his wife and daughter." He nodded abruptly and motioned with his hand, directing them to the front door.

"A recent police matter has come up with regard to the murder of your great-uncle Royce," Clarissa said slowly.

"I know nothing about him," Llewellyn replied. "He was dead long before I was born."

"Of course he was," Clarissa said soothingly. "But the police are wondering how many family members are still in the area. I can understand why you might not want to talk to me, but I can easily have Detective Baker come here and make it official."

Llewellyn nodded nervously. He directed them to a table in a corner away from everyone else, and they sat.

He began rubbing his forehead. "My father warned me not to set a business up here. He said that small towns have long memories, and there would still be people around who recognized the name and connected it with a famous murder. I just didn't expect it to happen so soon."

"Don't panic yet. You may not have to get involved at all," Clarissa assured him. "Where does your father live?"

"My father, mother, and two sisters live in the Philadelphia area."

"Do you have any contact with Doris and Elise?"

"When Uncle Royce was killed, my grandfather broke off all contact with them and pretty much forbade my father from ever reaching out to them," Llewellyn said. "Doris tried to get in touch with my grandfather during the first few years, but she finally gave up. I've never met them, and as far as I know, none of my family has either."

"What do you know about the murder?" Clarissa asked.

"Not much. My father will hardly talk about it. He considers it a family embarrassment. All I've been told is that Uncle Royce was a tough businessman and had an eye for the ladies. Somehow he rubbed the wrong person the wrong way and was shot."

"Do you know anything about Elise?" Ashley asked.

Llewellyn stared across the restaurant. "My father learned from my grandfather that she went sort of crazy after her father was killed. Her mother sent her away to school, but she went off the rails and ended up in some kind of psychiatric institution. I guess later on, she came back to Shore Side."

"Is there anything else you can tell us?" Clarissa asked.

He paused for a minute, obviously unsure whether to speak. "Look, I don't even know whether this is true or not, but my father let slip once that his dad had told him that Elise had a baby," he said.

"While she was in the psychiatric institution?" asked Clarissa, leaning forward in her chair.

"I don't know exactly when. My father thought that her mother made her give it up for adoption. I guess having a child without being married was a big deal in those days, and it would have been embarrassing."

"Was it a boy or girl?" Ashley asked.

"No idea. I don't think anyone in the family knows what happened to it." He stood up. "I'm afraid that's all I can tell you."

Llewellyn turned and headed for the door, the women following.

He smiled tightly as he held the door for them. "I hope to hear from you again . . . about the luncheon."

"I'm sure you will," Clarissa promised.

***

"So, what do you think?" Ashley asked as they drove back to the parsonage. "Did he tell us anything useful?"

"Hard to know," Clarissa replied. "That adopted child could be anywhere. It's a bit unlikely he or she would be here in Shore Side."

"But what if the child *did* reconnect with his or her family and lives in town? That would give us another suspect," Ashley pointed out.

"I suppose. I wonder how hard it is to get access to adoption records these days," Clarissa said. "If we could find the adoptive parents, maybe we could discover where the child is living."

"Detective Baker could probably tell us. I bet the police have all sorts of ways of finding these things out."

"I'll check. And we have to remember that this child was born over forty years ago, so he or she would be well into middle age by now."

When Clarissa pulled into the lot behind the church offices, she turned to Ashley. "You're done for the day," she told her assistant. "Why don't you head home?"

"I have my lunch in the office refrigerator. I think I'll eat here. Then I can avoid having to explain to my aunt why I don't want a ham sandwich."

Clarissa nodded. "I'll go over to the parsonage and eat a little bit of the huge lunch Mrs. Gunn has undoubtedly left for me," she said with a grin. "Then let's see if we can come up with any new ideas overnight, and we'll talk this all over again in the morning."

Clarissa walked across to the parsonage. On the kitchen table was a note that her lunch, a salad, was on the third shelf in the fridge. She took a portion of the large salad and sat down at the table.

She spent a few moments reviewing the questions she was going to ask during her visitations, and then decided to call Detective Baker about what she'd learned at the Florentina. After all, she'd promised to keep him more in the loop.

When he answered, she explained to him that Elise had given a baby up for adoption and that she wanted to know if he could discover the name and location of the child.

"I'll have to talk to the district attorney on this," Baker said. "I have a feeling that it would require a court order. The easiest thing might be to go have a chat with Doris and Elise. Maybe they would volunteer the information."

"Okay. It would be really helpful to know where the child is now."

"You think they might be the killer?"

"If the child has found and made up with the Llewellyns and feels like part of the family, he or she might be motivated to protect whichever one of them killed Royce," Clarissa said.

"I'll check into it," Baker promised.

The phone rang as soon as Clarissa set it down.

"Hi, this is Samantha Jones," said the voice on the other end. "Sorry I haven't been around to do my survey of the church, but the last few days have been awfully busy. I promise I'll get to it by the end of the week."

"No problem," Clarissa said.

"I do have that length of pipe I need to fix the sink in the parsonage," Samantha said. "I have a job in your neighborhood early this evening, and I was wondering if I could come over right after it to work on your sink. I know Mrs. Gunn really wants it fixed."

Clarissa went through her mental schedule. "I'll be here, so that should be fine. I might be working in the office, so if the parsonage is locked up, just come over and get me."

"Will do."

Clarissa ended the call and saw that she had to leave for her first visit. Taking her list of questions, a couple of pens, and a notepad, she headed out the door to her car.

***

Four hours later, Clarissa returned to the parsonage. Ashley had been correct; there was no way she could have booked more than two visits in an afternoon. Each had taken over an hour and a half, and that was only after excusing herself rather forcefully from both houses when they wanted her to stay longer. She was afloat in tea, and she felt she already had enough notes for a complete church history. She began to seriously wonder exactly what she had gotten herself into. But she had to admit that the people she met seemed delighted to have the minister come into their homes, and they obliquely commented that this was something Reverend Hollingsworth should have done a long time ago.

Although Clarissa wasn't very hungry, she decided that she had better eat after she changed into more comfortable clothes. When she waited until closer to bedtime, she often didn't sleep very well. So after changing, she heated up a small plate of meatloaf and mashed potatoes that she'd separated from the larger plate Mrs. Gunn had left, and ate while she leafed through the mail.

After eating, she found that she was too restless to relax, and she began pacing up and down the large living room in the parsonage. She had a nagging feeling that there was some connection in the Llewellyn case that was right in front of her eyes, and she was just failing to put it together.

Tired of pacing, she decided to go over to the office and rest her mind by transcribing her notes from her visits into a computer file. As she left the parsonage, she remembered that Samantha would be coming in later to repair the sink, so she wrote a note and taped it to the door to remind her that she'd be in the office. She walked across, unlocked the office door, and, heeding Detective Baker's warning, carefully locked it behind her.

Not bothering to turn on the light in her office, Clarissa began transcribing her notes, pausing along the way to polish them up a bit so they would sound like a historical narrative. She became so engrossed in her work that it was a couple of hours later before she looked up and realized that it had begun to get dark outside.

She stood up and stretched the kinks out of her back, and that was when she heard the thump of someone knocking on the outside office door.

She paused; was that Samantha? She listened for the call of the woman's voice, but the knocking just continued. That struck her as odd, and she felt an uneasy lump form in her stomach.

Her eye caught on the canister of pepper spray sitting on the corner of her desk, where it had remained ever since Ashley had given it to her. It probably *was* just Samantha, but she had promised so many people that she would be careful. Better to be safe than sorry, she thought, putting the small canister into her pocket.

Taking the keys from her desk because the inside lock also required a key, she walked into the outer office. Clarissa slowly unlocked the door, opened it a crack, and peered outside into the rapidly darkening night.

There she saw Wanda Bascomb standing on the stoop. Clarissa breathed a sigh of relief at the sight of the nurse, who waved a white envelope at her.

"Sorry to bother you," she said, "but I found this at work today, and I thought you might like to see it. It might be important in regard to Dave's murder."

Clarissa let her inside and took the envelope. She carefully opened it, wondering if she would get in trouble with Detective Baker for smudging prints. She slowly unfolded the piece of stationary.

The page was blank. She turned it over. The other side was blank as well.

"What am I supposed . . ." Clarissa glanced up and saw that Wanda now held a large knife in her right hand. Suddenly things fell into place. "You're Elise's daughter," she realized aloud. "There never was anyone in a hoodie."

"I knew you'd figure it out eventually," Wanda said menacingly. "When I followed you to the Florentina today, I realized that you were getting too close for comfort."

"Detective Baker knows everything. Killing me won't solve your problem," Clarissa warned her, backing up and grasping her keys tightly.

Wanda advanced toward her, the knife raised. "He'll never figure it out the way you did," she spat. "Anyway, I'll be long gone by the time they find your body in the morning, and there'll be no way they can charge my mother or grandmother. They had nothing to do with any of the murders—at least the recent ones."

Fumbling desperately with one hand, Clarissa managed to get a grip on the pepper spray in her pocket. Hoping she had the nozzle pointing in the right direction, she pulled it out of her pocket and fired it directly into Wanda's eyes.

The woman screamed and began flailing around sightlessly with the knife. Moving toward her unarmed side, Clarissa pushed her out of the way and ran out the door.

She had only taken a couple of steps when she was confronted by Doris Llewellyn, who was leaning on a cane with one hand, and holding a gun remarkably steady with the other.

"Don't make a move, or I will shoot you," the old woman warned.

"You're going to shoot me anyway," Clarissa gasped, frozen in place.

"No, I'm going to let Wanda do the job with her knife once she recovers enough to come out here. You didn't hurt her, did you? She's precious to me," Doris growled.

"She's fine," Clarissa said regretfully.

"You really should have stopped your amateur investigating before I had to go this far," Doris sighed. "When Wanda saw you talking to Noah Llewellyn, I knew eventually you'd put two and two together."

"If *I* can, the police will."

"I plan to send Wanda far, far away, and the police have nothing on Elise or myself."

"Poor Elise," Clarissa said, stalling for time.

"Yes, I've been protecting her for years. When that David Ames told her about Royce's relationship with Maggie Preston, Elise was devastated." Doris' lip trembled. "She stole her father's gun from his office desk and waited for him to come home. I was upstairs and never knew. As soon as he walked in the door, she shot him. By the time I got downstairs, she had collapsed on the floor beside her father with the gun still in her hand."

"And David Ames saw her do it."

Doris nodded. "The demands for money started a few days later. They weren't unreasonable, and so I paid them. When David went into the hospital, we couldn't believe our good luck that Wanda was working on his floor. We decided that he would never leave the hospital alive. Once Wanda overheard his conversation with you, she suspected that he was going to pass on his secret to Jack Spurlock. So we simply decided to speed up David's timetable."

"But why kill Jack?" Clarissa asked. "He knew nothing about the murder."

"When he came to the hospital with you to see Ames, he said that he already knew everything that had happened in the past. We couldn't risk that he might figure out who had killed Royce."

"So you killed him for insurance."

Doris sighed. "Can you imagine how tired we were of paying blackmail after fifty years?" she demanded.

There was a coughing and sputtering behind her, and Clarissa turned to see Wanda staggering out of the office. Unfortunately, she still held the knife firmly in her hand.

"Don't try to run, my dear," said Doris. "I was a very good shot in my youth—Royce taught me—and I believe I still am."

Clarissa knew she was between two people determined to kill her. She thought her best chance was to try to overcome Wanda and get the knife away from her. In the confusion she might be able to escape without being shot.

She was about to turn and charge toward the nurse when Samantha Jones stepped out of the surrounding darkness behind Doris and quickly twisted the gun from the old woman's hand.

"Drop the knife," Samantha said to Wanda, aiming the gun at her. "I'm a pretty good shot as well." There was no hint of compromise in the veteran's voice.

Reluctantly, Wanda let the knife fall from her hand.

Keeping a close eye on both Doris and Wanda, Samantha passed her cell phone to Clarissa. "I think it's high time we called the police, don't you?"

Chapter Twenty-Seven

"So Wanda Bascomb was the granddaughter, and she killed both Ames and Spurlock to end the blackmail of her mother?"

Clarissa nodded in response to Ashley's question. They were sitting in her office, discussing the previous night's events. Doris and Wanda were in police custody, and Elise was probably being transferred to a mental institution as they spoke.

Clarissa was indebted to Samantha for saving her life. No matter what the rest of the church board said after her probationary period, Clarissa was all for her being the church sacristan. She'd feel a lot safer with Samantha around, that was for sure. Who would have thought Shore Side could be so dangerous?

"Something snapped in Elise when she found out her father was cheating on her mother," Clarissa explained to Ashley. "He went from being someone she idolized to someone she hated. So she stole the gun from his office, and shot him when he came home the next night."

"And Ames was up to his neck in this," Ashley said, shaking her head. "He told Elise about her father and brought the whole thing about. And *then* he happened to be at the house when she shot him."

"As far as I can reconstruct it, he had a few drinks and went there to confront Royce for firing him," Clarissa said. "He happened to get there just in time to see Elise shoot her father, and he'd been blackmailing the family ever since."

"It's hard to feel sorry for him," said Ashley.

"True. But murder is always wrong."

"I suppose. What did Detective Baker say when he showed up? Was he angry at you?"

Clarissa looked somber. "He was pretty upset that I had almost been killed. But he came close to congratulating me for solving the crime. A reporter and photographer from the county newspaper showed up, as well. It was quite a scene."

"I bet you'll be famous," Ashley said.

"I hope not. I'd rather have it all disappear."

"Well, it sounds like things worked out pretty well for you this last week. You solved a major crime, and you have two hunky guys interested in going out with you. What are you going to do to celebrate?"

Clarissa smiled. "I'm just going to try to relax."

The door to the office flew open then, and Andrew Corrigan stepped inside. He had a newspaper held up in front of him like a banner.

"Have you seen this?" he asked accusingly, waving the paper at the two women.

Ashley took it and read the headline out loud: "'Private Eye Pastor Solves Murder.' Hey, this is pretty good press. It should pack them into the pews on Sunday."

Clarissa moaned.

"How could you take chances like that?" Andrew demanded. "You could easily have been killed."

The door flew open again and Tyler charged into the room, holding the same newspaper. He stopped in his tracks at the sight of Andrew.

"What's going on here, Clarissa?" Tyler said, staring hard at Andrew.

Andrew eyed the other man. "Who are you?"

"I'm Tyler Hamilton, and I'm Clarissa's fiancé."

"*Former* fiancé," Clarissa corrected.

"Who are you?" Tyler said, glaring at Andrew.

"I'm Andrew Corrigan, and I'm her *current* boyfriend."

"That remains to be seen," Clarissa added.

Behind the two men, Clarissa could see Ashley grinning and bringing her fists together in the imitation of two rams butting heads.

Both men opened their mouths to speak again, but Clarissa had had enough.

"Gentlemen," she said loudly in her I'm-giving-a-sermon voice. "I think it's time we sat down and had a discussion."

Suddenly solving three murders seemed like a piece of cake.

THE END

ABOUT THE AUTHOR

 Glen Ebisch was a professor of philosophy for over twenty-five years. Quite recently he retired from teaching at a small university in western Massachusetts. For much of that time he has also written mystery fiction, starting with books for young adults and later writing for adults. He has had over thirty books published. All are amateur sleuth mysteries and suitable for any reader.

He lives in western Massachusetts with his wife. His hobbies include reading, travel, and going to the gym. He and his wife frequently spend time in Wells, Maine, and Cape May, New Jersey, for their needed dose of the beach.

Made in the USA
Monee, IL
25 March 2021